PRAISE FOR RACHEL LEE
AND *UNDER SUSPICION*

"A well-plotted story....Rachel Lee has written from a
unique perspective and balances romance and suspense
very carefully, giving each of them equal time."
—Sue Waldeck, *Road to Romance Reviews*

"Rachel Lee expertly lets readers see through the eyes of a
mastermind criminal. This added bonus enhances the
high intensity that radiates through this exciting novel.
This one left goose bumps by the time I came to the
dramatic conclusion."
—Suzie Housley, MyShelf.com

"Ms. Lee struck the perfect balance....Clarence Tebbins
alone would make *Under Suspicion*
worth reading!"
—Nancy J. Silberstein, *Romance Reader*

"An extremely suspenseful mystery....Ms. Lee has
a gift for building tension and suspense to terrific
levels and sustaining those levels, which can be even
trickier....Mystery lovers will enjoy
Under Suspicion immensely."
—Heidi L. Haglin, Likesbooks.com

ALSO BY RACHEL LEE

Before I Sleep

After I Dream

When I Wake

Under Suspicion

LAST
BREATH

RACHEL LEE

WARNER BOOKS

An AOL Time Warner Company

WARNER BOOKS EDITION

Cover design by Diane Luger
Cover illustration by Franco Accornero

Warner Books, Inc.
1271 Avenue of the Americas
New York, NY 10020

Visit our Web site at www.twbookmark.com

Ⓦ An AOL Time Warner Company

Printed in the United States of America

First Paperback Printing: May 2003

10 9 8 7 6 5 4 3 2 1

For Fathers Austin Mullen and Eric Peters,
both of whom are among the best priests God ever
put on this earth.

ACKNOWLEDGMENTS

My very deep thanks to Father Eric for answering my questions and sharing so freely with me the joys and burdens of the priesthood. Any errors are mine alone.

AUTHOR'S NOTE

The Diocese of Tampa is purely the creation of my imagination. It is not intended in any way to resemble any real diocese, nor are any of the characters based on real persons.

PROLOGUE

The afternoon of the murder, nothing seemed amiss at St. Simeon's Parish in Tampa, Florida. Except for the presence of Chloe Ryder at a children's class.

Father Brendan Quinlan sat at the baby grand piano in the parish hall, banging out the accompaniment to "Trust in the Lord" with all his usual verve. What one child had described as "really cool shades" bobbed on the end of a nose set in a rather puckish face. Tall, too thin, and as loving and outgoing a man as God ever created, he had the dozen kids in the room gathered around him, singing at the top of their lungs.

On other occasions he'd been known to bang out the blues, or jazz, or anything else that struck his fancy. Parish parties were some of his favorite events. Tonight, however, he was participating in an RCIC—Rite of Christian Initiation for Children—class, and the music had to be more appropriate. For now anyway. There was no telling what he might play for these students—ranging in age from eleven to fourteen—by the end of the two-hour class.

He'd already led them in a rousing chorus of "Jesus Christ Superstar," but now he was going for the giggles.

They had reached the second verse, and he could already see the anticipation on the faces around him as they all sang:

> *Be not wise in thine own eyes*
> *But trust the Lord and beware of evil.*
> *And it shall be health unto thy navel. . . .*

He answered the expectation by lifting his hands from the keyboard, prying his clerical shirt open a little between two buttons, looking down, and saying, "Navel?"

A chorus of "Navel?" answered him, followed by giggles and laughs. Even kids this age bought into the joke.

Then his fingers hit the keys again, and all the kids joined him in the conclusion without missing a beat.

> *And marrow unto thy bones.*
> *Proverbs three: five six seven eight.*

He finished off with a jazzy version of the closing chord as the children begged for another one.

But there was an agenda tonight, as there always was, and Mary McPhee, one of the teachers, started urging the children back to the long tables that faced the whiteboard.

"Later," Brendan promised. "We'll do another song after class."

Steve King, a twenty-two-year-old who was about to graduate from the University of South Florida up the road, began passing out small squares of white paper. Brendan was very fond of Steve, knowing all the troubles the young man had been through, and was working with him to help him decide whether he had a true vocation as a priest. A handsome young man with light brown hair and eyes that were always warm, no matter how pained, Steve was always one of the first to volunteer when help was needed.

Two of the youngsters ran up to give Brendan hugs. Working with children, to his way of thinking, was the best part of being a parish priest. Their delight in life was always a fresh breeze through his soul.

Tonight the class had an unusual visitor, Chloe Ryder. Chloe was a lifelong member of St. Simeon's but she usually reserved her volunteering to the St. Vincent de Paul Society, a group devoted to aiding those in need of food and shelter. It had surprised Brendan when she'd offered to tell a story to RCIC after one of the students had expressed interest in origami. Chloe always seemed to be folding a piece of paper in her hands, turning out cute little animals and mythical beasts.

Chloe was an astonishingly beautiful young woman with blond hair and a perfect figure who owned her own law firm. She wasn't married, but Brendan figured that had to do with the still, silent core in her, a core that sometimes seemed as cold as liquid nitrogen.

She wasn't looking cold tonight though. She took her seat in front of the class and held up a large piece of white paper. "Tonight," she said, "I'm going to teach you how to fold a crane. Cranes are special, and while I show you how to fold, I'm going to tell you a story. After the demonstration, I'll work with you to help you fold yours, okay?"

All the heads nodded.

"Okay," Chloe said, and smiled. "This is called *sembazuru* in Japanese. It means 'thousand cranes.' It's a story that involves a little girl who was injured in the bombing of Hiroshima. Have you heard of Hiroshima?"

Some had, some hadn't, so Chloe explained. "Back in the

Second World War, we dropped an atomic bomb on a Japanese city called Hiroshima. A lot of people were killed, and a lot were made very sick by radiation."

Heads nodded, and Chloe started folding her paper. She continued with her story, and with each fold she held the paper up so the students could see what she had done.

"A little girl about your age—twelve—named Sadako Sasaki got sick with radiation poisoning. While she was in the hospital, she started using her medicine wrappers to fold into cranes."

More folds held up for the students to see.

"Finally, one day, someone asked Sadako why she was folding all these cranes. And she said that she thought if she folded a thousand of them, God would listen to her prayers.

"At first she prayed for her own healing, but as she saw the children around her sicken and die, she changed her prayer. She started praying for world peace."

Another fold.

"Sadako only finished 650 cranes before she died. But her story was published in newspapers all over the world, and people started folding and sending paper cranes to Hiroshima. When they built a memorial to the people who had died, a statue of Sadako was on top of it, holding a folded crane. And from the statue flowed streamers of origami cranes that had been sent in by people from all over the world."

She held up the completed crane. "Cranes just like this one. Even today people around the world still get together to make paper cranes, string them together, and send them to the memorial. And tonight we're making a string of cranes for world peace."

Brendan saw the moistening of Chloe's eyes as she told

the story, and saw a few other eyes in the room grow moist. His own throat tightened. "That's a beautiful story, Miss Chloe."

"It's true." She gave a small smile. "Okay, kids, let's get to work on yours."

Even with all the help, one boy of about twelve couldn't get his crane to come out right. Frustration clouded his face, and he looked on the edge of tears. Brendan sat beside him and put a hand on the boy's shoulder.

"Having a little problem there, Jimmy?"

"It won't work right, Father."

"How about I help you?"

Jimmy held up the piece of paper. "It's a mess!"

"It doesn't matter. It's just a piece of paper." Brendan accepted a fresh sheet from Mary, who was moving around the room, ready to step in as needed. "See? Now we have a fresh one."

"I'm just stupid. I can't do it."

Brendan's heart squeezed. He wondered how many times this boy had heard that accusation from an adult in his life, and wondered how he could step in. "You're not stupid. Not at all. You're just trying to do something new for the first time. Even grown-ups have trouble with that. Here, I'll show you how."

But somehow—accidentally on purpose—Brendan's folds turned into a paper airplane. "Hmm," he said, and tossed it away. It floated across the room, causing Jimmy to laugh. "I guess that wasn't it. Let's try again."

After Brendan committed a few more atrocities, and had Jimmy and other students in stitches, he wrote "dunce" across his last creation, a paper hat, and put it on. "Okay. I'm crying uncle over here. Chloe, help!"

Chloe was laughing, too. That was something Brendan had rarely if ever seen, a cause for celebration in itself. She joined them and with gentle prompting walked Jimmy through the making of a crane. He was so thrilled that he immediately wanted to do another one. Mary gave him another piece of paper, and Chloe kept an eye on the progress.

"We should send these to Japan when we're done," Steve said, watching the boy's progress.

"Yes, but not until after we hang them over the baptismal font for Saturday night," Brendan said.

While the dove was the traditional Christian symbol of peace, he knew the Catholic Church had a long history of incorporating—some called it consecrating—symbols from other cultures. He saw no reason not to adopt that pattern here. It would add to the children's feeling of belonging as they were welcomed into the faith at the Easter Vigil. And anything that encouraged children to feel like St. Simeon's was "their" church was fine with him. It was a decision he was prepared to defend if someone complained to the bishop.

Chloe was now using fine thread to hang the cranes from a frame made of balsa wood rods. As she lifted and twirled the rods, the birds seemed to flap their wings in flight. For Brendan, it called to mind Christ's baptism, and the Holy Spirit descending in the form of a dove. Yes, he would be comfortable standing up to the bishop if the whispering campaign continued.

For a moment, Brendan's face darkened. He was new to the diocese, and to St. Simeon's, but after twelve years as a navy chaplain he wasn't new to politics, gossip, furtive comments murmured in the chain of command. It didn't take a rocket scientist to figure out that the half dozen "friendly calls" he'd received from the chancery over the past six months had been responses to complaints. At times he felt like a marked man, however welcoming his parishioners seemed to be.

"What's wrong, Father?" Steve asked.

And that was Steve. The young man had an unerring emotional radar, able to pick up on subtle changes of voice, posture, or expression. It would serve him well in the priesthood, Brendan thought. Steve would be an excellent confessor and counselor.

Brendan cracked one of his trademark smiles. "Oh, it's nothing. I just think too much sometimes." He turned to the kids and brightened his voice. "How about another song? I know just the one."

To a chorus of unabashed agreement, another example of the gleeful faith he found so refreshing at St. Simeon's, he strutted back to the piano and began to hammer out a series of jazz chords, before he took up the song.

> *"O when the saints . . . go marchin' in*
> *"O when the saints go marchin' in."*

Steve King added a walking bass voice to those of the children.

> *"O Lord I want to be in that number,*
> *"When the saints go marchin' in."*

Steve was still humming the tune hours later, after the Holy Thursday celebration of the Last Supper, after hours of prayer at the Blessed Sacrament, after cleaning and locking up the parish hall. The evening's activities had been both beautiful and deeply moving, and he hadn't wanted to leave.

Walking to his car, he even started to sing out loud. The children's excitement had been contagious, and he found himself doing a little soft-shoe across the parking lot. "When the saints go marchin' in."

It was his own voice, and the rhythmic shuffle of his feet on the squeaky, damp grass that betrayed him. He never heard the footsteps behind him.

Nor the gunshot that killed him.

The man with the gun stood over Steve, unaware that he was watched. He waited, making sure the kid was dead, then turned to melt away into the shadows. Next was the priest. But first . . . first he was going to make that man's life a living hell, the way his own had been.

He was going to get even, in spades.

As he disappeared into the night, the watcher slipped away and made a quick call on his cell phone. "We got a problem," he said. "The cannon is loose, and there's a mess."

CHAPTER 1

Victor Singh's eyes scanned over the instruments, then out at the horizon, as he pushed the yoke forward and to the right. This was the critical moment. Up until this moment, he had been on a routine flight path, following instructions from air traffic control, crossing Tampa Bay, avoiding the landing and takeoff patterns for three major airports while gazing down at dolphins leaping in the wake of a fishing boat below. Just another small, private plane out circling so a pilot could log hours to keep his license current. But at this moment, he broke the pattern and heeled his aircraft to the south. The wide runways of MacDill Air Force Base came into view through the windshield. He focused on a smooth descent to one hundred feet. Attack altitude. Thirty seconds after his hard right turn, he crossed the perimeter of the airbase, aiming at the long, three-story, cement-block building, and pulled the lever beside his chair.

He shut down the flight simulator software. Thirty seconds. That's all he would need to enter the halls of glory.

At ten-thirty in the morning on Holy Saturday, St. Simeon's church was full of people. It was a joyous time,

Father Brendan thought as he watched the candidates and their families swirl around. This was the rehearsal for tonight's Easter Vigil Mass, and the baptism, first communion, and confirmation of the candidates. Most of the forty initiates were adults, joining the church for a variety of reasons. A dozen were older children who were joining with their families, the children who just the other day had been making origami cranes. One or two were adult Catholics who were receiving belated confirmations.

With them were family members who wanted to watch and small children who couldn't be left alone at home. It made for a pleasant melee, and Brendan couldn't help smiling, even if the director of religious education, Sally Tutweiler, a middle-aged matron with screaming red hair, was getting hoarse from trying to be heard over the commotion.

Finally, Peggy Randall, the church pianist, banged out a loud, dissonant chord on the piano. Even the three-year-olds stilled. For a moment.

Sally, having figured out she wasn't going to succeed by raising her voice, darted up to the ambo—the podium on the right of the altar—and took advantage of the microphone. "All right, everybody. Let's get to it. Catechumens in the front row, candidates in the next three rows, families all together please. Sponsors, sit next to your candidates. Parents, please restrain your small children. We don't want anyone to get hurt."

Another hubbub ensued as people headed for their designated pews. A baby started crying angrily. A boy of nine shoved a girl of eight, eliciting more wails. A father grabbed the boy's arm and drew him away, scolding quietly. The boy looked mutinous. Ah, people, Brendan thought happily. For all their faults and foibles, they were wonderful.

At last there was relative silence in the church. As much silence as there could be when a hundred people gathered and among them were young children.

"We'll begin with a prayer," Sally announced to the gathering. "Father Brendan will lead us. Father?"

He'd been standing toward the back, and now he made his way toward the altar, glad on this day of all days to be a priest and a pastor. There was so much joy in the church at this time of year, with the new people being welcomed into the faith and the resurrection about to be celebrated. His eyes lifted to the crucifix, the corpus covered in a purple Lenten shroud, and he felt the fatigue of the Lent season begin to seep away as Easter prepared to take its place.

Before he reached the altar, a little girl, maybe five or six, broke away from her mother and ran up onto the altar. Her mother called out in a horrified voice, but Brendan didn't mind. Gone were the days when only a priest or an altar boy could step into those sacred confines. He liked it when children wanted to explore the altar, and was more than happy to tell them all about everything up there.

But just before he reached the first step, the little girl called out, "Mommy? Mommy, why is the cross bleeding?"

Brendan froze. Everyone in the church froze. He saw the shock and disbelief on Sally's face, could feel the swiftly indrawn breaths from behind him.

A miracle? Brendan felt his heart slam. He'd hoped his entire life for a miracle, but now that he faced the possibility of one, he suddenly realized that a miracle could be a terrible thing. No, it had to be desecration of some kind. Suddenly angered, he took the two steps in one stride and swept swiftly around the altar. The little girl looked up at him with huge eyes.

"Why is it bleeding?" she asked.

He wanted to tell her it was a bad joke, that the dark stain on the floor was a bit of paint, but the coppery smell that suddenly assailed his nostrils told him otherwise. Copper and rot.

Oh my God!

Slowly, his neck almost refusing to bend, he looked up at the shrouded corpus and saw small stains where the nails in the hands were.

"Marci," said the mother, sounding frightened now, "come back here at once."

The little girl, with wide, brown eyes, looked up at him for another second. Then, apparently reading something in his face that frightened her, she turned and ran back to her mother.

The silence in the church was now as profound as a tomb. For endless seconds, Brendan warred with disbelief and shock. He had to do something. Finally, gathering a stray cogent thought or two, he turned and looked at Sally.

"Sally, move the rehearsal to the parish hall, please."

She nodded, her face as white as paste.

"I'll be over in a few minutes, all right?" He faced the crowd and raised his voice to be heard. "We, uh, seem to have had an act of vandalism," he said with remarkable steadiness. "So I'm going to ask you to move to the parish hall for rehearsal while we get this, uh, cleaned up." He managed what he hoped was a smile and not a grimace. "I'll rejoin you in a few minutes, but Sally will lead the opening prayer. Don't worry, she's as qualified as I am."

Some uncertain laughs greeted his poor foray into humor.

But no one moved. Curiosity, or dread, held them in their pews.

"Sally?"

Thus prompted, she seemed to come out of her trance. "Yes, let's go, everyone. Sponsors, lead the way, please. Joe, you have a key, don't you?"

God bless Sally. Brisk now, though still pale, she started shooing people out the side doors. A lot of heads craned to look at the crucifix, but no one disobeyed Sally and her catechists.

When the door closed on the last of them, Brendan forced himself to turn to the cross. Some part of his mind was praying almost frantically, but he was hardly aware of it. Anger filled him, anger and fear. No miracle, he told himself. He wouldn't be that fortunate. Or that cursed. Some idiot had gotten hold of some animal blood and. . . .

He never completed the thought. He'd bent down to loosen the shroud around the feet of the corpus, and had lifted it just a little.

Instead of wooden feet, carved so lovingly, the feet he found were swollen. Purple.

Somebody had been crucified in his church.

The call to 911 went surprisingly well, considering that the dispatcher couldn't seem to grasp the meaning of "crucified." Not that Brendan could blame her. He called from the phone in the sacristy, and felt as if he were caught in some kind of nightmare, speaking words that surely couldn't be his own. The dispatcher seemed to react the same way. Finally, he broke it down for her.

"Somebody," he said slowly, fighting to keep his voice calm, "has nailed a body to the cross in my church."

That got through to her. "Is he dead?"

"I believe so." He couldn't bear to imagine anything else. Nailed. Shrouded. Hanging there for who knew how long . . . Oh, God, what if that body was there during last night's service?

"Don't touch anything," the dispatcher warned him. "We'll have a car there in ten or fifteen minutes."

It sounded like ten or fifteen years. Brendan went to lock the church so no one else could come in. Turning the keys one by one. Locking himself inside with a corpse. The horror of it was beginning to reach him fully, to feel like an icy grip around his heart.

He had to tell Father Dominic what had happened. He had to make sure the assistant priest would fill in for him at the rehearsal. He had a feeling the police were going to want to talk to him for quite a long time.

And he didn't want to leave the body alone. Not like this. Someone needed to pray for the poor soul. Keeping his eyes averted from the altar, he went back to the sacristy and phoned the rectory next door.

"Father Dominic Montague."

For the first time in the ten days since Dominic had come to the parish, Brendan was glad the assistant priest was twenty years older—even if his experience seemed largely limited to jockeying a desk at the Diocese of Tampa. Because of his years, he would probably keep a cooler head.

"It's Brendan, Dominic. I need you to go over to the parish hall and take over for me at the rehearsal."

"The parish hall?"

"I had to move everybody out of the church." Brendan drew a deep breath and looked up at the icon of Our Lady of Guadalupe that had been donated by the Thursday Rosary

Group. "There's, uh, been a serious desecration at the church." He couldn't bring himself to say *murder.* The word wouldn't come even though he didn't know what else it could be. "I'm . . . waiting for the police."

"What happened?"

"Trust me on this. You don't want to know. You'll find out soon enough. Will you take over for me?"

"Of course I will. Anything special you want me to do?"

"Sally will handle almost all of it; that's her job. Me, I just show up to say the opening and closing prayer and lend an interested presence, if you follow me."

"I follow. Consider me on my way."

"Thanks."

Brendan hung up the phone and realized he was sweating profusely. Not because the church was warm, because it wasn't. Thanks to the modern miracle of air-conditioning, the church, even when the Tampa heat did its worst, was usually as cool as a cave.

Or a tomb. He shuddered, letting the tension run through him, giving himself a moment actually to *feel* what was happening here in this sanctuary, in this holiest of places. To accept the fact that one of the worst evils of all had crossed the threshold and made a mockery of one of the holiest symbols of his faith.

Evil. Human evil to be sure, but evil all the same. It should never have trespassed here.

But it had. And he had a duty to perform. Returning to the sanctuary, he sat in the front pew and began to pray for the repose of the soul of the person who hung on the cross.

Strangers crawled all over the church and altar, strangers in uniforms, taking pictures, dusting everything for fingerprints. The body still hung on the cross, and very little had been disturbed yet. Even the shroud remained in place, concealing the victim.

Once Brendan had given his brief statement of events, he had been forgotten. He was, in a way, surprised they hadn't told him to leave. Not that he would have gone. He was already on his fifth rosary for the victim. The repetition of the rosary, like a mantra, helped him meditate on God. Although right now he was finding it difficult to concentrate.

A man in a suit paused beside him, saying nothing, as if respecting Brendan's silent prayer. When Brendan looked up, the man slid into the pew beside him, flashing a badge. "I'm Detective Matthew Diel. Tampa homicide."

"Brendan Quinlan," Brendan replied.

"I know, Father."

Detective Diel, though only in his early to mid-thirties, had a careworn look. He had dark eyes, thick dark hair, and a nose that had been broken once. He also had an interesting scar slashing his cheek, almost a groove. Brendan wondered about it, but didn't ask.

"So," said Matthew Diel, flipping open a notebook, "you found the body?"

"I guess. Actually, a small child claimed the cross was bleeding. We were having our Easter Vigil rehearsal in here. I came up to investigate and found the body."

Diel nodded as if he already knew this. "How many people were in here?"

"Conservatively, about a hundred. They should all still be at the parish hall, if you want to check on that."

"Who has access to the church?"

"You mean with a key?"

Diel's dark eyes, devoid of feeling, settled on him. "I'm assuming you keep the church locked when it's not in use."

"Actually, we keep it open from six-thirty in the morning until eight at night on weekdays. Then we lock it up. On weekends it's usually opened around two on Saturday afternoon, except for special days like this. We probably unlocked the doors around ten this morning. And on Sunday morning we open at six-thirty, and close at four in the afternoon."

Diel nodded once more, as if the exact schedule wasn't important, but he did scribble it down. Interesting man.

Then Brendan realized he hadn't given the information the man really wanted. "This week was different."

Diel's head lifted. "How so?"

"It's Holy Week." Seeing that Diel's face betrayed no comprehension, he continued. "We had the Mass of the Last Supper Thursday evening at seven-thirty. It was over a little after nine. We followed it with adoration."

"Adoration?"

Brendan wondered how much he was going to need to explain to this man, then decided to go with the bare facts. Let the man ask what he wanted to know.

"We place the consecrated host out where it can be seen by everyone. So they can pray in its presence. So we can keep a vigil with our Lord." He added, "It's in remembrance of Jesus's suffering in the Garden of Gethsemane. We keep a vigil the way the apostles did."

"Who was here?"

"Father Dominic Montague and I, and any number of other people. They came and went as time allowed. Dominic and I stayed until midnight, when we locked the host away."

"Did anyone stay after that?"

"No. In fact, I locked the church up myself."

Diel scribbled for a minute. "What about last night?"

"We had the Stations of the Cross last night at seven-thirty. We locked up about ten."

"So the church is always locked overnight?"

"Always."

"Who has the keys?"

He rattled off the list: himself; Father Dominic; the facilities manager, Merv Haskell; the liturgist, Amelia Morgan; the parish secretary, Lucy Gallegos; Sally Tutweiler, the Director of Religious Education; and the sacristan, Mona Rivera. "I think that's it. You might check with Merv Haskell, though. He'd know if anyone else has a key. He's in charge of them."

"And if someone lost a key?"

"If they reported it, he'd know."

"What's Mr. Haskell's number?"

"I'll have to check my Rolodex. Listen, would it help if I called Lucy to come in? Like most good secretaries, she knows everything." He gave a wry, humorless smile. "I'm just the pastor."

Something in Diel's gaze flickered, and a faint smile came to his lips. At last, a human response. "That would help," Diel said.

Brendan started to rise. "I want to be here when you take the body down."

Diel's eyes snapped to his face. "Why?"

"Because I want to . . . take care of it. That person deserves some spiritual care, however late it may be."

"You can't—"

"Of course he can, Matt," said an edgy female voice from behind them.

Startled, Brendan turned to see Chloe Ryder standing in the aisle behind them. Stunning in white shorts and a dark blue polo shirt, Chloe looked like the original ice queen. He was a man, like any other man, and he noticed attractive women. But Chloe . . . There was something about her that was so hands-off he often wondered what her story was. Not that she would tell him. He wondered if Sister Philomena even knew, and Sister Phil and Chloe were apparently best friends.

All he knew about Chloe Ryder was that she'd been a cop once, and now was a lawyer. He'd heard whispers that she had something awful in her past, but no one seemed willing to let him in on the gossip. Which, he reminded himself, was a good thing. He shouldn't even be curious.

Her blue eyes were sometimes as cold as chips of ice, but right now they showed an amazing heat. Rage. This was such a completely new side of her to Brendan that he almost failed to greet her.

"Well, well, well," said Matt Diel, rising and facing her. "Chloe. It's been a while."

"Not long enough," Chloe said flatly.

Brendan looked from one to the other and wondered at the electricity he felt between them, not unlike the tingle in the air before a lightning strike. Antagonism?

"You know we can't let him touch the body," the detective said.

"Sure you can."

"And it's none of your business."

Chloe stepped forward, her face mere inches from Matt's. "Oh, it's my business all right. It's my parish, my church. My priest wants to bless the victim. That's the victim's right."

"If he's Catholic."

Chloe made an impatient sound. "He is. Why else would he be nailed to that cross?"

"The murderer . . ."

"Oh, the murderer may be Catholic, too. But so is the victim. You mark my words."

"I can't have anybody messing with the DB. Forensics—"

"Forensics is going to mess with the DB. And you know damn well that if they make a note of Father Brendan's viewing the body and blessing it, it isn't going to mess up a thing, Matt."

"Oh, hell." Diel sighed. "How did you hear about this?"

Chloe almost smiled, just a little lift of one corner of her mouth. "I have a scanner."

"I should have known. Okay, okay, I'll talk to the criminologists."

"Do more than talk."

"Don't turn this into a religious issue."

"It *is* a religious issue."

To Brendan's surprise, Matt Diel actually grinned. "You're still tough as nails."

Her answering smile was chilling. "It's how I get by."

CHAPTER 2

As Matt walked back to the altar, Brendan looked at Chloe. "Thank you."

She shrugged. "I'll hang around, Father. I know how to deal with these guys. I used to be one of them."

Which was the most forthcoming thing she'd ever said to him. He wondered if he would ever know her.

"I need to make some calls," he said. "The bishop." Oh, God, the bishop! "And Lucy."

"Sure. Go ahead. I won't let them take him away before you get back."

"Thank you," he said again, suddenly very grateful that this woman was made of steel. Right now he needed someone like her to depend on. "Do you think they can be done in time for Vigil?"

"I'll ask Deil. I think so. If they hustle."

He wondered if it mattered. If he would even be able to make himself hold the Vigil in this church, after this. "It might be better to use the parish hall."

"Maybe. Up to you, Father. But you better decide soon, because the people who were going to help decorate the altar are starting to arrive, and the cops are sending them away."

"How'd you get in?"

"I have my methods."

He imagined she did. And for the first time in his life, he was grateful to escape a church.

The relief followed him across the small courtyard to the rectory, where he sat at Lucy's desk and used her Rolodex to call her and Merv, and tell them to come in immediately. They were both home, thank heaven, and upon hearing what had happened, they promised to be right over.

The bishop, well, he had to deal with the bishop's gate-keeper, a priest he had never really liked. A man who would undoubtedly hold it against him personally that something so revolting had happened at St. Simeon's.

He did take some small satisfaction, however, in the way the monsignor's breath sucked in when he heard what had happened. This unhappy crucifixion might have happened at St. Simeon's, but the diocese would have to deal with it. That meant Monsignor Crowell, the alligator at the gate, would have to deal with the public relations nightmare. Sometimes there *was* justice.

"What the hell is going on over there, Quinlan?" Crowell barked.

"I told you, Monsignor."

"What you *didn't* tell me is why things like this are happening in *your* parish."

It sounded like the navy all over again, Brendan thought. Having spent twelve years as a navy chaplain, he'd discovered that anything remotely related to his faith, the chapel, or his congregation was always his fault. He didn't bother to argue. However, having spent half of those twelve years on a ship, seasick every one of them, he figured he was better off right now. Just on that front alone. Which gave him some patience.

"Monsignor," he said as gently as he could, "my parish can hardly be responsible because some sick, evil person decided to commit an act of such enormity."

"No? Well, I might point out that nothing like this has happened anywhere else. And nothing like this ever happened before you arrived here."

"I should hope not," Brendan said. Thinking of the poor soul in the church reminded him that there were worse things than Monsignor Crowell. "I would hate to think this is a diocesan practice."

"Quinlan!"

"Sorry."

"Your levity will be your undoing."

Brendan suspected that it already had been, with Crowell at least. Could he help it if he dealt with stress through humor and music? Or that he loved a good joke? Well, of course he could help it. He just refused to allow himself to be turned into a dour, judgmental, bitter man. The Catholic Church already had enough of them.

"I wasn't being humorous, Monsignor. I was being honest." There, let the old boy chew on that one. "Of course nothing like this has happened before. And, God willing, it will never happen again. But unfortunately, it *did* happen. I presume you want me to make every effort to help the police?"

The answer should have been a prompt "yes." This was, however, the church hierarchy he was dealing with, and in his experience if the hierarchy could find a way to be secretive, it would do so on principle. He was sure they didn't want a loose cannon like him shooting off his mouth without supervision. Or maybe up there they thought of him as a loose "canon." The pun brought a grim smile to his mouth.

"Let me talk to the bishop, Quinlan."

The bishop, the Most Reverend Arthur A. Rourke, was a kind and gentle man who probably had no idea that he was surrounded by a moat of politically motivated alligators. Then Brendan sighed inwardly. He was being unfair and he knew it. Most of the people in the chancery weren't like Crowell, who, he would bet, had his eye firmly fixed on cardinatial red.

"Of course, Monsignor. But I will point out that the police are here *now,* and they want to talk to some of the parish employees."

"Well, of course they must cooperate," Crowell said, as if realizing he was walking perilously close to a cliff edge. "I imagine no one knows anything anyway."

"Except for the murderer or murderers, I'm sure you're right."

"Just see to it that no one talks to the press. Any information will have to come through the diocese."

"I assumed so. I'll warn everyone."

Without saying good-bye, Crowell hung up. He always ended conversations abruptly, at least when dealing with Brendan.

Sitting at Lucy's desk, in an all-too-rare moment of solitude, Brendan closed his eyes and allowed himself to feel the gravity of this day, of the event that had unfolded in his church. Allowed himself to feel some of the grief and shock that any mind could be so twisted, that any human being had been killed such a way.

He hoped to God he'd never seen the victim before in his life.

Unfortunately, he was not to be so lucky.

As he was coming out of the side door of the rectory into the courtyard, Brendan ran into Father Dominic Montague, who was coming in through the back gate, ostensibly on his way back from the parish hall.

A tall man with graying hair and eyes the color of gunmetal, he was an imposing figure. The kind of figure Brendan had often wished he were. Everything about Dominic suggested that he was destined for the hierarchy. Monsignor at the very least. So what was he doing as parochial vicar under a much younger man? Brendan couldn't figure it out, and his network of friends didn't have a clue. And if Dominic knew, he wasn't saying either.

"What's going on, Brendan?" he asked bluntly.

"There's been a crucifixion in the church," Brendan answered with equal bluntness. As soon as he spoke, he wanted to call the words back. They showed nothing of his usual tact or consideration. In fact, they sounded almost like a joke.

That was Dominic's initial reaction. He could see the flicker of impatience in the older man's gaze, then saw realization dawn. "You're not kidding, are you."

"I wish to God I was. Is the rehearsal over?"

"All except the cops trying to get everyone's names, addresses, and phone numbers. It's making them all very uncomfortable. And people are demanding to know what's going on."

"Oh, man." Torn, Brendan hesitated. On the one hand, there was the victim in the church. On the other, his newest flock members were being needlessly upset. What would any of them know about this? They'd all arrived in the church this morning *after* Sally and her teachers. "Let me see what I can do. Is there a detective over there named Matt Diel?"

"No detectives, just uniforms."

"All right, hang on a minute."

From the courtyard, the entrance to the church led directly into the sacristy, where priests robed for Mass. From there, he walked directly onto the altar. Detective Diel was still there, he saw, making notes and talking to one of the criminologists. Chloe was still there, too, sitting in the front pew, her arms folded, her gaze watchful, looking, he thought, like a Valkyrie ready to spring into action.

"Detective Diel," Brendan called out.

At once the detective turned. He said something to the criminologist and came over to Brendan. The body, thank heaven, was still shrouded, though men were now on ladders poring over the huge wooden cross.

"Yes, Father?" Diel seemed amiable enough, but Brendan didn't trust the friendliness.

"I want to know why your men are upsetting all the people in the parish hall."

"We need to know who they are. We might need to question them later."

"The church can provide that information. But you need to stop upsetting them. They're supposed to come back into this church tonight for their Rites of Initiation. I don't like you scaring my flock away."

"I don't like people being murdered either," Matt said flatly. "But it happens anyway."

"Can you give me one good reason why you need to treat these people like criminals?"

"There's been a murder."

Point non plus. Brendan felt irritation rising in him. "You have no reason to think any of them are involved."

"Father, they were here when the body was found. One of them might have been here for . . . another reason."

Brendan's face set against the anger he was feeling. "Do you really think a new convert would want to do something like this? Why would they be here if they felt that way? This was a thrust at the heart of the church."

Matt nodded. "It could also be directed at *you,* Father."

That set Brendan back on his heels. He didn't know what to say.

"This is a bizarre way to murder someone," Matt continued almost conversationally. "It screams *message.*"

"Yeah," said Chloe, joining them. "It does. But it could just as well be a message to anyone in the parish."

Brendan told himself not even to think about that. He had more important concerns. "You have a crime to investigate, but I have a parish to shepherd. Your men are getting in the way of that."

Now it was the detective's turn to look taken aback. "I'm doing my job, Father. I'm sorry it's making your people upset, but whoever's hanging on that cross was probably pretty upset too. Sometimes it's an upsetting world." He turned to Chloe. "You of all people should know that."

"Don't you *dare,*" Chloe snapped. "Don't you dare disrespect the victim and my priest and my parish by making this about me. You can question these people as well on Monday as you can today. The parish has their names."

Matt seemed about to say something but cut himself off

with a shake of his head and turned to Brendan. "Okay. I'll stop taking names and numbers. As long as you promise me you can get them for me if I need them."

"Call my secretary Monday morning. And be nice to her. She's not as easygoing as I am."

Chloe gave a half smile. "Go, Father," she said.

Matt scowled at her, and Brendan felt the electricity swirling between them again, a snap and crackle that was almost tangible.

"You're grasping at straws," she told him flatly. "This wasn't done by someone who's been working hard for the last nine months to get into the church."

"Hey, Matt?" called one of the criminologists from the ladder to the right of the cross. The hand was now uncovered, and Brendan felt his stomach turn over.

"Yeah?" Matt answered, turning.

"We're not going to get the body off this thing. We'll have to take it all down together."

"Why not?"

"You wanna come up and look at these nails?"

Matt shook his head. "No thanks."

"We'd need the cross anyway."

"So take the whole thing down."

Some part of Brendan felt he should object. The cross, after all, had been the gift of a parish member nearly fifty years ago when the church had been built. It was as much a part of St. Simeon's as the stained-glass windows and outdated confessionals. It had survived the post-Vatican II upheavals, when churches began to take down their statuary and move their crucifixes from the altars in search of total ecumenism, to the point where many new churches were identifiable as Catholic only by the sign at the driveway.

But he also knew that cross could no longer stay in St. Simeon's. Not after this.

It hung by chains from the domed ceiling over the altar, and came down with little trouble except for its weight. Four men had to grip it from the bottom, and the men on the ladders steadied the cross beam. But down it came, in fits and jerks, until it was lying on the floor of the altar area.

"Oh, Blessed Mother," whispered a voice behind Brendan. He turned and found Sister Philomena LeBlanc standing a little behind him, dressed in her usual jeans and T-shirt emblazoned with the parish logo. Sister Phil, as everyone called her was a tall, rail-thin redhead who liked to make her third-grade students laugh by describing herself as a stop sign. She always had a smile. Or usually did. Right now she was staring in horror.

Reaching out, she took Brendan's hand. "Chloe called me. Are you all right, Father?"

"Oh sure, Sister," he said, on autopilot. He was thinking about the body on the cross, about the unfortunate victim. About what he needed to do. Without another word, he approached the body. Kneeling beside the cross, he began to murmur prayers for the dead. Too late for an anointing. He felt bad about that. Phil came to kneel across from him, joining his prayers. For a minute, everyone in the church observed a moment of silence.

Then someone—Brendan didn't notice who—leaned over and lifted the shroud from the face.

His world tumbled, shock slammed into him until he couldn't breathe. He knotted his hands together until his knuckles turned white, rocking slowly on his knees, murmuring, "No no no no no . . ."

It was Steve King.

CHAPTER 3

"Y ou sanitized the area?"

"Completely," the watcher answered. "We mucked it up so much, nobody is going to be able to tell where that kid was murdered."

"What did you do with the body?" the second man asked.

"No," said the first man. "I don't want details."

It was always this way, the watcher thought. They'd set their ugly little balls rolling, but they didn't want to sully their hands or their minds with the detail work. It was left to people like him to take care of things and keep their noses clean.

"You can read about it in the paper," the watcher said finally.

"Not the paper," said the second man.

Hell, what did these idiots think was going to happen? You couldn't murder people and not get in the paper. Not unless you made them vanish completely, and vanishing wasn't in their plan. Not at all.

"I took care of it," the watcher said flatly. "Nobody's going to figure out what really happened."

"That's all that matters," said the first man, giving a stern look to the second. "Any idea why the cannon did this?"

The watcher shook his head. "No. You picked him because he wanted the priest. It's anybody's guess why he took this kid down."

"Well, so long as he can finish his job . . ." The second man's voice trailed away.

Yeah, thought the watcher. Keep your eye on the ball and never mind the messy trail of bodies in its wake.

Maybe he was in the wrong line of business.

With some difficulty, the cross had been carried out, the body of Steve King still attached. Because the press had already gathered out front, the crucified body had been thickly shrouded in black plastic.

Matt Diel, who'd already yanked all the information he was going to get at this time from the criminologists, turned to watch Chloe Ryder. She sat in the front pew, folding delicate little animals out of small squares of white paper. A collection was growing on the wooden seat beside her.

She appeared to be oblivious to the doings around her, but Matt knew her better than that. If he knew her at all, that was. She was an enigma to him, and had been since they'd met during their days in uniform. She'd had a good nose, and he'd figured back then that they'd both be homicide detectives someday. Instead, Chloe had left the force under a cloud, and he'd made the squad.

And now she was sitting in the front row of this church, driving him nuts with those endless paper creations when he knew damn well she wasn't missing a thing. And still, damn her, every bit as beautiful as ever.

Except colder now. She hadn't been cold when he'd

known her. Right now he felt as if he'd get frostbite if he came within six feet.

But he'd never been one to be deterred by a little danger. So he marched over there. She was plugged into this parish, and she'd better be willing to talk.

He sat in the pew behind her, hoping to unnerve her as she was unnerving him. No such luck. She didn't even glance over her shoulder at him, nor did her fingers pause as they continued to make tiny folds.

"Okay," he said, an indirect acknowledgment of her attitude. "What do you know about the vic?"

"A little." She kept right on folding, didn't look at him. Now he wished he'd taken a seat beside her. "Twenty-two," she continued. "About to graduate from USF with a degree in business administration. Seriously considering going to the seminary in the fall."

"He wanted to be a *priest?*"

She held up a tiny white unicorn and turned it around, as if trying to decide if it was complete. "You're letting your prejudice show, Matt."

"It's not prejudice. It just beats me why any kid that age would want to give up all the fun in life."

"Women, you mean?"

"And other stuff."

"I see." She set the unicorn down, apparently content with it, and pulled another square of paper out of her purse. "I'm sure a lot of priests don't see it as giving up all the fun in life. In fact, I read a study not too long ago that says the majority of priests are very happy in their work."

"Really."

"Really."

Stonewall. God, she was a good stonewall. "What else do you know about him?"

"He was kind. A good young man. Well respected in the church. A great volunteer. He was working his way through school. A job at some fast-food place, I think."

"But you don't know which one?"

She shook her head.

"Parents?"

"Dad's dead. About eight years ago. Mom's in prison. Hit-and-run DUI with serious bodily injury. You'll find that Steve King was taken out of the home a couple of times because he was abused. Apparently she'd go on drunken binges, beat him up, get sent to rehab, and stay clean for a while."

"Yeah, I get the picture. So he was running away."

Now Chloe did turn and look at him, but the victory felt hollow. "The church doesn't want people who are running away. It's not a good place to hide."

He didn't answer that. All he felt was another surge of antagonism toward her. That bothered him, too. He couldn't figure why he kept wanting to shake her out of her icy composure. What the hell difference did it make to him?

"Was he gay?" He didn't know where the question came from, and it was out before he even realized it.

"Stereotyping, Matt?"

He felt defensive. Thinking "outside the box" was one of his strong points. "What the hell do you mean?"

"Oh, just that nobody would want to be a priest and give up women for the rest of his life unless he was gay, right?"

He leaned forward until his face was just a couple of inches from hers. He met those glacial blue eyes of hers and ignored their chill. "Let's get something straight here. I'm working a murder case. I want to know every possible thing that might have caused somebody to murder that poor kid. Are we straight on that?"

"Sure." Her inflection revealed nothing.

"So get off your high horse and quit acting like I'm threatening your turf here. I'm trying to find out what kind of fucker would nail that young man to a cross. And if it hasn't crossed your mind yet, it's certainly crossed mine that it was one hell of a barbaric act."

Her gaze never wavered. "He was gay."

"Drugs?"

"I don't know where he would have fit them in. He was motivated enough to be getting ready to graduate *summa cum laude,* he worked enough to support himself with some student loans, and he seemed to be here all the rest of the time. He was clean, Matt."

Matt nodded and settled back in the pew. "Not a lot of motivation for a murder."

At last Chloe's expression changed. For the first time he saw something like grief in her face. "No," she said quietly. "There was no reason at all for anyone to want to murder him."

But both he and Chloe knew that couldn't be true. There was almost always a reason for killing, however shallow or crazy it might be. Most of the time, the motive leapt up and bit him on the nose: greed, fear, hatred, anger.

A murder like this, though . . . Matt looked toward the altar, the absent crucifix as vivid to him as if it still hung there. A murder like this required something more than simple motivation. There was a message in this one.

He looked down at his pad, at all the scrawled notes. "Who should I talk to about the vic?"

"Father Brendan. He was Steve's spiritual counselor."

"What's that?"

"Basically, he was helping Steve decide if he had a true vocation."

"Gotcha. Who else?"

"Merv Haskell, he's the facilities manager. Steve helped out a lot. And Sally Tutweiler, the Director of Religious Education. Steve was one of her catechists."

"Anything else?"

Again she looked at him. "He was an Eagle Scout, Matt. Until recently, anyway. I think he sent back his badge after that court case."

Matt sighed heavily. "He *had* to have done something to really piss somebody off."

Chloe shook her head. "Maybe he just got in the way of somebody who's pissed off at the church. Or at someone in the church."

"How long has Father Brendan been here?"

"A little over six months."

"Smooth sailing?"

"Most everybody seems to like him. But you know how that goes."

"What about the other priest . . ." He flipped through the pages of his book. "Dominic Montague."

"He got here about ten days ago."

That brought Matt's head up. "Where from?"

"The chancery. He was on the marriage tribunal."

"What's the marriage tribunal?"

"They decide whether to annul a Catholic marriage."

"What if they say no?"

"Theoretically, the Catholic never marries again. Or commits adultery and can never receive the sacraments again."

"I'm surprised *he* wasn't the victim."

At that Chloe astonished him with a small smile. "Does make you wonder, doesn't it?"

Lucy Gallegos, the parish secretary, had cried freely, but was now sitting with reddened eyes, staring blindly at nothing at all. Sister Phil patted her back and wished there was some magic word of comfort she could offer. Everyone liked Steve. *She'd* liked Steve. She'd never taught him, but he'd graduated from St. Simeon's high school, and she'd gotten to know him when he was still a student, during those rough years before he was able to leave home and make it on his own. During the rough years when he'd wrestled with his sexual preference.

The phone rang and Lucy answered. "St. Simeon's . . . yes, it's true." She paused for a moment, listening to a question, and let out a silent sigh. "Yes, tonight at seven-thirty. And all the masses for tomorrow are still as scheduled in the parish bulletin." Another pause. "Yes, we're all shocked. Thank you, I'll tell him."

She hung up the phone and turned to Phil. "I guess I'm going to be answering the same questions over and over today."

There was, Phil thought, at least the merest trace of the feisty Lucy she'd come to know and love over the years. Lucy was never quite so happy as when standing her own in a staff meeting or, lately, against the few malcontents who came to her with gossip about Father Brendan. If a celibate priest and a married grandmother could be the proverbial match made in heaven, Lucy and Brendan were that match.

"How's he holding up?" Phil asked with a nod toward Brendan's office.

"About like you'd expect, Sister. He's trying to be brave and get through the weekend. But I'd hate to be his pillow-case come Sunday night."

"Should I pop in to say hi?" Phil asked.

One of the benefits of a close working relationship between pastor and parish secretary was that Lucy not only knew Brendan's schedule, but his heart and needs as well.

Lucy shook her head. "He's probably rewriting his Easter homily right now. He can't ignore what happened, or he'll seem cold."

"And leave too many unanswered questions to gossip," Phil said.

"Exactly. So he'll have to find a way to work it into the Easter readings, without turning his Easter homilies into a eulogy. I'm guessing he'll be at it most of the day. You know how he agonizes over homilies anyway."

"I sure wouldn't want to have to write this one," Phil agreed.

A movement outside caught her eye, and she looked out the window to see Chloe exchanging words with the detective. Judging by the set of Chloe's jaw, they weren't pleasant words, and they seemed to be growing more heated.

"I'll let you get back to your work," Phil said, with a gentle squeeze of Lucy's shoulder.

"Blessed are the peacemakers?" Lucy asked, following Phil's gaze out the window.

Phil was already turning to the door. "Blessed are they who keep their friends from saying something they'll regret later."

"If you want me out of here by five o'clock, then stop interfering and let me get back to my job," Matt said, his voice echoing around the courtyard as Phil emerged from the rectory.

Chloe's eyes flicked over to Phil before returning to Matt. "Do your job. Just don't listen to rumors, okay? If you want the straight scoop, talk to those of us who spend time with him."

"Rumors are part of a cop's business, Chloe. You know that. It's my investigation to run. And I'm going to run it my way."

With that he brushed past Chloe, barely acknowledging Phil with a nod, and stormed back into the church. Chloe muttered a curse and turned to her friend.

"What a troll."

Phil knew better than to ask for elaboration. If Chloe wanted to talk, she would. If she didn't, nothing short of torture would get another word out of her. Instead, she chose an open-ended line of approach. "How are you holding up?"

"This is going to be a nightmare," Chloe replied. "Now some busybody got hold of one of his men and said Father Brendan and Steve were lovers."

Unwelcome anger surged in Phil. "Some people have no shame."

"I don't know who I'm more angry with. The . . . *thing* who did that to Steve, or the one who seems to want to nail Father to the cross with him."

Phil nodded. Few people alive knew Chloe well enough to gauge her moods. Phil thought she was one of them. And while her friend's anger was readily apparent, there was more beneath the anger in those glinting blue eyes. This was personal, beyond simply having happened in Chloe's parish. Ancient history between Chloe and the detective, perhaps? That was Phil's guess, but she knew how likely it was that

Chloe would come out and explain. It wasn't going to happen.

"Those rumors float around all the time about the clergy and religious," Phil said. "As far as most people are concerned, half the priests and nuns are gay, and the other half are sleeping with each other. I'm sure this guy is smart enough to recognize that."

"Don't bet on it. And if it gets out that the cops are even suspicious enough to check it out, you know what that's going to do to Father Brendan. You of all people should know."

The remark cut, but Phil bit back her reply, reminding herself that Chloe had never said an unkind word to her. She could be terse, and often opaque, but she'd never been unkind. Phil applied the doctrine of charity, taking it as a given that Chloe hadn't meant to hurt her, and thus had another agenda in mind.

"What do you want, Chloe?" she asked simply.

Chloe's eyes had shifted to the rectory. "Someone's going to have to do damage control. Father hasn't been in the diocese long enough that the people downtown will swarm to his defense. You've been through this before."

"In my case it was true," Phil said. "And I had to move halfway across the country to leave the rumors behind. I'm not sure I'd be much help."

There was another concern, one that Phil didn't voice. If she got too deeply involved in the investigation, would her own past come out? As a nun, she was celibate, so her sexual orientation was irrelevant. Still, she knew how some people thought. Especially parents. As a teacher, she knew what that could mean.

"I don't blame you for being reluctant," Chloe said, as if

reading her mind. For someone who was such a sphinx her-self, her insight into others constantly amazed Phil.

"Look, Phil," Chloe continued. "I'd hate to see you hurt again. You know that. But I don't trust Matt Deil to get this right, and Father Brendan doesn't have the contacts to cover his own ass."

"He wouldn't think to call them in if he had them," Phil said. "He's not the political type."

Chloe nodded. "So we have to do it for him. And I'm going to be . . . busy on another angle."

Phil's eyes narrowed. "You're going to investigate it on your own, aren't you?"

"Somebody has to do it correctly. Matt's got one thing right—this *is* a message crime. But he's looking for all the wrong messages. The kind of person who'd do . . . *that* . . . isn't going to stop there. That was only the beginning."

Phil felt a chill creep down her spine and let out an in-voluntary shudder. Almost without thinking of it, she crossed herself. "And deliver us from evil."

"Sometimes," Chloe said, "we have to help deliver our-selves."

Dominic Montague picked up the phone in his personal office and dialed the private number he'd been given for Monsignor Crowell, a line only the monsignor answered. "Dominic," he said cryptically when Crowell answered the private line. "You heard?"

"Damn straight I heard," Crowell answered. "And I've heard more. Quinlan and that youth were lovers."

Dominic closed his eyes, disgust and anger filling him. "Why the hell wasn't I told this before I came down here?"

"Because *you* were supposed to get the proof without appearing to have any bias. Quietly. Now we've got a public mess on our hands, and the Church gets another black eye."

Dominic understood the Church's methods of operation. A great effort was made to avoid public scandal and keep private the failings and foibles of the priesthood. In cases where a priest was alcoholic, such secrecy made sense. Send the guy away to rehab and bring him back, saying nothing except that he'd been ill. But there were some cover-ups that stuck in his craw, and this was a type that made him want to choke.

"Do you know it for a fact?"

Crowell snorted. "If I knew it for a fact, what would I need *you* for? But now the cops are asking if Quinlan has any history of homosexuality. How would I know? He's been in the diocese less than a year."

Such, thought Dominic with irony, were the problems of institutional secrecy. He found himself wishing for his relatively quiet job with the tribunal. He'd never been cut out to be a parish priest. He was a man who preferred the company of books and others like himself, not the world at large, with all its messy problems. Although some of the stories he'd read in connection with annulment proceedings had been pretty sordid.

But even less than being a parish priest did he like being a spy. And he'd been sent to St. Simeon's to spy on Brendan Quinlan because the complaints against him were attracting attention at the chancery. Naturally, he hadn't been told the source or type of complaint. He'd just been told to "get down there and find out what the devil is going on."

After ten days here, he didn't know "what was going on," but he had a fair idea of what he did know. And as much as he hated to annoy Monsignor Crowell, who could be a formidable enemy, he was bound to speak the truth. "I haven't seen one thing out of line down here. Brendan works his tail off, Monsignor. If he has a lover, I couldn't begin to imagine where he fits it in."

"Maybe he's behaving because you're there, and he doesn't know you yet."

Dominic felt his jaw tighten. "You know, if the cops are asking if Brendan's gay, then they're suggesting that the young victim was his lover. And they're playing with the idea that Brendan might have killed him."

"Ta-da!" Crowell said sarcastically.

"I'll tell you something, Monsignor. Getting a body up on that cross dead would have required more than one person. Or a supernatural act. Getting it up there alive would have been impossible."

"Our Lord was crucified—"

"Our Lord," Dominic said firmly, "was crucified by a group of armed Roman soldiers. Not by one single man."

Crowell harrumphed.

"It occurs to me, Monsignor," Dominic said quietly, "that you may be barking up the wrong tree." Then, without waiting for the blast that was sure to come in response, Dominic hung up the phone.

And felt better than he had in the entire two weeks since he'd heard he was being sent here and why. Even if it did mean he'd never see his cozy office at the chancery again.

The killer bought both of the major local newspapers that day. And he couldn't believe that the murder wasn't getting even a mention anywhere. It had been two days. It should have turned up somewhere today, even if only as a small mention. They had to have found the body Friday morning.

The news should certainly have been on the TV last night. Standing in front of a Catholic church and talking about a body found in the parking lot was a sure bet for a good visual.

But nothing.

Uneasiness began to prickle at the nape of his neck. What if the kid wasn't dead? But no, he'd made sure of that. Very sure. So . . . what if someone had seen him do it? What if they'd taken the body away?

But why would anybody do that? Why?

His hands were shaking as he put the newspaper down. Something was wrong, terribly wrong. But he had to be sure to get that effing priest before it was too late.

CHAPTER 4

Chloe found Brendan shooting hoops at ten o'clock that night behind the school. She stood just outside the pool of light and watched him run, dribble, shoot, run, dribble shoot. She could hear his labored breathing, and when he swung around quickly, she could see the sweat fly from him.

Around and around he went, missing more shots than he made, which told her a lot. Brendan played a mean game of basketball. Three-pointers were his meat and drink. Right now he looked like a man trying to drive himself to the brink of exhaustion and beyond.

The church kept the outdoor basketball court lighted all night long for the benefit of kids who had nothing else to do. Usually, any night of the week, this court would be busy until well after midnight. Tonight, except for Brendan, it was empty. Word had spread. Nobody wanted their kids playing late at night in a place where someone had been killed.

Finally, she stepped into the light and gave him a chance to notice her. At first he seemed inclined to ignore her, but finally he stopped, caught the ball and tucked it under his arm, and faced her. He wiped the sweat from his face with the hem of his sodden T-shirt.

Chloe spoke. "You're a fool, Father."

His answer was unexpected. "So it seems."

"You shouldn't be out here alone."

"It'll be as God wills."

"Really?" She stepped closer. "I seem to remember Christ saying that we shouldn't tempt God."

"Ah. A Catholic who reads the Bible."

"Smart-ass."

The comment seemed to get through to him. He tossed the ball over to a corner of the fenced-in court, to lie with a couple of other balls that waited for the neighborhood kids. "I deserve that."

"Maybe. You need to stop hiding from this."

He swung around to glare at her. "I'm not hiding. I'm surviving."

"Maybe. But I don't think you know what's going on."

He dashed away some more sweat and came closer. "What do you mean?"

"Someone's out to get you."

He stood for a few seconds, looking at her, his expression a mixture of exhaustion and pain too great to bear. "I don't see the connection."

"You would, if you knew that one of the first things someone told the cops was that Steve was gay. And that the cops are asking about your orientation now."

"I have no orientation. I'm a celibate priest, remember."

"Smart-ass," she said again.

For an instant, she thought he was going to swear at her. Instead, he headed for the bench and grabbed a towel, using it to scrub his face. "They can say all they want. Steve was gay. Everyone knew that. Maybe they think that's why he was killed. Like that kid in Wyoming, God rest his soul."

"Father, stop thinking like a priest. Stop thinking like a good person. Don't you get it? If Steve was killed because he was gay, who'd have the best motive? Someone who needed to hide the fact that he was Steve's lover. Someone with an *urgent* need to hide that fact."

Brendan stilled for a moment. Then he asked simply, "What do you think, Chloe?"

"I think you could be framed. There are elements in this world who'd love nothing more than to nail another Catholic priest for sexual misconduct. And I know cops. They have a tendency to build the most obvious case once they think they know what happened."

"How do you know I didn't do it?"

"Because I've seen the way you look at me sometimes."

The night was suddenly so silent that even the traffic sounds seemed to fade away. Brendan was clearly rendered speechless, and he just gaped at her.

"Oh, it's not obvious," Chloe said. "Don't worry about it. You're not like most men, who talk to my chest. But you're a heterosexual male. I'd bet my life on it."

"Damn," Brendan said, and flopped onto the bench. "You've just succeeded in making me extremely uncomfortable."

"Good. You need to stay that way."

"I'm sorry," he said quietly.

"Don't be. We Catholics understand our priests are human. It doesn't bother me. You're not predatory. Which is another thing those cops probably can't distinguish. I know you wouldn't hurt a fly. They'll probably never believe that."

"Thanks, I think. You know, in the old days, they taught priests never to look a woman in the eye. The eye contact was supposed to be too seductive. In my experience, the eye is the safest place to look."

Chloe gave a little laugh. "Yeah." But her humor faded as quickly as it arose. "The thing is, Father, you need to watch your back."

He sighed and reached for a bottle of water. As he unscrewed the cap, he said, "You know, I've been getting a little paranoid already. I don't want to get more so."

"Paranoid why?"

He shrugged. "There seem to have been some complaints to the chancery about me. I keep getting these sideways phone calls from downtown."

"Well, I'm sure there are some idiots in the parish who'd prefer an old-fashioned priest who ruled the church like a dictator."

"There's a right-wing element everywhere. They want to go back to the way it always was. Completely ignoring the fact that it wasn't always that way." He sighed.

"What kind of complaints have you been hearing?"

"The interesting thing is that they're never really specific. Just general questions about what's going on down here. What am I doing? I feel like I've got somebody breathing down my neck, but I don't know why."

"Not good." Chloe tipped her head back and looked up at the emptiness of the artificially lighted night. "I want you to listen to me, Father. You've got to watch your back." She lowered her head and looked at him. "That crucifixion was a message. I can't say for sure yet that it was a message to you. But it was a message. This isn't done with."

"Dear God." His shoulders slumped. "I hope I die before I ever see anything like this again."

"You may, Father. Are you hearing me?"

After a bit, he looked up at her. "I hear you."

"Be careful what you say to anyone, especially the cops. You're in their sights right now. Even an innocent comment could put you behind bars."

"But what can I do except tell the truth?"

"Say as little as possible. Trust me, I'm going to look into this."

"Thanks, Chloe."

But she had already melted away into the night.

Chloe was just stepping out of the shower when the phone started ringing. By the time she'd wrapped a towel around herself and another around her wet hair, her voice mail had picked it up. But then it started ringing again.

As a criminal defense attorney, Chloe never gave out her home phone number or address. The types she dealt with were often not the kind of people she wanted to show up unannounced on her doorstep.

She padded to the phone by the second ring, and checked the caller ID. *Diel, Matthew.* She hesitated, not wanting to talk to him, but then she grabbed the receiver before the fourth ring, when the phone company's voice mail would take over the call.

"What do you want?" she asked without preamble. She could hear him sigh.

"One of your most charming features, Chloe, is your incredible talent for rudeness."

"I'm just getting to the point fast. You called, I'm tired, what do you want?"

"I want to know if you're going to buck me on this investigation."

"Why would I do that?"

"Because you hate me?"

Chloe settled onto the couch and tried not to shiver as the air-conditioning turned on, sending a draft of cold air over her wet, bare shoulders. "I don't hate you, Matt. I never have."

"Okay. You're just supremely indifferent."

She didn't answer.

"You didn't answer my question. Are you going to mess with me on this?"

"I'm just going to make sure you don't get tunnel vision."

He sighed again. "I get less tunnel vision than most. You of all people ought to know that."

"Maybe." She didn't care for references to her past. "I'm not going to mess with you unless you start to mess up."

"How the hell are you going to know if I mess up?" The question was challenging.

Chloe lifted one foot and looked at the goose bumps that were running down her legs. "You ever heard of quid pro quo?"

"Yes. I'm not stupid because I'm just a dumb cop."

She ignored his irritation. "I'm going to suggest a little quid pro quo. One hand washes the other. I tell you what I find, you tell me what you find."

"You know I can't discuss an investigation."

"Sure you can. Nobody will know except me."

He was silent for a few moments. "So you want to do a little horse trading? What have you got to trade?"

"Not on the phone." She could tell he was on his cell

phone, by the way it faded and crackled, and there was no guaranteed privacy on a cell phone.

"Kramer's Diner on Fletcher. Fifteen minutes."

"Thirty."

"Okay, thirty. And you better have something to share."

Thirty minutes later, Diel watched Chloe walk into the diner. Isolation seemed to surround her, making it look as if she existed on another plane, despite the students and a couple of drunks who filled booths. He'd managed to get away from them, into a quiet corner, and a tip to the waitress had given him at least a reasonable guarantee that she'd try to shuffle any newcomers to the far end.

When she slid onto the vinyl bench across from him, he noticed her hair was damp. She'd probably just gotten out of the shower when he called. The realization made him feel things he didn't want to feel for this ice queen, but the image of drops of water sparkling on her skin made him shift uncomfortably.

The waitress came over immediately. "What'll it be?"

"Coffee, decaf," Chloe said. "Wheat toast, dry."

She'd always eaten like a sprite, as if her body needed little mortal sustenance. Matt was not so lucky. He needed to eat, but rarely had the opportunity to do so except in quick gulps.

"A full stack with maple syrup. Coffee, leaded."

Then they were alone, facing each other like old antagonists. Which they were. Silent, unspoken tension rose between them.

"So," he said, wanting to ignore the discomfort she always made him feel.

"So." Ever so slightly the corners of her mouth tipped up. "You first."

He shrugged. "Okay." He figured if she didn't have anything, this would be their last meeting. He was willing to trust her. "The vic was dead before he was crucified. Shot in the back of the head. Small caliber, probably a .22. There's powder on his scalp."

"So it was an execution?"

"Or he didn't hear the perp come up behind him. We'll know more after the full autopsy." Matt shrugged. "Now you."

"There's a whispering campaign against Father Brendan. There've been complaints to the chancery, vague ones. I wouldn't trust a lot of what I hear, if I were you."

Matt looked at her, ruminating. "Why do they hate him?"

"Anybody's guess at this point. The Church is a funny place, Matt. There are people who are willing to do almost anything to return to the Middle Ages. There's still a powerful right wing that hasn't recovered from Vatican II."

"And he's too modern?"

"For some, I'm sure. And not modern enough for others. Like most priests, he's walking a fine line all the time. We may be one body in Christ, as they say, but we have all the failings of any group of human beings."

"But why would that involve the kid?"

"I didn't say it did. I just want you to be aware that there are agendas out there."

He sighed. "There always are, Chloe. Tell me something I don't know. So there have been complaints about him to the chancery?"

"Apparently so."

"About what?"

She shook her head. "Even he doesn't know. He keeps getting vague phone calls asking him what's going on down here."

"You talked to him?"

"Of course."

"Are you his attorney?"

She almost smiled. "If I were, I wouldn't be telling you this. Apparently there have been enough phone calls that he's been feeling a little paranoid."

Matt mulled that over. It *could* be tied in with the kid, but he didn't say so. "I'll keep that in mind. What else?"

"Nothing you won't find out if you get a subpoena."

"Save me the grief. I haven't got any reason to get one yet."

"I know." Again that faint smile, as if she enjoyed having the upper hand. "He was a navy chaplain for twelve years. His jacket is full of commendations."

"How'd you find that out?"

"I have connections who have connections at the chancery."

He nodded. "Okay. What else?"

"He spent two years in a monastery before being assigned here."

That made Matt lean forward. "Why would he do that?"

"You'll have to ask him."

"Damn. Why should he tell me?"

"Because," she said, as his plate of pancakes was placed in front of him, "he's an honest man."

"Yeah, right." Matt snorted. "Diogenes never did find one."

"Well," she said, a soft smile tracing her lips, "Diogenes apparently didn't look in St. Simeon's."

* * *

The early edition of the paper started hitting the streets around four in the morning. Hardly anyone was up and about, and the delivery trucks drove through streets nearly empty of traffic. At each newsstand, they stopped and loaded a stack of fresh papers, and cleared out yesterday's edition, if any were left.

Home delivery drivers tooled around in their vans and trucks, tossing plastic-wrapped papers on driveways and lawns as the eastern sky began to brighten.

It was not the kind of Easter Sunday edition most people wanted to see. Yes, beside the masthead was the greeting *Happy Easter* in purple ink, but below it the headline screamed news that seemed to come from another world:

MAN CRUCIFIED IN CHURCH

Below it, in sharp color, was a photo of the façade of St. Simeon's Church, surrounded by police cars and crime scene tape.

Dominic had set his alarm early, and so reached the front stoop long before Brendan stirred out of his room. He pulled the paper from the plastic, read the story with a deepening sense of evil chill, then hastily bundled it into the trash can behind the rectory. If Brendan wanted to see what the news hounds had to say, then he was going to have to go out and buy a copy. Otherwise, it was Dominic's considered opinion that Brendan did not need to see that headline or story sitting beside his morning coffee cup. He offered a brief prayer asking forgiveness for his act of charitable deceit.

Then he went into the kitchen to make the pot of special blend coffee that always started their day. The Starbucks coffee was Dominic's introduction, a small self-indulgence. He was a diocesan priest, which meant he hadn't taken a vow of poverty, and hence if his family chose to send him money, he could indulge in a few things of this nature.

Brendan, however, was an ordinal priest, a Jesuit who took his vow of poverty seriously. If he laid claim to any possessions at all in the world, they were probably the clothes on his back, and the old basketball autographed by Larry Bird. The ball had, Brendan explained, belonged to his father, who had lived, bled, and died Celtic green.

Dominic had watched him on more than one occasion take money out of his pocket and give it to someone in need. Brendan wore clerical clothes that were frayed, apparently replaced only when someone in the church noticed that he needed some new ones. His shoes, according to Lucy Gallegos, had been resoled twice since he had come to the parish. Dominic suspected that he used his entire meager stipend for haircuts, gas, and gifts to the poor.

Which was admirable, and Dominic felt no resentment of Brendan's charity. But he did rather like the way his nominal superior appreciated the change in coffee brands. He'd also noticed that Brendan wasn't averse to having a biscotto with his coffee, if one happened to be there. Just one, though. Never more. A moderate man.

It was, Dominic thought as he poured himself a cup of fresh brew, probably not surprising that Monsignor Crowell disliked Brendan. In a church that coddled its priests, seeing to all their needs, an austere man like Brendan might niggle at some consciences. Especially Monsignor

Crowell's, for the monsignor had a taste for the finer things in life.

Ah, well.

All he knew for sure was that he felt good about getting rid of the newspaper. Brendan's pain was clearly bad enough.

Another man awaited the early edition eagerly. The killer, restless all night and worried that he might have failed, was wide-awake and pacing the floor of his pleasant suburban home, trying to keep quiet so as not to disturb his wife. When he heard the clatter of the truck at the corner, he waited only a few minutes before darting out to go get a copy.

Inside again, his hands shook as he turned on the light and unfolded the paper.

So sure was he that the story would be a small one, he almost missed the screaming headline.

But when he saw it, his knees gave way.

The watcher, having a calmer conscience at the moment—after all, he hadn't had anything to do with the kid's death, not really—didn't get his paper until the rosy spring sun was washing away a fine mist from overnight.

In the absentminded way he usually did, he bought it at the stand in front of the convenience store without looking at it. He tucked it under his arm and went inside to buy his large cup of coffee, cream, no sugar. Then he strolled back to his motel, where he sat at a rickety table in the corner of his room. Only after he had removed the cover from the coffee and stirred it twice did he open the paper.

What he saw made his heart stop.

Then the phone started ringing.

*　　*　　*

"What the hell were you thinking of?" demanded the voice on the other end, a voice with a face he knew, but no name.

"I didn't—"

"No, obviously you *didn't* think! My God, this was supposed to be quiet, not sensational. What do you think you're doing?"

"I didn't—"

"I don't want to hear your excuses, dammit. Do you understand the meaning of *covert?* My God, man, the police are going to be all over this. The cannon won't dare do a thing for weeks if not months, and I need that fucking priest *gone*."

The watcher, recovering at last from his own shock, shouted into the phone, "I didn't do it!"

"You expect me to believe that?"

"Believe what you want, but I'm not crazy. I know my job. I took the damn body away from the church. It should have been found in an alley!"

Silence answered him. And silence filled him.

Because they both knew what this meant.

Someone else knew what was going on.

CHAPTER 5

The biscotto went untouched. The coffee was barely sipped. Brendan appeared to be the mere shadow of the youthful, vibrant man he had been only yesterday morning. As a priest, Dominic felt he ought to have some comfort to offer. But all the platitudes of his priesthood seemed thin this sunny Easter morning. Promises of eternal life and resurrection couldn't take the pain from a wound caused by such an atrocious act, and he knew it. That comfort would come later.

He considered offering to take all the Masses this morning, then decided Brendan needed to be busy, needed to be immersed in all the grace and sanctity the rite could offer.

With little more than a distant nod, Brendan rose from the table and left. Minutes later, Dominic heard him leave through the side door for the church. First Mass wasn't for an hour yet. The pastor must want to pray.

Dominic sat at table for a while, but his thoughts moved far away from his concern about Brendan. For the first time it struck him that he and Brendan had been soundly asleep only yards away when that heinous act had occurred.

The evil chill he had felt earlier returned, stronger this

time, running down his back like ice water, and clinging like wet, dead leaves.

St. Simeon's had padded kneelers in all the pews. Many of the newer churches skipped them, for monetary reasons or because the congregation didn't want them, but St. Simeon had been built when such things were never omitted. Since kneeling during Mass had been introduced only in the nineteenth century, Brendan didn't particularly care whether his parishioners stood or knelt during the consecration, as long as they were respectful, just as he didn't care if they showed up in shorts and T-shirts, as long as they came.

But kneeling . . . kneeling was sometimes the only way he felt right about approaching God. Kneeling went back to his childhood, and to his seminary days, and to the two years he'd spent at the monastery, mending his soul. Kneeling was uncomfortable after a while, especially on knees battered by years of playing basketball, but he needed that discomfort. He needed to enter into some of the suffering of his Lord.

And right now, the pain in his protesting knees felt like a small measure of atonement. Because he felt guilty. Guilty for the death of Steve King, even though he had no direct hand in it. He was second-guessing himself, wondering if he could have made any difference. He assumed the young man had to have been murdered Friday night. Certainly after everyone was gone. But then he recalled that he hadn't seen Steve at all on Friday. Might he have been murdered on Thursday night. After the adoration?

The thought made him shudder. If that was the case, then he could certainly have prevented the young man's death simply by staying after the adoration to help him close up. But to think he'd probably been lying soundly asleep in his bed when that young man's life had been taken, when the church had been desecrated . . .

He put his face in his hands, wrestling with an anguish too huge to bear.

It wasn't the first time in his life he'd faced a terrible personal loss, but this was one area of life where experience didn't help at all. Besides, this was so heinous, every time he thought of it, he felt punched.

He was facing an evil greater than any he had ever faced before. It was not only the loss of Steve's life that ripped at him; it was the manner of it. That any mind could be so cruel, so blasphemous, so . . . *evil.*

He lifted his head, looking up at the altar, but there was no cross, no corpus, to remind him that others had suffered such evils. There were only satin banners, hung swiftly yesterday by the facilities manager to cover what would have otherwise been a distracting hole behind the altar. White banners embroidered in gold with doves and rays of light.

But there was nothing there for him. For the second time in his life, he had entered the dark night of the soul, when God was out of reach, hidden from him when he needed Him most.

Cut loose from the most important mooring in his life, Brendan felt as if his mind were tumbling down a bottomless dark tunnel, where questions gnawed at him like hungry mouths. How did he know it wasn't just all bullshit? How did he really know there was a God? How could he be sure Jesus had ever existed? How was all of this any different from the rites and panoply of a pagan shaman?

How could any merciful God allow such things to happen?

The questions weren't new to him. He'd faced them before. He'd even answered them countless times from the comfort of his faith . . . when he felt it.

But this time . . . this time they gnawed harder, filling him with a clawing sense of abandonment worse than any he had known. His faith had shriveled in the night hours and was now blowing away on a frigid wind that ripped through his soul, gutting him.

Leaving him utterly alone and dangling over an abyss of despair.

His spiritual director at the monastery had told him once that faith was a matter of acting as if, even when one didn't feel it. So when the time came, as the first people began to enter the church for the early Mass, he rose and went to the sacristy, vesting himself as he had countless times over the last fifteen years. The actions should have felt familiar and comfortable, but this morning they felt strange and awkward. As if he were doing something for the first time in his life.

Just as he finished, Dominic entered the sacristy from the rectory-side door, letting in a breath of fragrant, humid morning air. "I'm concelebrating," he said.

Brendan didn't question or disagree. He didn't have the heart to do either. He waited for his assistant to finish dressing, then they walked in silence to the back of the church, where the altar servers were already waiting.

People were still entering through the narthex doors, and greeted the priests. Some faces were tired, others were bright and smiling. Ordinarily, Brendan would have loved chatting, but this morning his face felt like wood. He couldn't even make himself smile.

The sheer pointlessness of it all was weighing down every muscle in his body. His legs felt like lead as they processioned up the aisle to the altar. His arms felt weighted in cement as he raised them in the opening blessing. His heart . . . . his heart was gone.

The readings seemed to pass in a blur as lectors came up to the ambo and departed. Then the Alleluia. His lips moved with the words, but no sound came out of him. How he got through the Gospel reading he had no idea. But then it was time for the homily. A homily he had constructed before yesterday's horror. A homily that had been written by a different man. He didn't know if he could do it. But he also knew he had to, nor could he ignore what had happened.

He paused, looking down at the sheaf of papers before him, covered with his awkward scrawl. Then, drawing a deep breath he looked up, seeing a sea of expectant faces.

"Yesterday," he said, his voice cracking briefly, "yesterday a terrible thing was discovered in this church. A terrible, sad thing. Many of you know that we have lost young Steve King, one of our most devoted parishioners. Many of you knew Steve, knew he was planning to dedicate his life to the priesthood. Many of you have heard what was done to him."

A murmur passed through the congregation, and Brendan felt as if it passed through him as well. A quiet wail of sorrow. He drew another breath, forcing himself to continue, when every cell in his body was suddenly demanding that he run from this place and never return. But he knew what his duty was, even if his heart was gone, even if he didn't believe it himself.

"Today, more than ever, we must cherish our belief in the resurrection. Today, more than ever, we need our faith." Bitterness, corrosive and hot, began to fill the void left by the absence of his faith. He fought it down. This wasn't for him, this was for these people.

"Today commemorates the day that Christ taught us there is no death. That for those of us who believe, there is eternal life. Steve has moved on, and I have no doubt his rewards are great." *Liar.* He had every doubt at this moment in time. "Today," he finished, "is the test of everything we believe. May God bless you all."

Then, his prepared homily utterly ignored, he returned to his seat to the rear and far side of the altar. A moment later he rose to lead the renewal of baptismal vows, but with a nudge of his elbow, he signaled Dominic to do it. His fellow priest did so at once.

Brendan couldn't even bring himself to mouth the familiar words, or say "I do" in answer to the age-old questions. It was gone. Everything he had lived for was gone.

Dominic took the rest of the Masses that morning. He had to. Brendan refused to say them.

"I'm not worthy," he told Dominic after the early Mass was over, after he had failed even to stand out front and greet the departing congregation.

Dominic paused as he was removing his stole, and looked at him. "Why aren't you worthy?"

"I don't believe."

Dominic never for an instant believed that was a permanent state of affairs, but he didn't say so. Forgetting for the moment his need to vest fully for the coming Mass, he sat beside Brendan on one of the folding chairs and put his hand on his shoulder. "That doesn't matter, Brendan. You know that. The worthiness of the celebrant has no bearing on the consecration."

Brendan shrugged. "It would still be blasphemy."

Dominic arched one salt-and-pepper eyebrow. "Really.

So let's see. You've lost your faith but still believe in blasphemy?"

Brendan merely looked at him from hollow eyes.

"Okay, Brendan," Dominic said after a moment. "Okay. I'll take the Masses. But you have to promise me one thing."

Again, just a look, no verbal response.

"Promise me you'll stay right here until I'm done."

One corner of Brendan's mouth hooked up mirthlessly. "I won't do anything stupid."

"No, I know you won't. But you'll make me feel a hell of a lot better if you just hang around."

Brendan shrugged. "Whatever."

"Okay." Dominic squeezed his shoulder, then finished garbing for Mass. A few minutes later, he left the sanctuary, leaving Brendan alone with his demons.

But Brendan was facing a particular demon, one he didn't like at all. Almost as soon as the word "whatever" came out of his mouth, he felt a river of self-loathing, rapid and violent, race through him.

He was acting like a whiny child, shirking his duty, and wallowing in self-pity. He had no business behaving this way. He knew better than to give in to these feelings. Whatever the guilt he might bear in Steve's death, for not making sure the young man wasn't alone late at night, it was no excuse for abandoning his responsibilities. No matter what questions of faith he might be feeling, he still had priestly duties to fulfill.

And no matter how much anguish he might feel, he had no right to indulge it at the expense of others.

Rising, he began to vest as a concelebrant, determined

that however unworthy he felt, all he could do in atonement was to fulfill his appointed duties.

Vested, he emerged onto the altar just as Dominic was beginning the blessing. Dominic caught his eye, and smiled in approval.

By the time they reached the consecration, when he lifted the chalice while Dominic lifted the host, Brendan even began to feel a small measure of comfort in the ritual, even if it was only the comfort of familiarity, of awareness that he was merely another link in a two-thousand-year-old chain of priests who had performed this sacred ritual. He was only that, one small link, of no significance at all.

His eyes looked out over the congregation, seeing the bored faces, but more importantly, seeing the rapt faces. They were the ones who mattered, those rapt faces. Those who felt the miracle unfolding here in their very hearts. They mattered.

Then his eyes lit on one face, and his hands faltered. For an instant, he was in danger of dropping the chalice. That face! He'd never thought to see that face again. Fighting for equilibrium, he closed his eyes a moment.

When he reopened them, the face was gone. He must have imagined it.

With shaking hands, he replaced the chalice on the altar. It was lack of sleep and grief, he told himself. That and nothing more.

It could not possibly be anything else.

CHAPTER 6

After five years, Chloe Ryder's law practice was doing well. She even had a partner, and it was to her partner she turned.

"I need time off, Naomi."

Naomi Blancher, a slender, dark-haired woman, looked over the tops of her reading glasses at her. "What's wrong?"

"Nothing. I just need time to . . . work on something. I'll be in and out, helping with case research and so on, but I need my time to be more fluid."

"You're asking me to take your court appearances."

"And client meetings, as far as you can."

Naomi frowned. It wasn't an unfriendly or disapproving expression, but rather a thoughtful one. "That's a lot to ask, Chloe. You know what a DUI practice is like. You used to do it."

Chloe had, at first. Driving under the influence was the bread and butter of many criminal defense attorneys, a client base that invariably had enough money to pay for a routine defense of their stupidity. It also caused a lawyer to spend an extraordinary amount of time in courtrooms for hearings and trials. But she'd been able to move beyond that with time, so that now she left the routine DUIs to Naomi and handled only the major cases: possession, trafficking, embezzlement, DUI manslaughter, and even, right now, a contract murder case that she believed was a frame job.

"I know. But I need some slack here, Naomi. A . . . friend of mine has a problem."

"Could he become a client?"

"I hope not. But if he does, it'll be pro bono." That was for sure.

Naomi's frown faded and was replaced by a grin. "Isn't that always the way? Okay, okay. Have Leah and Marcia put their heads together and see how much they can juggle you out of." Leah and Marcia were their staff.

"Thanks, Naomi. I owe you."

"Trust me, I'll take you up on that. I'm getting desperate for a vacation anywhere they don't have telephones."

"I know the feeling."

In the front office, Chloe told Marcia and Leah what she needed. Both women were worth their weight in gold in talent, knowledge, and drive.

"Well," said Marcia, immediately switching her computer screen to Chloe's calendar, "you at least picked a good time to do this, boss. You've got a light week. Remember? You wanted time to do research on the Vazquez and Milburry cases."

"Great. But I may need more time than this week. Just see how much you can loosen my time without overburdening Naomi and losing any clients, okay? Then let me know what I've got left. Right now I need to get to an autopsy."

As Chloe departed, Marcia turned to Leah. "Did she say autopsy?"

Leah nodded. "I didn't know lawyers went to those."

*   *   *

Which was pretty much what Matt said when he was walking into the Medical Examiner's office and found Chloe already there. "You can't attend the autopsy."

"No?"

Matt closed his eyes, an expression of long-suffering patience crossing his features. "Look," he said, opening his eyes again, "even if you had standing or authority to be present, it wouldn't be allowed. This guy was a friend of yours."

Chloe, who was seated in one of the institutional chairs in the reception area, simply shook her head. "I'm not going in. But I want to hear everything you know when you come out."

"You know it won't be final."

"I don't care. I want to know."

He dropped onto one of the seats beside her. "Where's the quid pro quo?"

"It'll come."

"So now I'm supposed to go on blind faith?"

She gave him a wry little smile. "It'll do your soul some good, Matt."

"Haven't you heard? Cops don't have souls."

Then he was gone, heading inside for the least favorite part of his job. No matter how many autopsies he attended, he never got over the smell.

Chloe waited patiently, knowing it might be hours yet, but certain that if she weren't there when Matt came out, he'd find a way to avoid her. Since she hadn't been able to find out exactly when the autopsy had begun, she had no idea whatsoever when Matt might emerge . . . or whether he'd even stay to the end. So much couldn't be determined until later, with the aid of tests and microscopes, but it was the big picture she was after.

To her relief, her wait wasn't all that long. Matt emerged a half hour later, looking a little green, and with a jerk of his head signaled her to come outside with him.

The morning was turning cloudy, the breeze stiffening with the hint of a cold front. By tonight they might need light jackets. Chloe found herself hoping so. Despite having lived her entire life in Florida, she felt that the cool season was too short. She liked the way chilly air invigorated her.

Side by side they walked to Matt's nondescript sedan, a beige, slightly older model that wouldn't be noticed anywhere it went.

He leaned back against the car and folded his arms.

"Well," she said finally, giving him what he wanted, her impatience.

"The kid probably was killed Thursday night."

A shiver of surprise went through her. She'd been assuming, as had they all, probably, that he'd died on Friday night.

"Yeah," he said, as if he shared her shock. "I wasn't expecting that." He rubbed his chin and stared off into space. "Bullet to the base of the brain. Death was instantaneous. Decay leads the coroner to think the vic was dead at least twenty-four hours."

"But he's not sure?"

"Not yet, but he's pretty good at these things. So someone had to have come back and crucified the guy on Saturday morning."

Chloe looked at him. "Why?"

"Because he couldn't have been there that long before he was found. I mean . . ."

Chloe interrupted him with a shake of her head. "Here's a little quid for your quo. That cross was shrouded Friday morning. It's routine. Steve could have been hung there anytime after three-thirty or so in the afternoon, and before the seven-thirty service began, as well as later at night. Although given the number of people who drift in and out of the church on Good Friday, I'd bet he couldn't have been put up there before nine-thirty on Friday night. After the Stations of The Cross. But that's still a thirteen-hour window." But what if Steve *had* been hanging there during the Good Friday services? She wanted to shudder at the thought. "And nobody that I can find has seen Steve since Thursday night."

"You've been calling around?"

"Of course." She stuffed her hands into the pockets of her suit jacket. "What do you think I've been doing? The last anybody at church knows, he offered to stay late to clean up the parish hall. End of trail."

"And he doesn't have a roommate or anything."

"In retrospect, it's odd nobody missed him at Good Friday services." Then she shrugged. "But it's a busy time, and people don't always show up for these things, even wannabe priests. He might have had to work, he might have been a little sick. Nobody would really remark on it."

"Except maybe a certain priest everybody said the kid was so close to."

Chloe kept her face expressionless. "Do you have any idea how busy a priest is at this time of year? There could have been a lot of reasons Steve didn't show up on Friday evening. He might have gone to another church. It's not a required service anyway. Given all the pressures Brendan's under during this season, and given all the reasons Steve might not be there, it probably didn't even cross his mind to wonder."

"Thus speaks the defense attorney." He cocked a brow at her. "So tell me, Chloe. Why'd you go from being a cop to a criminal defense attorney?"

She looked him dead in the eye. "Because I worked with cops and prosecutors."

He astonished her then with a hearty laugh, one of those belly laughs of good humor that she still remembered from the old days. "Touché," he said, letting the insult pass.

But then, why wouldn't he? She knew all too well the time he had stood up against corruption. She supposed she ought to give thanks that Matt Diel was heading this investigation.

"Okay," he said presently, "what've we got? We got a kid who was shot, then crucified, probably sometime early on Friday morning. He may or may not have been on the cross most of the time in between then and Saturday morning. Nobody had seen him since late Thursday."

"What else did the M.E. note?" Past experience had taught her that more had been discovered in today's autopsy. She wondered why Matt was making her drag it out of him.

Matt shrugged. "Well, he wasn't killed in the church. There was grass and dirt in his mouth, under his nails, and on his clothing."

Her lawyer's mind immediately leapt on an apparent logical problem. "But you said he died instantly."

"He did. Postmortem paroxysm, not uncommon, especially in brain injuries."

"Oh." She studied the pavement beneath their feet and thought about what she had just learned. "Somebody went to an awful lot of trouble to muddy this trail."

"So it would seem. To muddy it, or send a message."

She raised her head to look at him. "What else?"

"What makes you think there's anything else?"

"I know you, Matt. You always hold something back."

He sighed. She wondered what he was thinking, if he was remembering.

"What the fuck," he said finally. "Okay. Whoever did the nail job did it without breaking any bones."

Chloe fought to conceal the shock she was feeling.

"Me too," Matt said, as if she were an open book. "Not to mention the M.E. He's kinda thrown by that. What he said was, 'Do you know how many small bones there are in the hands and feet?' "

"Yeah." Chloe knew. She'd taken an anatomy course, thinking it would be useful as a cop. "But it's possible."

"Yeah, it's possible. With a knife. Not with nails like those. The bones don't even appear to be nicked."

"Cripes. But it could be done."

"Yeah. On purpose. The thing is—" He broke off and looked around, making sure there was no one nearby, then he leaned close, lowering his voice. "The thing is, Chloe, that even if those nails had found the path of least resistance and slipped between the bones, there should have been some scraping. Something. The M.E. said those nails were driven with surgical precision."

Chloe studied the pavement for a minute or two. "So we're looking for someone with a medical background."

"Maybe. Or just some damn lucky fool."

"There's another thing, Matt."

"What's that?"

"Nobody's found the corpus."

"The what?"

"The body of Christ that was hanging on the cross to begin with. Carved from solid wood."

Matt sighed. "You had to do that, didn't you."

"Do what?"

"Give me another headache. You just can't resist."

"Well, look at it this way. I didn't commit the crime."

His dark eyes met hers. "Yeah. We gotta take our consolation where we can find it, right?"

Dominic had the morning Mass, so Brendan sat alone in the rectory, in the dining room, with his cup of coffee. He was still sitting there, thinking too much, when Merv Haskell, the facilities manager, rapped gently on the doorframe.

"Father? Lucy said it was okay if I talked to you."

Brendan shook himself out of his dangerous lethargy and managed a faint smile. "Sure, Merv. Come on in. Help yourself to the coffee and biscuits. Biscotti, I guess they are."

"Thanks, Father." Merv filled a mug and joined him. A retired parishioner with enough energy for a thirty-year-old, Merv was a popular man in the parish. He was also, to Brendan's way of thinking, an extremely useful brake on priests like himself, who weren't always the most practical of men.

"Father," Merv said after a delicate moment, "we can't find the corpus."

In the haze of grief, anger, despair, and, frankly, self-pity that had been filling him since Saturday, Brendan hadn't even thought of that. Now the back of his neck prickled. "Anywhere?" he asked, knowing it was pointless, but needing to say something.

"It's not on church grounds. Sister Phil and I spent all afternoon yesterday looking for it. I thought maybe it would turn up in the school or hall. I mean, that thing was *heavy*. Who'd want to take it away?"

"Someone who didn't want his crime to be discovered too quickly."

"True." Merv nodded, passing a hand over his bald head. It was a characteristic gesture, that smoothing of hair long gone, and evinced his discomfort. "The thing is, we have to have a corpus. That new directive . . ."

Brendan rose from the table, clasped his hands behind his back, and paced to the window. The day outside was insultingly beautiful. "Ah, yes. The return of Christ to the church."

"Father?"

"You know, Merv, I'm a post-Vatican II Catholic."

"Yes, Father."

"I'm too young to really remember the Mass in Latin. But I'm not so young I don't remember a time when all Catholic churches had a crucifix on the altar. Don't you find it a little bit strange that we now have to be *told* we must have a corpus?" In the burst of ecumenism, many Catholic churches had abandoned statues of any kind.

"Well, yes," Merv admitted. "We're Catholics."

"Exactly. And while many non-Catholics may be deluded enough to think we actually *worship* those statues, the fact remains, we know better, don't we, Merv?"

"Yes, Father."

"So we never should have bowed to that pressure."

Merv was silent, apparently wondering where this was going.

"I love the fact that St. Simeon's is old enough to still have statuary. I loved that beautiful crucifix behind the altar."

"So did I, Father."

"But you know what, Merv? We are never going to have another like it, not while I am pastor here. I couldn't bear it. In fact, I don't want that cross to go back up, even when or if we get it back."

The old pendulum clock on the wall ticked away the silent seconds. Finally, Merv said, "I understand, Father."

"Thank you. But you're right, we need to have the corpus. So do me a favor, Merv, whatever you decide to do about it, please ensure that it's . . . different."

"Yes, Father." Merv left, taking his coffee with him. Moments later, the phone rang and Brendan answered automatically. "Father Brendan."

A whispery voice came across the line, pouring into his ear like corrosive acid.

"You're next, Father."

CHAPTER 7

The meeting held that evening in the rectory parlor wasn't convened for spiritual purposes. Brendan was there, of course, but so were Sister Phil, Chloe, and Matt Diel.

Brendan had been troubled by the call that morning. Initially he'd been inclined to dismiss it as a crank call, but as the day had worn on, it had niggled at him more until he finally mentioned it to Phil, who had stopped by after school let out for the day. It was she who had sent up the flares, calling Chloe at once. Chloe had then called Matt. Dominic had wanted to be there, but he was needed at the hall for a meeting of a grief support group.

"I'm probably making too much out of a crank call," Brendan said, giving a half smile. "I'm just jumpy."

Matt spoke. "I'd agree with you except for what's happened here. Yes, it may just be a sick twist, taking advantage of the situation to scare you. Then again . . ." He didn't need to complete the sentence. "There's been a possibility from the outset that this was a message crime, which makes it possible that you were the intended recipient."

"A message saying what?"

Matt shrugged.

Brendan studied him for a moment. "You also think there's a possibility I'm making up the phone call."

Matt merely looked at him.

Brendan sighed. "I'm glad I don't live in your world."

Chloe smiled faintly as she watched Matt bristle.

"Somebody's got to live in my world, Father," he said simply. "Because not everyone out here believes in yours."

"I wasn't putting you down, Detective," Brendan said kindly. "I'm just remarking that I'm glad I don't have to live in a world where I have to question everything and everyone. Where I have to suspect every statement may be a lie."

Matt leaned forward, placing his elbows on his knees. "You'd better listen to me, Father. Because right now you *are* living in my world. You need to be suspicious of everyone. *Everyone*. Because if that phone call wasn't a prank, if it was from the killer, then you've got somebody after you. A very vicious somebody with one hell of a grudge."

Brendan drew back slightly, as if in distaste over what Matt was saying, but he never wavered. "I'm not sure I know how to be so suspicious."

"Then you'd better start learning."

"He's right, Father," Chloe said.

"I'm not saying he isn't. It's just that I don't . . . think that way."

Matt straightened. "Then we'll do it for you. From this moment forward, you don't go anywhere alone. Not anywhere."

"Now wait. I can't possibly perform my duties that way."

"You're going to have to. I can't assign a cop to guard you, not based on that one call. But you can find someone else to be with you. Night and day."

"I'll help," Chloe volunteered.

Phil immediately chimed in. "So will I."

But Brendan was shaking his head. "I need to make visits to the sick. People need to make confessions in private. There's no way I can function if I'm never alone."

"Sick calls?" Matt said. "You mean go to people's houses because they claim to be sick?"

"Yes."

Matt shook his head. "No way. The killer could call and set up a meeting that way."

Brendan's jaw set in the firmest line Chloe could ever remember seeing. "I will continue to function as a priest. These people's souls are more important than my life."

Matt looked at Chloe. "You talk some sense into him."

"He's talking perfect sense."

"Yeah, right." Matt returned his attention to the priest. "The next thing you have to do is put your thinking cap on. I want you to think over your entire life and see if you can't figure out why someone would hate you so much. Somebody, anybody, who might have a grudge."

"I'm sure there are plenty of those," Brendan said, almost smiling. "I'm a priest, after all."

"Yeah, well, then I want a list."

"I can't do that."

"Oh, for pity's sake!" Rising from his chair, Matt threw up a hand. "If that call was for real, then you're in deep shit, Father. And all I'm trying to do is save your life."

"I understand that, Detective," Brendan said firmly. "I do. But I can't betray confidences. I am a priest . . . first, last, and always."

* * *

Outside the rectory, Matt drew Chloe down the street until they stood in a puddle of light from a streetlamp, well away from prying ears.

"That man is crazy," Matt said flatly.

"No, he's not," she answered, her voice tight with irritation. "He doesn't live in your world, Matt."

"That's hogwash, and you know it. We all live in the same world. The exact same world where kids get nailed to crosses, and people carry out vendettas, and men beat their wives—" He broke off abruptly, realizing that was somewhere he shouldn't go.

Chloe appeared to ignore his last statement. She was focused, with the intensity that was always daunting, on the current problem. "Listen to me, Matt. Just listen. You're dealing with a priest."

"He's just a man."

"Shut up," Chloe said bluntly. "Shut up, and for once in your life, just listen. He's a *priest*. A truly dedicated priest. He's not just any ordinary man. Priests hold some things far higher than life. Priests have died rather than break the seal of confessional, and if you think I'm kidding, read some of the lives of Catholic saints. And most of the good priests I know consider any confidence offered to them to be equally sacred. Even if he *knew* who did this, he couldn't tell you, not if he came across the knowledge through a confidence shared with him."

"That is so much crap."

Chloe looked away from him, compressing her lips and staring off into the distance. "It's that attitude, Matt, that makes it impossible for me to deal with you."

He drew a sharp breath, realizing she was talking about

him now. About *them,* and what once he had hoped would be. And he didn't like what he was hearing.

"We're talking about the spiritual here," Chloe said after a moment, her tone quieting and even softening a bit. "We're talking about a man who considers his pledge to God, his immortal soul, and the immortal souls of everyone else to be more important than his own life. More important, even, than catching a murderer. We're talking about a man who is willing to die for his beliefs. A man who is willing to follow Christ through Gethsemane and onto the cross."

"I'm willing to die for what I believe in," he said, almost harshly.

She astonished him then, reaching up to touch the scar on his cheek with gentle fingertips. "I know you are." She dropped her hand. "But you see this as a war between the good guys and the bad guys. Father doesn't."

"No? How does he see it?"

"He sees it as a battle for salvation, where there are only good guys, and other good guys who haven't yet realized how to be good. He believes that everyone is worthy of salvation. That's a far cry from believing some people deserve death."

"Oh, horseshit. The man believes in hell. What's different about that? How can you separate that from capital punishment?"

"It's very simple, Matt."

"Yeah."

She half smiled at him. "Yeah. You see, you believe a single act can deserve the ultimate punishment. No redemption allowed. Father Brendan believes in redemption. So long as there is breath in the body, the soul can be saved. And that's why he'll die first."

She paused for a moment, looking up at the few stars whose sparkle made its way through the ambient city light, then turned to him. "The difference, in a word, is hope. Father Brendan lives in a world that sparkles with hope. A world that literally drips with the promise and security of God's love. It's not a perfect world. He sees the same ugliness the rest of us do. I'm sure he's heard his share of hurt and pain and selfishness and horror in confession. He's seen families ripped apart and grieving. He was a navy chaplain for years. He's had to see a lot. But he sees it through eyes of grace. Through eyes of love. Through eyes of hope. And that's why this is so difficult for him."

He looked at her. At the passion and conviction of her words, and the wistful sadness in her eyes. She was talking about something she admired and did not have for herself. It hurt to watch.

"Chloe, he may have to be a priest, but I have to be a cop. That puts you in a difficult position."

At that she smiled. "And that's life, Matt. We all have our roles to play."

"You'll keep an eye on him?"

"You know I will. And I'll get some help in doing it. But there are places protectors won't be allowed to go. And you need to deal with that, Matt." She started to turn away. "Good night. I'll call you in the morning with any information I might get."

He walked away, not wondering where her loyalties lay, but how she could cling to them with all that had happened to her. And whether he would have to shred them to stop a killer.

* * *

Chloe went back to the rectory, trying with each step to settle the emotional turmoil Matt had managed to stir up in her. She vastly preferred to observe the world from a distance and feel as little as possible. Feelings only hurt. And Matt had, indirectly, caused her to face some feelings she definitely wanted on ice.

In the rectory she found Phil and Brendan still in the parlor, joined now by Dominic, who had finished with his duties for the day. Dominic, she thought, was a question mark. A man sent by the chancery who had little or no pastoral experience. A man who might well be in the pocket of someone in the diocese who didn't care for Brendan. The thought wouldn't have occurred to her last week, but tonight it did, after what Brendan had said about the calls from the diocese. Dominic might be here as a spy, or worse. She was cynical about church politics. While there were plenty of good men of the cloth, there were plenty who were more interested in power than souls. She didn't know which group Dominic belonged to.

Phil had made some tea and poured her a cup as she sat in the remaining armchair. No sofa in the rectory parlor, only armchairs. Old armchairs with worn upholstery.

"Thanks, Phil."

Phil smiled, an expression that lit up her face. She might refer to herself as a stop sign in order to make the children laugh, but when she smiled, you forgot her beanpole build, her freckles, and her flaming red hair. All you saw was light.

"Okay," Chloe said, taking charge as she was wont to do, "we need to protect Father Brendan."

"I already said—"

"I know what you said, Father. But within the limits of priesthood, we can still protect you. We won't go into the confessional with you, but we can still be in the church nearby. When you go to visit the sick, somebody can ride shotgun and remain outside."

Brendan looked down at the floor, sighing heavily. "I don't see any reason to go overboard. One phone call, which might be a prank, isn't reason to put me under full-time guard."

Dominic spoke. "One phone call, which might not be a prank, following a terrible murder in the church, is ample reason. I agree with Chloe, Brendan. This is not the time to be foolhardy. I was assigned here to help with the pastoral duties, and I'm willing to take on the majority of home visits."

"Some parishioners might not be happy about that."

"Then let them be unhappy," Dominic said firmly. "A priest is a priest, and my anointings and absolutions are as valid as yours."

Brendan looked wryly at him. "At the very least."

"So I'll take over what I can. Eucharistic visits can be made by Eucharistic ministers. I'll handle any anointings and confessions in private homes."

"As long as there isn't a conflict." Brendan sighed. "All right. All right. I think this is extreme, but apparently none of you will be happy unless I agree."

"It's only a temporary measure," Phil said. "Until the killer is caught."

Sorrow again shadowed Brendan's face. "That poor young man." He looked at Chloe. "Do the police have any leads at all?"

"None they're sharing with me. Yet. But I can tell you one thing, Father. It might make this a little easier for you.

Steve was shot in the back of the head. He never knew what hit him."

"He was dead before he was crucified?"

"Absolutely. There's no doubt. He died instantly from the gunshot."

"Thank God for small mercies." Brendan bowed his head a moment, as if saying a silent prayer.

"And now," said Chloe briskly, "the best thing you can do for yourself and for Steve is to try to remember if there's anybody in the world who might have a serious grudge against you."

Brendan raised his head and looked at all of them. "Do you know how appalling it is to consider the possibility that someone might have done that to Steve to get even with me? Do you have any idea how that sickens my soul?"

Dominic leaned forward. "It's appalling. I know it is. But sometimes we have to look into the jaws of hell. Steve's murderer has to be found. Not just because he killed Steve. Not just because he might be after you. But because he might go after others. What's more, Brendan, what hope is there of saving his soul if he isn't found? If he keeps this sin locked forever in his own heart, he'll never be saved."

Brendan nodded slowly. "You're right. I know you're right. But to tell you the God's honest truth, I never thought anybody hated me that much. And I hope to God I never did anything bad enough to make someone willing to do this."

Chloe shrugged. "None of us wants to believe a thing like that. If it's any consolation, Father, this killer, or these killers, are sick twists. It might not have taken all that much to trigger them."

Phil nodded agreement. "I received death threats at my last assignment. And I didn't do anything at all."

"You see?" Dominic said. "It might just be some small thing, Brendan. A small thing. Or it might be nothing at all. But you need to think about it anyway."

But Brendan's attention had turned to Phil. "I'm sorry," he said. "You should never have been treated that way."

Phil shrugged and smiled one of her patented smiles. "Nobody ever should be treated that way. But it happens."

Chloe spoke. "So help us, Father. Help us in any way you can."

"I will," he said. "Of course I will. But right now . . . right now I need to go to the church and pray."

He was not allowed to go alone. Phil and Chloe accompanied him and sat behind him in the pews. He reminded himself to keep his prayers brief, because both of them needed to get home to sleep, for they had work in the morning. So did he, but he was used to getting very little sleep for long periods.

He tried not to look toward the altar, toward the changes that were a reminder of what had happened, but his gaze was drawn there nonetheless, as if by a powerful magnet. His heart squeezed with anguish, and he fell into deep, questioning prayer, demanding answers from God.

God rarely answered, of course. The Divine Plan was inscrutable, leaving a man with little to cling to except shreds of blind faith. And right now, the usual answers about how suffering drew one closer to Christ, about how every agony yielded grace and eventually became a source of strength, weren't working for Brendan anyway.

This time he wanted, *needed,* to know why. He needed a reason. He needed some explanation of why such a beautiful young life had been cut so short in such a terrible, meaningless fashion. It wasn't that he hadn't seen young lives cut short before. He'd lost count of the times he'd buried a young person who had died in an accident, or a fight, or from illness.

But there was something about this time, something so horrible, that he needed an answer.

No voice thundered from on high. No bush burned in the night for him.

But suddenly, as if from nowhere, a gentle peace filled him. It was as if unseen, loving arms wrapped around him, as if a quiet flood of tenderness filled his heart, driving away all the pain and horror.

That night, he slept easily for the first time since the murder had been discovered.

Victor Singh paused to wipe the sweat from his brow with a thin towel, then went back to work with the cordless saw. His white T-shirt was smudged with black, from hours of wrestling with old tires. He was nearly done with the saw. Then he'd feed the tires into the chipper to produce a mulch of old rubber.

He could have bought the mulch. It was commonly used in playgrounds and parks, in place of cedar shavings. But his contact had said no. That would leave a paper trail. Instead, he'd had to go to landfills, looking for battered junk cars from which he could salvage the tires. He hadn't needed many—two dozen or so, his contact had said. That would make enough mulch.

A mulch which, when burned, would produce a thick, acrid, oily smoke. That smoke itself might be enough to cause respiratory problems for an old person, or a young child, or someone who was ill already. But that wasn't the point. It was merely a medium. A way to make his real pay-load hang in the air to cause maximum damage.

It was, he thought, terrifyingly simple to make a chemical weapon.

CHAPTER 8

The killer looked across the breakfast table at his wife, who was reading the newspaper. He was annoyed, because she had gotten to it before he had, and he was impatient to learn if there was any follow-up information about that kid's killing.

"Terrible," Jo said. "It's just terrible."

"What is?" he asked between his teeth. He was so tense he could barely sip his coffee.

Jo looked at him, her graying hair still a mess from bed. "What is your problem this morning? You sound like you want to kill somebody."

His heart slammed, even though he knew she was totally unaware. "I'm just irritable," he answered. "What's so damn terrible?"

"The crucifixion of that young man. Can you believe anyone would do such a terrible thing? Such a blasphemous thing."

Count on Jo to find it blasphemous. Living with a Bible-thumping Fundamentalist was not the best way to spend more than thirty years. "Obviously someone did it," he answered shortly. "Do they say who?"

Because he knew he hadn't done that part. And he was going nuts from wondering who had seen him. And why they had done this to the body.

Jo turned a couple of pages and read, leaving him ready to strangle her as he waited.

"No, they have no leads. But they *do* say he was dead before he was nailed to the cross."

The killer gritted his teeth. "That's all?"

"That's all they're saying." Jo turned a couple of more pages, reaching the op-ed page. "Blasphemy," she said again. "Even if it *was* a Catholic church."

"Well," he said, "you might remember that our son was Catholic."

"Oh, that was just rebellion," she said blithely, folding the paper so she could read more easily. "He'd have come back into the fold eventually. People always return to their roots."

The killer didn't have any roots in religion, but he didn't bother to point that out. It would only lead to another lecture about the state of his soul.

Jo looked up at him with a smile. "Would you like the sports section, dear?"

"What makes you think the priest knows anything?" the watcher demanded of the two men in the sun-filled room with him. The nameless men. "If he did he's had more than two years to blow the whistle."

The taller of the two men turned toward the window and puffed on his cigar. The other, seated on a mass-produced cheap hotel chair, rapped his fingers on the veneered tabletop. "He knows. He just doesn't know he knows."

The watcher felt a surge of annoyance. "How can you be

sure? Look, if I'm going to keep this going, you've got to tell me more. You say there's a deadline. You say there's a priest who knows something, and you're using a loose cannon to remove him so there won't be a trail. But then you say the priest has known all along. It's not adding up."

The man with the cigar turned from the window. "This wouldn't be a good time to get an attack of conscience," he said. The words chilled the air in the room.

"I'm not getting an attack of conscience," the watcher said. "I'm with this plan, you know it. Have you ever had reason to question my loyalty?" But he was sweating a little around his hairline. He hated getting crosswise with these guys; he knew what they were capable of.

The man with the cigar turned back toward the window, as if forgetting all about the watcher. The other man drummed his fingers again: *shave and a haircut, two bits.* A familiar rhythm. Once a lifesaving signal for the man at the table. The watcher knew that much about him.

"No, he's right," the man at the table replied. "He's right. There's an unexpected wrinkle here, which," he added, looking at the watcher, "we're investigating."

"Thank you."

"The priest," continued the man at the table, "was a close confidante of one of our operatives a few years ago."

"He turned the guy," said the man at the window.

"We had to eliminate the operative," added the man at the table.

"Why didn't you just take out the priest, too?"

The man at the table shook his head. "We couldn't get to him. By the time we found out about the priest, he was in a monastery, in seclusion. Those monks guard each other better than the Secret Service guards the president." He gave a raspy laugh. "Hell, we couldn't even get to have a word with him. He was observing a vow of silence, they said. He didn't talk to anybody, and he never came out of the monastery."

"So he wasn't really a problem."

"Not then. But then we discovered he's left the monastery and is here . . . in Tampa. And that's too much of a damn coincidence. Even if he hasn't figured things out for himself yet, he will once things start happening. And he'll know too much."

"Exactly," said the man at the window. He blew another cloud of smoke. "We've got nine days to eliminate him. The plans are in motion, and we can't call them back. I want that priest out of the picture." He turned and smiled coldly. "And I don't give a damn about your back."

The watcher had always known he was the only one who cared about his own back. Nothing new in that. He had to figure out a way to get the cannon moving.

"How's it going?" Matt asked, when he and Chloe met for coffee at a doughnut place the next evening. They hadn't spoken since the night before at the rectory.

"Well, being a bodyguard was never my goal in life."

He grinned, a charming smile that once had drawn her like moth to a flame. "That's what you get for sticking your nose in where you shouldn't. You *could* just let *me* handle this case."

"Sure. I imagine you've already broken it."

His smile faded. "Play nice, Chloe. For once, just play nice. You got anything for me?"

"Only that I don't think I could survive the pace that Father Brendan keeps. He started at seven this morning, and he's booked until ten tonight. Then he comes back to the rectory to make phone calls."

"Someone's with him?"

"All the time, so far. You got anything for me?"

He shook his head and wagged his finger. "Wait. I'm not done questioning you. Are you carrying?"

She nodded. "I have a Glock. And a permit to carry."

"Good. What about the rest of your people?"

"I seriously doubt that either Father Dominic or Sister Phil would consider carrying a gun."

"Yeah, you're probably right." He shook his head. "Better if they don't. They don't have the training. They'd only hurt the wrong person . . . or themselves." He paused for a moment, in thought. "Okay, another question. Is it easy to get Father Brendan on the phone?"

"No, it's not. He's so busy, you usually have to leave a message or a voice mail for him."

"No cell phone?"

"Well, yes, but only the office staff have that number. He has a pager, too, but same thing. A priest can't be interrupted while he's tending to parishioners, so voice mail it is."

"So it's unusual that he even got that phone call."

"Are you trying to say something?"

He shook his head. "I'm not saying anything. I'm just thinking out loud. Ordinarily the caller would have been dumped to voice mail."

"Yes, usually."

"What about emergencies?"

"Well, then of course, the staff would call him."

"At night?"

"At night, he answers his own phone. He has a private line, and there's also an emergency rectory line. If there's an after-hours emergency, the answering machine gives out that number."

Matt pulled a pad out of his pocket, along with a pen. "Let me run through this again. The offices are in the rectory?"

"Only the parish secretary's and the priest's private offices. The rest of the offices were moved to a new wing at the parish hall five years ago."

Matt made a note. "Doesn't that cause a problem, her being in one place and everyone else over at the hall?"

"It doesn't seem to. She's basically a secretary to the priests."

"Okay. So we have the phone being answered over at the hall?"

"Yes, unless someone calls the rectory directly. Then they get Lucy. Or they get the emergency number."

"Where's the emergency number answered?"

"There's a phone upstairs in the priests' residence area, and another one downstairs in the kitchen."

"And their private phones?"

"In their bedrooms and offices."

"Okay, I think I get the picture."

"What are you thinking?"

He sighed. "Only that my plan to have Father Brendan trace these calls is probably a waste of time. If he gets another one, it'll probably land in his voice mail."

"Probably. Unless the guy calls the emergency number at night."

Matt picked up his coffee mug and took a deep drink. He frowned. "It's getting cold." With a finger he signaled the waitress, who replaced his cup with a steaming mug. "Hmm." He looked down at his pad and doodled something.

"I don't know if tracing will work if the call is transferred. I'll have to find out. How secret are these unpublished numbers?"

Chloe smiled. "Not secret at all. Ever since he got here, Father Brendan's been scrawling the number for his private line on every business card he hands out. I think 90 percent of the parishioners have it. And the rectory number is no secret at all. If you want it, you've got it just by calling after hours and copying down the emergency number. Or simply by asking for it. You have to understand, priests aren't trying to be inaccessible."

"Tell him about the trace anyway. He can do it by pushing star-five-seven. You never know. We might bag our guy."

"Of course. Now it's your turn."

The corners of his eyes crinkled with a suppressed smile. "I knew that was coming. What have I got? Very little. We're waiting for all the reports to come in. You know how it goes. And so far I haven't found anyone who's seen or heard anything."

"I hate these cases," Chloe said flatly.

"Me too."

"Some total stranger walks up, kills a kid, and there's nothing. Nothing at all."

"Well, except that the body was moved. More than once."

Chloe's head snapped up. "How do you know that?"

"The criminology lab found some fibers that don't match the clothing the vic was wearing. Like rug fibers, only cheaper. Then there's gravel and dirt that they don't think go with the grass I told you about earlier."

"My God." Chloe looked thoughtful.

"Yeah. Now it may just be that somebody moved the

vic's body to the church in a car trunk. But we've still got the gravel and dirt. The lab thinks it's from a recently paved surface, something paved with oil and gravel mix."

"That doesn't fit anything at the church."

"I know. There wasn't a whole lot of it. It *could* have been in the trunk when he was moved. I'll tell you frankly, Chloe, that I don't like the possibility that body may have been moved *twice*."

"It doesn't make any sense. I mean, if you're going to transport a body in a trunk, why the hell would you take it out, then move it again?"

"I don't know. Unless we've got more going on here than a murder."

Chloe's wheels were clearly spinning now, and she turned to look out the window beside them, into a parking lot that was nearly empty. Traffic whizzed by on the road out front. "Then there's the entire problem of how Steve was put up on that cross. That would take more than one person."

"Exactly. I watched them take him down. No way only one person could have done it. I'd say three at a minimum."

"Or an act of God."

Matt started to laugh, then broke off abruptly and looked closely at her. She wasn't kidding. A chill ran down his spine. "Don't go spooky on me."

Chloe looked at him. "I'm not going spooky. I'm looking at the senseless death of a good young man who was destined for the priesthood. Who's to say that the message in this crime wasn't being delivered by a power greater than us?"

"Oh, Christ." Matt shifted uncomfortably on the bench. "If you want to think that was a miracle . . ." He couldn't even finish. The thought appalled him too much.

"I'm not saying it was. I'm just saying . . . I believe in miracles. If it *was* an act of God that put Steve there, I can guarantee you one thing."

"What's that?"

"We'll never know. Anyway, I'm going forward on the assumption that there are bad guys involved, and that we can track them down. I'm a human, Matt. I know the evils we're capable of."

He felt better. At least she wasn't going to run off on some hoodoo religious tack on him. She'd be useless to everyone if she did.

"Fair enough," he said finally. "Just don't give me the willies again."

She smiled faintly. "You could use a little religion in your life, Matt. For a Catholic, everything in this world is a sign of the grace of God."

"Even what happened to the King kid?"

"Even that. Some good will come out of it somehow."

"Yeah, I know what good will come out of it. I'll nail the sick twists who did it. And that's all the good I need."

CHAPTER 9

The call to present himself at the chancery ripped a hole in Brendan's day. He wasn't given an option of choosing a better time, or setting a mutually convenient appointment. He was simply told to show.

He left Lucy scrambling to rearrange his appointments and get Dominic to fill in for him, and climbed into his car for the drive downtown. Somehow, somewhere in the back of his mind, he had known this was coming. There had been too many calls from Monsignor Crowell in the past few months, and with what had happened over the past weekend, things were bound to come to a head.

For this trip, he had even managed to ditch his shadows. Since he'd been working at the rectory for a change, none of his self-appointed bodyguards had been with him to argue.

He wasn't sure how he felt about that. On the one hand, it was nice that people cared enough to put themselves out this way. On the other, it was a relief to be going somewhere by himself. He spent so much time in the company of others that his car was an escape, a place of solitude.

He could listen to music of his own choosing, or just take time to think things over and clear all the junk from his head. Because he certainly accumulated enough junk in the course of a day. Of course, like most priests, he was wonderfully forgetful when it came to information that people wanted to keep private. It was a talent developed over years of hearing confessions from people he still had to be able to greet with warmth and love only minutes or hours later. The worst secrets died a rapid death in his memory cells.

Today, however, there was little room for anything except discomfort about the interview he was facing. It was strange to him that he'd been in the parish only six months and for some reason was facing serious opposition. He honestly couldn't think what he had done to make any of his parishioners so upset with him. Of course, he knew he must have done something, however minor. He wasn't holding himself free of responsibility. But it troubled him that he had no inkling of who or why. Perhaps today would clarify the issues and give him a clue so he could mend fences. He hoped so.

But regardless of his hopes for the meeting, he was well aware that Monsignor Crowell didn't like him. Which meant there would be a great deal of unpleasantness along the way as he tried to discern what was really going on.

He was kept cooling his heels in an anteroom for twenty minutes. Not surprising. He'd been around the block enough times to recognize an exercise of power for the sake of power. He'd seen it frequently in the navy.

But at long last, he was summoned into the monsignor's august presence, into an office full of enough antiques and icons to suggest it was an extension of the Vatican. The room, however, failed to intimidate him. How Crowell chose to spend his own money was Crowell's business. Brendan vastly preferred his own situation, where he had next to nothing to spend, and what he had could be given where it was needed.

For reasons known only to himself, Crowell had chosen to wear a cassock in a diocese where cassocks were relegated to the backs of closets as impractical. He also wore a pectoral cross big enough to blind. It was as if he were trying to remind Brendan that the full weight of the church stood behind him.

Brendan took the chair Crowell waved him to. Pleasantries were exchanged in the briefest possible fashion.

"Let's get straight to business, shall we?" Crowell said, steepling his hands.

"Yes, of course," Brendan replied. Trying to look more relaxed than he felt, he settled back and crossed his legs.

"I'm sure," the monsignor began, "that you've noticed this office has had to make a number of calls to you in the past month or so."

"Yes, I have. But they were all very vague, Monsignor."

"Deliberately so. However, I have called you here today because a serious charge has been leveled against you. I thought, in your interests, that we would keep it just between the two of us for the moment."

"You're very kind." But Brendan's normally somnolent radar was beginning to beep. Loudly.

"I also want to give you the chance to make a confession. We can work this out, Father. There are programs available to help priests like you."

"Like me?" Brendan's heart began to beat faster. "What do you mean?"

But Crowell chose not to answer directly. "The important thing here is to avoid scandal for the Church. I'm sure you agree with me."

"Always."

Crowell smiled. "I knew you would. We want to handle this as quietly as possible, and help you to regain your spiritual purity."

Brendan's heart was still beating rapidly, but now it was beating with anger. "I'm not aware that I've compromised my spiritual purity in any significant way, Monsignor."

Crowell arched both eyebrows. "Then the situation may be more serious than I thought."

Brendan couldn't quite keep a touch of acid out of his voice, although he tried. "It might be very helpful to me if you would tell me what it is I'm supposed to have done."

"The Church has many homosexual members, Father. That is of no concern to us as long as these people remain chaste."

Brendan began to sense where this was heading. "Monsignor, I am chaste. I have always been chaste. I have never once broken my vow of chastity."

"But you may have stretched it a little?" The eyebrows rose again.

"No. Never."

Crowell sighed. "I wish you wouldn't make this difficult for us, Father. We have reports to the contrary."

"What reports? From whom?"

"They were made in confidence."

"Of course." Brendan stood and walked a few steps before turning again to face Crowell. "I repeat, I have never broken my vow of chastity. And I am not gay, not that it should matter, given my vow."

"Please sit, Father. I don't care to have you towering over me."

Brendan sat, but on the edge of the chair this time.

"We have," Crowell continued, "received complaints about your relationship with this young man who was so unfortunately murdered and crucified."

"The poison of dirty minds. He was planning to enter the priesthood, and I was guiding him."

"Yes, yes. I believe you." But it was evident that Crowell did not. "However, there was that in your relationship which led some to believe otherwise."

"Monsignor, I can't help what others choose to believe."

"Yes, you can. You can be more circumspect for one thing."

Brendan gritted his teeth, but managed a nod.

"But to get to the heart of the issue. This morning we had a very disturbing phone call from a man who says that not only were you having an . . . affair with young King, but that you had one with a young man when you were in the navy. That young man also died under unfortunate circumstances."

"What?" Brendan was out of his chair like a shot. "May I remind you, Monsignor, that bearing false witness is a mortal sin?"

"Calm yourself, Father," Crowell barked. "And sit."

Like a dog, Brendan thought. He was being talked to like a dog. Which Crowell evidently believed he was. He sat, biting his tongue.

"These are serious charges, Father. The diocese cannot afford to ignore them. In reviewing your file, I note that you did indeed leave the navy very abruptly. Then you went into seclusion for two years."

"That was only part of—"

"Father, hold your tongue. You can deny all of this, but it remains that it looks bad. And the police are asking about your relationship with young King as well. It would be unfortunate for the diocese and the Church if this came out in the papers."

Brendan knotted his hands together, biting back words of self-defense, reminding himself that he had taken a vow of obedience. It was the one vow he'd ever broken in his life, but now was not the time to break it again. As calmly as he could manage, he said only, "Yes, Monsignor."

Crowell rocked back in his chair a bit. "That's better. Now, since you deny all of this, I suppose we're going to have to have an investigation. I'll speak to the bishop about it. But in the meantime . . . in the meantime, Father, I expect you to keep a low profile and do nothing, I repeat, *nothing* untoward. And if this comes out in the papers, we'll have to remove you immediately."

"Yes, Monsignor."

"Then we understand one another." Crowell smiled. "I hope you are what you say your are, Father. For the sake of your eternal soul."

If Brendan's eternal soul was at risk, it was only because of the uncharitable thoughts he harbored toward Monsignor Crowell on his way back to the parish. Words like *pig, snake,* and *jackass* even passed his lips. Vile, vicious rumors treated as facts, and all of them, of course, spread anonymously. There was a reason Paul included gossip among his list of repugnant sins in his Epistle to the Romans. Then he reminded himself of what Paul said at the start of the next chapter: "Therefore you have no right to judge, for you do the very same things." He was surely not so holy that he could judge anyone, not even Crowell.

Still, the interview stuck in his throat like a fish bone. Yes, he went out of his way to welcome gays and lesbians in his parish. They were children of God, and needed the grace and nourishment of parish life every bit as much as anyone else. Truth be told, he agreed with the many Catholics who thought it was high time the Church fully recognized gays and lesbians, although he didn't see that likely to happen anytime soon. And yes, Steve King was gay. He was also celibate, or so he had told Brendan. And even if he weren't, it could in no way excuse the horror that had been committed upon him.

As for Brendan himself, well, the rumors were simply ugly lies. And of course, in Crowell's eyes, Brendan was guilty until proven innocent, as if there were any way he could *prove* that he was both straight and chaste.

"The bigger question," Dominic said as they sat across the table in the rectory having a late-night snack, "is who is spreading these rumors, and why. I think this confirms the detective's suspicions. Someone is out to get you, my friend."

"I try not to be paranoid," Brendan said, although in fact he was becoming *very* paranoid.

"This isn't paranoia. This is a fact. Someone is out to ruin you."

Brendan sighed. He was weary to his very soul. "I'm so tired, Dominic. I feel like every homily is a lie. I feel like . . . like I'm casting pearls before swine."

"You are," Dominic said. "In part. Look, I haven't been at St. Simeon's long, but I've been here long enough to know that the vast majority of the people here would kiss the ground you walk on. I've never seen such warmth. If I'd known it was like this, I wouldn't have spent most of my priesthood in an office downtown. But there are five thousand members in our parish. You can't expect to please all of them."

Brendan nodded. "I know. Maybe I'm just worn-out from Lent and the rest of it."

"Maybe so. Or maybe, just maybe, in addition to being a priest, you're also a human being. With human frailties and weaknesses and needs. And human grief."

"That's no news flash, Dominic. I know I'm human."

Dominic tapped his head. "Up here you know, yes. But you need to know down here." He tapped his chest. "You need to accept that you're angry and hurt and frustrated, and you feel deeply wronged. And that there's a very good reason for that. Because you have been. Christ told us to be as cautious as serpents and as gentle as doves. You're a good dove. But you need to learn some caution. Find a rock and stay under it until this mess blows over."

"But you can't—"

"You'd be amazed what an old man can accomplish in a good cause," Dominic cut in. "I'll handle the parish. You keep your head down and let Chloe and that detective handle this. I have a feeling they'll do just fine."

"I have a feeling they'll do more than fine," Brendan said with a half smile.

Dominic winked. "Yes, that too." He paused a moment. "By the way, what happened when you were in the navy?"

Brendan drew a deep breath and pushed the remnants of his sandwich away. He rose and shook his head. "I learned how wrong I can be. How very wrong I can be."

Chloe and Sister Phil were playing cards at Chloe's house, a couple of blocks from St. Simeon's. They liked to play rummy as a background to their chats, and as usual,

Chloe was cleaning up. Beside them on the dining table was a bowl of Chex Mix and a couple of glasses of cola.

The house itself was small and snug, not the kind of place one expected for a successful attorney. But Chloe wasn't ever what anyone expected. She seemed quite content in her small, comfortable, and slightly shabby home. Phil had an apartment that she shared with a couple of other sisters, but she liked the relative peace of Chloe's house. For her it was sometimes a great escape.

Tonight their conversation was neither idle nor peaceful, and finally Phil put her cards facedown on the table. "Okay," she said, "I'm not supposed to tell anyone, but I'm going to tell you anyway."

Chloe looked up, forgetting her own hand. "What?"

"Lucy told me that Father was summoned to the chancery today by Monsignor Crowell."

"And?"

"I don't know. Lucy said Brendan seemed angry when he got back, but he didn't say anything."

Chloe arched one eyebrow. "So you naturally called the chancery."

"Well, of course. Not that it did me any good." Phil reached for a handful of Chex Mix, allowed by genetics to be scornful of such things as calories and fat content. "Nobody seems to know what's going on. Whatever it is, Crowell is evidently playing it very close to the vest." Phil wrinkled her nose. "I don't trust that man."

"Why not? I don't know much about him."

"No reason you should. You're just a parishioner. But the word at the chancery is that Monsignor is a very political creature who has his eye on the corridors of power."

"Which corridors?"

Phil crunched and swallowed. "Oh, the corridors at the Vatican."

"Whew."

"Exactly. Whew."

"How likely is that?"

Phil shrugged. "The Church is both human and divine. Unfortunately, the human sometimes gets in the way of the divine. Does brown-nosing and money make it easier to ascend? Of course. Is it the only way? I hope not."

Chloe surprised her with a small laugh. "God forfend."

"Exactly." Phil's green eyes sparkled humorously. "Actually, I'm sure it's not. Look at our bishop. Bishop Cruz is one of the kindest, most godly men in the Church. I'm sure he had to be politic on his way up, but the goodness of his heart is unquestioned. Will he ever be a cardinal?" Phil sighed. "I doubt it. Let's just say I don't think he's politic enough in some quarters."

"Well, I like him better as our bishop."

Phil grinned. "I agree."

"So, do you think Bishop Cruz knows about Monsignor Crowell?"

"Probably. But at this point he probably hasn't heard anything to worry him too much. I mean, this is part and parcel of the Church hierarchy. Some people play power games, political games. Unless they overstep in some egregious way, nothing is going to happen."

Chloe nodded and put her cards down. "But if Crowell is stepping on Father Brendan . . ."

"In the first place, we don't know what happened in that interview. It may have been about Steve's murder, and certainly the diocese is going to have concerns there, Chloe."

"Well, of course."

Phil shrugged. "Unless I can find out something concrete, we can only speculate."

"I'll ask Father."

"I don't know that Lucy would appreciate that."

"Hey, I'm on a case. I'll tell him I found out through other sources. Which will be true."

Phil laughed. "Okay, okay. Now for the interesting stuff?"

Chloe looked surprised. "What do you mean?"

"What's the story with you and that gorgeous police detective?"

Chloe's face darkened, and Phil found herself regretting her lighthearted teasing. She shouldn't have mentioned it at all. "Chloe . . ."

But Chloe waved a dismissing hand. "We have a history, that's all. An old, old history."

"And not a completely happy one, I gather." Phil hesitated, then plunged on. "Forgive an old nun who has to live some things vicariously, but . . . was it romantic?"

Chloe looked at her, her eyes gone as glacial as the North Pole. But then the expression softened just a bit. "You're not an old nun by any means. And it wasn't romantic. There was . . . no time for that."

"I see. So I'm just supposed to sit on my hands and wonder forever?"

Chloe smiled faintly. "I'm afraid so, Phil. I'm afraid so."

Phil sighed and reached for another handful of mix. "Nobody ever told me how positively boring it could be to live a religious life."

"Boring? You're kidding, right?"

Phil shrugged. "Nobody ever tells me the really good stuff. They don't want to sully my ears."

Chloe couldn't help smiling. "Trust me, Phil. There's nothing that would sully your ears in my relationship with Matt. It's just too painful to talk about."

"Sometimes sharing pain can make the load lighter. But whatever. I'm here if you ever want to talk. Just tell me one thing. Is the guy married?"

"No."

Phil nodded. "Okay, I'll shut up." But she wondered if Chloe realized how much she had just revealed. An uninterested woman wouldn't know Matt's marital status. Inwardly, Phil smiled.

CHAPTER 10

For good or ill, keeping secrets was as natural to a priest as breathing. Over the years Dominic had been party to many secrets, but they had never been secrets of a kind he had had the least desire to share. They had been ugly little secrets, sometimes even horrifying, he had read in petitions for annulment. They involved people he didn't know and would probably never meet. They were already past by the time he read about them, and while they sometimes made his heart ache, he had never felt the least urge to discuss them.

Thus it shocked him that he felt compelled to tell someone what Brendan had told him about the interview with Crowell. The compulsion kept him awake late into the night, and when he finally did sleep, it wasn't for long.

The seal of the confessional was not on their conversation; he knew that. But it didn't make any difference. Words spoken to a priest were assumed to be confidential, and Brendan would never imagine that Dominic might share them elsewhere.

But throughout the dark hours of the night, the compulsion grew. One of his favorite mystery novels was *The*

Rosary Murders by William X. Kienzle. In it, Father Koessler asked the perennial question: If someone tells you in confession that he has poisoned the communion wine, what can you do? There was, of course, nothing, unless you could find a way to spill the wine.

A horrendous dilemma, and one Dominic was eternally grateful that he'd never faced.

But now he felt he was facing something along similar lines. It was clear to him that someone wanted to destroy Brendan, and it was not simply Monsignor Crowell. He was sure, in his very bones, that Crowell hadn't invented the complaint, however gleefully he might use it against Brendan.

So what now? This information might be important to the police investigation, especially since it seemed to link what was happening now with something that had happened while Brendan was in the navy. A clue in the past might lead to a resolution now . . . and might save Brendan.

But even though the seal hadn't actually been on their conversation, it was implied. Troubled, Dominic wrestled with the problem for most of the night.

In the morning the problem was no more clear, nor was his head, foggy with lack of sleep. He had the morning Mass, and he vested with less agility than usual, things slipping from his fingers. He was sure that when he left the sacristy he looked as if he'd slept in his robes.

The usual forty or so people were present, many of them the heart and soul of St. Simeon's. They were faces he already knew well, in just a few short weeks, not only from daily Mass, but from their presence around the parish hall and offices as they volunteered their time and talent.

But one face was not usually here. Chloe, like many in

the parish, had to be at work or on her way to work at this hour of the morning. Today, however, she sat in the front pew.

It was like a message from God. As soon as Dominic's gaze lit on her, he knew what he needed to do. When he gave her the Eucharist, he murmured, "I need to see you after Mass."

She nodded, meeting his gaze briefly, then moved on to the chalice of wine.

After Mass, there were the usual number of people who wanted to speak with him. Some simply wanted to socialize for a few minutes. Others had problems they wanted to share. Many expressed concern for Brendan and asked how he was getting along. If there was malice in this parish against the pastor, none of these people evinced it.

But then, those who went to daily Mass were without a doubt some of the best people in any church.

Chloe, thank goodness, waited patiently until he was able to signal her to follow him into the sacristy. Once there, he stripped his vestments, speaking as he did so.

"I'm going to break a confidence here," he said, reaching for a hangar. "I'd appreciate it if you'd keep it to yourself. Primarily, don't tell the cops."

Chloe tilted her head to one side. "I can't promise that, Father. I'm not just a parishioner, I'm also a lawyer, which makes me an officer of the court. I can't be involved in anything that might be obstruction of justice."

Dominic sighed, finished hanging his vestments, then sat facing her. "I don't think this falls into that category. But I'll let you use your best judgment, then. Just understand that this was told to me in confidence, and the only reason I'm breaking that confidence is because I believe it might have some bearing on what's happening here."

Chloe nodded. "I'll treat it carefully, Father. As an attorney, I understand confidentiality as well as a priest."

He smiled wryly. "Maybe you do."

"I know I do."

"Very well. We're on the same page."

Chloe nodded. "Close enough. So what's going on?"

Dominic hesitated, trying to decide what was essential and what he could skip over so as not to divulge anything unnecessary. Finally, he decided to approach the matter as if he'd heard it from somewhere else.

"It's come to my attention," he said, "that another complaint has been lodged against Father Brendan at the chancery. From what I understand, this complaint alleges an improper relationship with young Steve King."

"That's already on the table, Father. Somebody spilled that to the cops."

"Yes, but there's more. Its seems this complainer linked the matter of King to an incident while Brendan was a navy chaplain."

Chloe became very still and very quiet. Dominic, who hadn't known her very long, wasn't used to this habit of hers, and he found it quite unsettling. In fact, it was downright unnerving how her blue eyes could suddenly seem icy enough to freeze anything they happened to gaze upon. At the moment, thank goodness, she wasn't looking at him.

"Father . . ." She spoke slowly, thoughtfully. "Are you telling me that Brendan was accused once before of having a romantic relationship with a young man?"

"I don't know if that's the case. I don't know if he was

accused or not. In fact, I know nothing about what really happened. I . . . tried to find out, and met with a dead end."

"Shit." Chloe spoke the word, then glanced at him. "Sorry."

"Quite all right. I believe I've used that word a time or two myself."

A small, mirthless smile lifted the corners of her mouth. "Thanks. Okay. I'll find out what's going on. Somehow."

"I'm just concerned that there may be a link, at least in the mind of someone who's threatening the pastor."

"There may well be. I don't know. It may be nothing but malicious gossip. But I'll check it out."

"Thank you. And, by the way, I don't especially care to know what you find out."

Chloe looked at him, her eyes seeming to penetrate past his surface to the not-quite-shiny state of his soul. "You weren't sent here just to be parochial vicar, were you."

It wasn't a question. Dominic, who thought he'd forgotten how to blush at least thirty years ago, felt his cheeks heating.

"You don't have to answer," Chloe said pleasantly enough. "Just guard his back, Father. Because regardless of what problems the Church hierarchy may have with Brendan, they at least won't kill him."

He nodded, unable to speak, and watched as this extraordinarily self-possessed and icy woman walked out of the sacristy.

Being asked to help Chloe with an investigation was often the high point of Phil's life. After fifteen years of teaching third- and fourth-graders, most of the problems she faced had become entirely too familiar. Chloe's occasional requests for her to do research of some kind were invariably welcome.

One of her favorite jobs had been driving down to a bad part of town and parking where a cop had supposedly been parked while watching a drug exchange. She thought she'd earned her fedora that day, because there was no way the police officer could have seen a drug transaction at the corner where it supposedly took place, through the sign he was parked behind.

But this request was different.

"Well, of course I have contacts in the chancery," she said in answer to Chloe's request, "but they aren't going to give me anything except gossip. Certainly not someone's personnel records."

"I don't need you to *get* them," Chloe argued. "I just need to know if there's anything in them about an incident involving the death of a young man while Brendan was in the navy. Since he was a priest at the time, there might be something there about it."

"I don't know, Chloe. Those records are *very* private. There's not only the question of you and me being privy to something that's so private, but there's the question of asking someone else to check it out."

"I understand that. But the simple fact is, Brendan's life is in the balance. And a complaint made at the chancery suggests that Steve's death was not the first time Brendan was associated with the death of a young man. If there's a link there, it could lead us to the killer."

The two women were sitting in Chloe's living room, sharing a pot of green tea on a sunny April afternoon that had turned unexpectedly chilly. For now, Brendan was safe under the watchful eyes of about three hundred people as he performed a wedding. In forty-five minutes, though, one of them needed to get over to the church to keep an eye on him.

Phil poured some more tea into her small Japanese cup and sipped it. This was a leap she wasn't sure she was ready to make, yet already her mind was considering ways she might achieve what Chloe wanted.

"The problem with me," Phil announced after a moment, "is that I can't resist a challenge."

"I know." Chloe laughed. "That's what makes you such a great investigator."

"And a fool. I could get really burned on this, and so could whoever helps me."

Chloe didn't say anything. That was the worst thing about Chloe. She didn't argue. If she'd argued, Phil would at least have had something to argue against.

"Oh, all right," Phil said finally. "I'll see what I can do. But I can't make any promises."

"You realize," Chloe said, "that if we don't get to the bottom of this, and quickly, someone might be inspired to call the police with the same story. If that were to happen, Father Brendan wouldn't have a lick of privacy anymore, not from the police and not from the press."

Trust Chloe to give her the good reasons *after* she'd made her decision. Still, it helped ease her conscience somewhat. "Do me a favor, Chlo?"

"Sure, Phil."

"Remind me to go to confession. Soon."

Chloe's laugh was little comfort.

The watcher called the killer and told him the priest was going to be gone from Tampa in five days. The killer heard this news with a sinking heart, even though he knew he was the cause of it. Those phone calls to the Tampa chancery offices had finally had an effect.

He hung up the phone and turned to his wife, who was watching some sitcom on the television. "I have to go out of town again."

She looked up, dismayed. Since the death of their son she'd begun to hate it when he traveled, even though she'd been alone before. It was as if she was afraid he was going to go away and never come back, just as their son had.

"Do you have to?" she asked, a hint of a whine in her voice.

"There's an emergency."

"When?"

"I'll leave in the morning."

She sighed. "How long will you be gone?"

"A couple of days. I'll call and let you know."

Then, as always, she went back to her television show, leaving him alone.

He went to his son's room, as he often did. In the years since Tom joined the navy, he and his wife had talked about converting the room into a guest room, but they'd somehow never gotten around to it. Oh, they'd started. They'd taken down the posters and the high school memorabilia, packing it all carefully away for Tom.

The twin bed was still a twin bed, though. They'd never bought the queen-size bed they'd talked about once with so much hope, speaking of a daughter-in-law and grandchildren. The bedspread was different though. His wife had gotten rid of the "ratty" NFL spread and replaced it with a peach-colored chenille.

But otherwise, the room was still the same. The same nicked wood desk was in the same corner, still bearing the scars of careless youth and one angry attempt to carve something nasty into it when Tom was eight. The shelves still held the books Tom had left behind, from Dr. Seuss to *Cliff Notes*. A copy of the King James Bible, battered from years of being carried to Sunday school and Bible study groups.

The room looked dingy and sad. But mostly it looked empty.

Sometimes when he sat on the edge of the bed, the annoying sound of the TV muffled by the closed door, he thought he could hear his son's voice, could hear his laughter, and his impatient, angry teenage retorts. Could hear him announcing with such pride that he'd joined the navy. It was as if the room had captured those sounds and held them, cherishing them.

He let the sorrow come to him, let it fill him and spill wetly from his burning eyes. His throat tightened until he could barely breathe, each gasp sounding pained.

I'll get him for you, Tom, he vowed silently, anger fueled by his anguish. *I'll get him for you.*

Then he sat there and sobbed like a baby.

The watcher sat in the cheesy hotel room—the big guys always got the slightly better hotels, while he wound up in the cheapest motel in the area—and stared at the telephone. He'd done it, he'd pushed the cannon, but he wasn't at all sure he was happy about it.

Sitting there, he did some painful thinking. It was rare that he allowed himself to do so, because painful thinking seldom led to answers, but it often led to exactly that: pain.

However, the choice of cannon in this instance was really beginning to bug him. It wasn't that he questioned the goal of his organization. After all, you couldn't fight terrorism with mealy-mouthed platitudes and endless investigations. No, you needed to fight them head-on, with every bit as much threat and weight as you could put behind your words. The business in Afghanistan was a surprising but welcome step in the right direction. However, the real nest of vipers was being overlooked.

So you gave a little push and shove in the right direction. All perfectly well and good. He approved of that.

He also understood the need to use a cannon that couldn't be traced back to them. But their choice this time . . .

He shook his head. He'd questioned it from the outset, although not too loudly, since loud complaints could bring the hammer down on his head. But he'd questioned it even then. Now the cannon had killed a kid, and was plainly running his own agenda. Not good. Not good at all, even if the big guys *did* say that it would make the cannon look even more like a crazed killer working for his own reasons.

The problem was, the cannon *was* a crazy man working for his own reasons. That made him difficult to control. That meant he might do something else stupid, something that could get him caught before he got the target.

Shit. He was going to have to keep a closer eye on this guy than he liked. He was going to have to expose his own back.

And that's why he didn't like painful thinking.

CHAPTER 11

Nothing," Phil said to Chloe. "There's absolutely nothing."

The two women were on the church basketball court. The team Phil coached had finished practice and disappeared to their various homes and other activities. She and Chloe were alone, tossing free throws for the heck of it, working up a good sweat, as the westering sun bathed the world in a golden glow. Dominic was with Brendan in the church hall, along with three hundred kids, who were getting their weekly dose of religious education.

It turned out that shadowing a priest wasn't the most difficult job in the world. The man was rarely alone.

Chloe dribbled the ball, then swished a three-pointer. "Then who's making this connection?"

"Darned if I know. I mean, Brendan's file is clean. All it says is that he went into retreat for two years after leaving the navy. Whatever the reason was, that was kept solely between him and his spiritual advisor."

"Hell."

"Tsk," said Phil, more out of habit than because she was offended. Older kids used four-letter words all the time, and she habitually voiced disapproval. The automatic response of fifteen years as a teaching nun. Dribbling the ball, she ran around the court and shot from behind Chloe. The ball sailed over the other woman's head, then bounced off the backboard.

"Sheesh," Phil said, "I couldn't hit the broad side of a barn tonight."

"Try again." Chloe headed for the bench and the towel she'd left there. The chilly air had gone as fast as it had come, and the night hinted at the humid, hot summer to come.

But Phil tossed the ball into the corner of the court, with all the other balls, and joined her at the bench, mopping her face with her own towel. "The thing is, Chlo," she said, keeping her voice down, "you're probably going to have to ask Father about this. He's the only one who knows what really happened, if anything did. Well, other than Crowell and whoever is pouring poison into his ear. And they're not going to talk."

"Shit."

This time Phil bit back the automatic sound of disapproval. "Well, it seems to me if you want the real skinny, you need to go to the horse's mouth."

"What if the horse doesn't want to talk?"

"Then you get nothing. Same as you've got now."

Chloe sighed, wiped her face again, and took a deep draught from her water bottle. "I don't want him to feel like he's being hounded."

"He *is* being hounded." Phil sat on the bench and plucked her damp St. Simeon Saints T-shirt from her skin. "Worse, he's being hounded by someone who probably wants to do the same thing to him that they did to Steve. God, you know, it hurts even to think about that."

"Yeah." Chloe sat beside her and rested her elbows on her knees.

"You got anything from the cops?"

"They're still waiting for lab reports. And they're still wondering what the relationship was between Brendan and Steve."

"Right." Phil reached for her own bottle of water. "Anybody with eyes can see how Brendan looks at you. He's het, or he ain't nothing."

"Yeah, that's what I told Brendan."

The water bottle paused halfway to Phil's mouth, and she gaped at Chloe. "You didn't."

"I did."

"Oh, my word . . ." Then a shriek of laughter escaped Phil. "Oh my, oh my. He must have looked like a deer caught in headlights."

"He did." Chloe shrugged. "Too bad. He's not obvious about it. He doesn't make me uncomfortable."

"No, but you've probably made *him* uncomfortable."

"Well, I was trying to get his attention."

"I bet it worked."

"I don't know. That man walks around in a haze of true goodness so thick I don't think he'd believe it if he had a dagger sticking out of his back. He'd convince himself he must have somehow bumped into it."

"Yeah, he's amazing, isn't he? Very otherworldly."

"It must be, because he doesn't strike me as pathetically naive. Not at all. It's an odd twist, the way he seems to have a good understanding of human nature, but seems unable to believe the worst about anyone or anything. I guess it's like I told Matt. He truly believes in redemption."

"Yes, he does." Phil sighed and sipped her water. "I'm pooped. Wanna clean up and get dinner?"

"Sure. But first let me check and make sure Father Brendan doesn't go wandering off on his own somewhere."

They hadn't even made it across the parking lot to the hall before Matt pulled up beside them in his nondescript sedan. The women stopped walking and turned toward him as he rolled down his power window and smiled.

"How are you ladies this evening?"

"Fine," Phil said, smiling back.

"Hot, sweaty, and tired," Chloe answered. "Do you have something for me?"

"I need to talk to you."

Phil looked at Chloe. "You go ahead. We can catch dinner another time. I'll just check on Father."

Chloe hesitated, but only briefly. "Thanks, Phil. I'll call you later."

Smiling, Phil waved and walked away.

"Hop in," Matt said.

"I wasn't kidding about being sweaty. You want that on your car seat?"

"You don't want to know what's been on my car seat. A little sweat won't hurt it."

So she climbed in on the passenger side, and felt the blast of air-conditioning turned on high. Almost at once her damp T-shirt felt like ice against her skin. Matt turned out of the parking lot, onto the residential street in the direction of Dale Mabry, one of the busiest streets in town.

"What's up?" Chloe asked.

"Let's get something to eat. I haven't had an encounter with food since early this morning."

"I'm not dressed for a restaurant."

"You'll be dry in five minutes, and anyway, I wasn't thinking fancy. I was thinking drive-through."

Typical cop, Chloe thought. Fast and greasy. It was a wonder any of them made it to retirement age. "As long as I can get some vegetables with it."

"No prob. I give you your choice. Fried chicken and coleslaw, or a sub."

"I'll take the sub."

He stopped at a place to get her a veggie sub, before hitting the chicken drive-through for his requisite dose of saturated fat. Then he pulled into a parking place behind the restaurant and suggested they sit at one of the picnic tables. Chloe was glad to; it had taken only a few minutes to make her feel that she was in danger of becoming an icicle.

"Okay," she said, as they sat facing each other and eating, "what's up?"

"Not much. King is so squeaky clean it's hard to believe. We tracked down his friends, his teachers, and even his mother. The only unkind words we heard was that he was too clean. Too straight. Sometimes a wet blanket because of it."

"I've heard of worse character flaws."

"Yeah, me too. Too serious, maybe, for his age, but given his background, not surprising."

"Anything else?"

"I got a look at the prelim on the autopsy. Still waiting for toxicology and all that, but physically there was one other interesting thing."

"What's that?"

"If he was gay, he was a virgin. If you know what I mean."

She knew what he meant. She put her sandwich down

and looked at him. He was biting into a chicken thigh with obvious relish. "So when are you going to give up on the idea that Father Brendan may have had something to do with his death."

"Oh, I gave up on that. Unfortunately, now I'm wondering again."

"Why?"

He wiped his chin and took a drink of cola. "Because I've been hearing rumblings that another young man of his acquaintance died under mysterious circumstances."

Chloe's heart skipped a beat. "Where are you hearing this maliciousness?"

He grinned. "From your frigging close-mouthed chancery, that's where."

"Really." Chloe's face as usual betrayed nothing. She'd practiced a wooden look for a long, long time. But her heart lurched, and her stomach sank. "From whom at the chancery?"

"I don't reveal sources."

"You know, Matt, I absolutely *hate* it when you're gleeful."

"Me, gleeful?" He grinned again. "What in the world makes you think that?"

"You've got that Cheshire-cat grin again."

"Sorry. I'll frown."

"Don't bother, it's too late. So some unnamed person is spreading nasty rumors. Big deal."

"Hey, this was from the chancery."

She leaned toward him, her sandwich forgotten. "Let me tell you something, Mr. Smarty-pants Detective. The chancery has nothing on Father Brendan. *Nothing.*"

Now he did frown. "How do you know that?"

"Because I have sources who checked his personnel file. There's not a peep in it about this so-called incident."

"Then somebody knows something unofficially."

"No, somebody knows a nasty rumor. And I'll let you in on another little secret. Somebody at the chancery has a big grudge against Father Brendan."

"How do you know that?"

"I just know." It was her turn to favor him with a Cheshire-cat grin. "Trust me on this."

"All right, then what's the grudge?"

"I'm working on that. I'll let you know."

"Grudge enough to kill?"

Chloe let her gaze wander away from him, to some distant point amid the trees that separated the restaurant from the houses behind. "I don't think so. But anything is possible. At this point, I'm not going to rule out anything."

"Except Father Brendan."

She looked straight at him. "Matt, if you knew the man at all, you'd realize he isn't capable of this crime. But you know what? I'm not ruling him out. I just consider him to be the least likely possibility of all."

"Fair enough. Truth to tell, I'm inclined to agree. There was something about that phone call I got about his past. . . ." He shook his head. "I can't put my finger on it. But I'm still going to look into it."

"Well, you won't get anything official out of the chancery. So let me try."

"Try what? Why should you get any further than I can?"

"Because I'm going to talk to the horse's mouth."

"Horse?"

"Father Brendan."

"Oh." Another smile lit his face. "You *do* like to take the bull by the horns. That's what I always liked about you, Chloe. Where angels fear to tread, and all that."

"Sometime," she said, wrapping up the remains of her sandwich for later, "you might try reminding me what I ever liked about *you*."

His laugh had always seemed to her to be warm and attractive. It still was.

That night at ten, Brendan thought he was done for the day. He even thought he could slip out alone and shoot some hoops without one of his shadows following him, and the good Lord knew he needed the time.

He didn't, however, make it five steps across the grassy parking lot toward the court before a voice accosted him.

"Father, you're not supposed to be out here by yourself."

He turned and saw Chloe marching toward him, looking every inch a warrior maid descended from Valhalla. "Don't you ever sleep?" he asked her.

"Sure. About as much as you do these days. If you wanted to shoot hoops, all you had to do was tell me."

He sighed and put his hands on his hips. "How'd you know I'd come out here?"

"Well, I hate to destroy your impression of my omniscience, but I was coming to the rectory to talk to you."

"So we'll talk. While I shoot some baskets."

"Sure."

But for a while, they didn't talk. She sat on the bench and let him wear himself out. He didn't seem quite as possessed tonight, not the way he had seemed right after the discovery of Steve King's body, but she got the feeling he was still looking for a state of exhaustion that would preclude thinking. That was fine by her. The less guarded he was feeling, the better.

The week had taken a toll on him, though. He'd visibly lost weight, and he was looking every one of his forty-three years and then some. He tired faster, too, as if he hadn't been eating enough to keep up his strength.

Finally, he dropped on the bench beside her and scrubbed his face with a towel.

"Basketball's a wonderful thing," Chloe remarked. "I was out here earlier with Sister Phil, practicing. It cuts you loose somehow, lets you get away. I guess most exercise does that."

"Yeah." He was panting but recovering quickly, the sign of good conditioning.

"You're not eating enough."

"So I hear."

"Well, it's not going to do anyone any good at all if you wind up in the hospital. Force yourself, Father."

"Just call me Brendan. I have a feeling that what you want to talk to me about doesn't involve a priest-parishioner relationship."

"No, it doesn't."

He waited. For a naturally gregarious man, he was sometimes very good at using silence.

Chloe, who didn't want to be at odds with him, gave him what he wanted. "So what's this thing about a young man you knew in the navy dying under mysterious circumstances?"

She'd shocked him. She could see it in the way he went utterly still. When he finally spoke, his voice rasped.

"Who told you that?"

"The cops."

"Oh, man."

"I've always thought," Chloe said slowly, "that it's unfortunate that being a priest doesn't allow you to swear. A good *Jesus Christ* would probably fit right now."

He gave her an almost smile, one that didn't reach his eyes. "Thou shalt not take the Lord thy God's name in vain."

"You know, I don't think that's taking the Lord's name in vain. I think taking it in vain is twisting what God has said and using it against others. Misrepresenting God."

"You might be right. However, I'll forbear if you don't mind."

"If 'oh, man' works for you, I have no problem with it."

He wiped his face again. "So I guess you want to know the story."

"It could be helpful. I'm not just being morbidly curious. I find it interesting that this rumor is making the rounds at this time. There may be a connection."

He nodded slowly. "Can we walk while we talk? I'm stiffening."

She hesitated, looking around. On the one hand, he'd be an easy target even with her beside him. On the other hand . . .

"Okay. But if I say duck, you hit the ground, okay?"

He looked at her, recognizing an unpalatable possibility, and finally giving it credence. "Fair enough."

They strolled around the grassy parking lot, far enough away from trees and buildings that Chloe felt she could have at least a reasonable chance of protecting Brendan from someone in the shadows.

"So," he said finally, as if accepting at last that she wasn't going to let him out of this, "somebody is spreading a nasty little rumor to the cops."

"Somebody at the chancery is spreading the rumor. You need to know that."

He sighed again and draped his towel around his neck. "I get the feeling they'd love it downtown if I'd just go back to the monastery."

"How do you feel? Is the monastery looking good about now?"

"Oh, occasionally I get wistful for the peace there. But the truth is, I didn't become a priest to hide from people. *Or* hide from life."

"No, that doesn't seem like you. I *am* curious about why you withdrew for so long, though."

He wrapped his hands around the ends of the towel. Hands that had been anointed, making him part of the apostolic succession that had continued unbroken since the time Christ. Hands that were empowered to raise the Host and consecrate it. Hands that could bestow blessings and absolution, or the final sacrament.

Hands that, as Jesus himself had said, could bind in heaven what was bound on earth, and loose in heaven what they loosed on earth.

But apostolic successor or not, anointed or not in the service of God, he was still a mortal man. And Chloe, like most Catholics, had no difficulty accepting that dichotomy.

"Well," he said, "I reached a crisis of faith. I needed to reestablish my relationship with God. It happens, you know."

"Of course it does. I've been there a few times, although I didn't have a monastery to hide out in."

"So it doesn't shock you that I came close to losing my faith?"

"Why should you be exempt?"

He laughed and tugged the towel a little, as if needing to flex his arm muscles.

"Did it have to do with this mysterious young man?"

"In part. But he was only the last straw, as it were. Things had been building."

"Can I ask what things?"

He thought about that for a moment. "Why not? What I say is confidential, isn't it?"

"Yes. If it makes you more comfortable, consider me your retained lawyer."

He glanced at her. "I can't afford a lawyer."

"Ever hear of pro bono? I do it all the time. So I'm your lawyer."

"Thanks." He favored her with a smile. "Not that any of this needs a lawyer."

"You never know."

He shook his head, as if wanting to knock away an unpleasant thought. "Have you ever heard of the theory of just war?"

"Very vaguely."

"Basically it holds that a war can be justifiable if it's fought solely out of self-defense, if no other means of protection is available, and if it's fought purely. You know, don't kill the innocents and all that. It's more complex, of course, but that's the basics."

"Okay. I can follow that. It's basically the same as self-defense in the law."

"Probably not very different," he agreed. "I agree with the doctrine, and of course I feel wholeheartedly that our servicemen and -women need their souls ministered to. But over time . . . let's just say I was finding it harder and harder to justify my continued participation in the military machine, however benign. I began to feel as if my presence there was a sign of approval. And it wasn't. I saw things . . . well, let's just say, not everything our military does would qualify as 'just' under the terms of the doctrine."

"Of course not. And that bothered you."

"Increasingly. I won't get into all the details, but let's just say that eventually I reached a point where I was questioning myself, my role, my Church, and even God's existence."

Chloe nodded. "Been there, done that. It's hell."

"That's exactly what it is."

He fell silent and they continued to walk for a while. As they started yet another circumnavigation of the lot, Chloe asked, "Now, what about this mysterious young man?"

Brendan stopped walking and faced her. "He committed suicide. And it was all my fault."

CHAPTER 12

For an instant it seemed to Chloe that the world hushed. The breeze seemed to hold its breath, and even the endless racket of tree frogs and bugs fell silent.

But of course, nothing hushed. The hush was internal, as she absorbed what Brendan had just told her. Finally, out of disbelief as much as anything, she asked, "How was it your fault?"

He sighed and looked up at the heavens, where a few stars managed to gleam through the perennial glow of city lights. "I failed to realize how close to the edge he was. I failed to insist that he get medical help immediately. I failed to insist he go to the emergency room."

"You know, mind reading isn't required, even of a priest."

"Maybe not. But something more than trite, reassuring, it'll-all-be-okay counseling is required. I failed that young man. I was wrong."

"Perhaps." She wasn't going to argue with his conscience; that was between him and God and his spiritual advisor. "But that doesn't make you responsible. And I don't see how a suicide can be connected with what happened to

Steve King, or even why anyone should consider it mysterious."

He sighed. They were once again near the basketball court, and he opted to return to the bench. She sat beside him, waiting for whatever he chose to say. She understood that he was walking a tightrope right now, between confidences that he could and could not share.

"Well," he said finally, "this young man was gay. In fact, he converted to the church because we don't condemn gays, only homosexual acts. He felt more welcome in Catholicism than in the religion he was raised in."

"That's a beautiful thing."

"Well, yes, but then there's the military policy of don't ask, don't tell. The last time I saw him, he feared someone had found him out and was going to blow the whistle. And I didn't realize how desperate he was."

She reached out and took his hand for a brief instant, squeezing it before she let it go.

"Two days later," Brendan said, "he was dead. And it all came out."

"I see. And the link someone is making is probably just that both Steve and this young man were gay."

"It's the only one I can see."

"How very ugly."

"Ugly?" He looked at her.

"That someone would be spreading gossip like this. That someone wants to be so hurtful."

"It happens."

"That doesn't excuse it. Bearing false witness is on the top ten of don'ts."

"Yeah. But so are other things, and they happen."

Chloe reached into the pocket of her shorts and found a

small square of paper, slightly rumpled but still usable. She began to fold a dove, neat, tiny, practiced folds.

"You really like doing that," Brendan remarked.

"It soothes me."

"I never think of you as needing soothing. You're always so . . . cool."

"Icy is the word you're looking for. I've heard it many times."

"How come?"

"Why am I icy, or why do I hear it?"

"Why are you?"

She finished folding the dove and set it between them on the bench. Once again she fished in her pocket and found another piece of paper. She began to fold a rabbit.

"Well," she said finally, "that's a long, ugly story, better left for another time. Suffice it to say, a man once used my feelings against me so he could abuse me. And when he turned up dead, even my friends thought I had killed him."

"Did you?"

"No. Although I'd gotten to the point of *wanting* to. A terrible sin. Anyway, thanks to one person, the charges were never filed."

"Did they find the killer?"

"No. Never."

He sighed. "So it hangs over your head forever."

"Something like that. Anyway, feelings are a weakness. I don't allow myself to have them."

"Chloe." He turned to her and waited until she looked him straight in the eye. "Feelings are also our greatest strength. Someday you might want to consider that."

She never answered. She walked him back to the rectory and made him swear he wouldn't leave it again until it was time for morning Mass. Then she climbed into her car and drove away.

The pain followed her, but as always, it followed far behind. It rode in the exhaust fumes of her car. She wouldn't let it into the passenger compartment with her.

"You didn't call me," Phil said accusingly the following morning as they met just outside church for Mass.

"Sorry. It was rather late."

Phil peered at her. "And you have no intention of telling me."

"Privileged information," Chloe said. "I can't. Suffice it to say, some rumormonger is drawing a pretty weak connection."

Phil groaned. "Sometimes I wish I didn't have to deal with priests, nuns, and lawyers all the time."

"So buddy up to a basketball player." But Chloe couldn't help smiling. "Sorry, Phil. I promised."

"I know, I know. But I *hate* being cut out of the loop."

"Everyone does."

"Well, you're going to tell that cop, aren't you?"

"Not until I have more solid information."

"I swear you can be the most frustrating person on the planet sometimes."

Chloe half smiled. "Believe me, I'm not. I've met worse."

"Yeah, right. And pigs fly."

Thus, in complete harmony, they went in to Mass.

After Mass, however, Chloe managed to get Brendan aside. "I need more information, Father."

"More?" He looked a little distracted, as if he couldn't

quite shift gears from talking jovially with his parishioners to considering the threats that faced him.

"About that young man who committed suicide."

"Chloe . . ." His gaze focused on her, as did his full attention. "You know I can't—"

"I need to know his name, and the date and place of his death. And that's not privileged, Father. That's public record." But she hated herself right then. For a few minutes, among the church members, he had almost looked like his old self. In a mere instant, he looked old and worn again.

"You're right," he said. "I could tell you that. If I knew." He sighed and did what was for him a rare thing: He stuffed his hands into his pockets.

"Well, you must know his name."

His expression became haunted. "I don't remember his full name. I honestly don't. It troubles me, Chloe. It's troubled me for a long time that I can't remember. I know he was Tom."

"But didn't you perform his funeral?"

"Oh, no. Evidently his family claimed the body and took it home. In fact, I only heard about his death weeks later, when someone told me about it."

He looked so distressed that she almost reached out to him.

"So many people," he said sadly. "Over the years . . . You know, I was transferred five times in my twelve years in the navy. I served on three different ships, seasick every minute of every day." He gave her a self-deprecating smile. "And there were all these young people. Amazing numbers of young people, most of whom were indistinguishable because they wore the same clothes, had the same haircuts, and had these very fresh, youthful faces. And while I got to know the members of my congregation by sight over time, there were many of them I never knew by anything except first or last name, depending. It was enough. I didn't need to know if Bill was Bill Blowden or Bill Corelli. I knew the face, and I had a name to go with it. They came and they went, and I got to know each of them a little, but the changes were so quick sometimes that things didn't get burned into my memory unless something spectacular happened. Or unless I did a lot of in-depth counseling."

"But wouldn't this suicide have made the young man stick in your mind?"

"It did. But I don't know if I ever knew his last name. He would have stuck in my mind regardless. He was a very troubled young man who was wrestling with some serious things. But I didn't need to know his last name to help with that, or to listen, or to provide absolution."

He looked down, and she could see his fists tighten in his pockets. "I feel bad about that. Really bad. It's one of the reasons I wanted to leave the navy and come to a parish. It was enough rootlessness. I wanted names to go with faces and long-term relationships that might last a lifetime."

"I can understand that."

His smile was humorless. "Can you? You seem to avoid them like the plague."

"Ouch."

"Well, it's my turn to make *you* uncomfortable. Anyway, to get back to the subject of your concern, I was already on my way out of the navy when Tom turned up in my life. He struck me as a fine young man who took moral and ethical concerns seriously. He had just come into the Church, as I recall, though it was one of the other chaplains who brought him in."

"Where was this?"

"Three years ago at Norfolk."

"And he died when?"

"Again, I'm not sure exactly what day, but it had to have been sometime in November, two and a half years ago."

"That should be enough."

"Why do you need to know?"

Chloe shook her head. "Because some police detectives won't take my word for anything. I've got to provide proof."

"Ah. Well, I don't see how this helps anything."

"It just makes it clear that the parallels are exceedingly thin. But you never know. One thing can lead to another."

"True. In fact, it always seems to."

Chloe called her office from her cell phone and got put through to Naomi.

"You owe me, girl," was the first thing Naomi said. "You owe me big-time."

"Okay, so I'll pay for your cruise to Antarctica, far, far away from phones."

Naomi was silent a moment. "How did you know I want to do that?"

"I have my methods."

"God, sometimes you're positively eerie. Well, it's too damn expensive."

"No it's not. I figure you're earning it. In fact, maybe we'll go together and tell all the drunks and criminals to give it a rest for a month."

Naomi laughed. "I wish. Okay, what do you need?"

"I need to track down a death and get as much info as possible on the circumstances."

"Oh, piece of cake. I'll put Dianna on it." Dianna was their part-time investigator.

Two minutes later, Chloe disconnected. Almost immediately, before she could do more than start her car engine, the cell phone rang. She picked it up and answered.

"Chloe Ryder."

"Well, well, Ms. Chloe," said the all-too-familiar voice of one Matt Diel. "What did the horse say?"

"What makes you think I spoke to the horse?"

"The fact that you're sitting parked in the lot of the church. What gives?"

"I don't want to talk about it on the airwaves."

"Fair enough. I'm parked across the street from the lot. Meet you at IHOP?"

"Can't you ever pick a place where cholesterol isn't the top item on the menu?"

"The day I eat alfalfa sprouts will be the day I cock up my toes."

She sighed loudly, on purpose, wanting to give him a little dig. "Okay, okay. Which IHOP?"

Fifteen minutes later, they were facing each other across a table in a booth.

"We've got to stop meeting like this," Matt said. "People are going to think we've got something going."

She eyed him sourly. "We never had anything going."

He raised his gaze to her, and for once there was nothing in his eyes except honesty. "We almost did. Once."

"A long time ago, in a galaxy far, far away."

"Maybe. But maybe it doesn't have to be."

She regarded him uncomfortably and didn't say anything.

"All right, I'm a dork," he said. "Always saying the wrong thing at the wrong time."

"Why do you say that?"

"So you don't have to. What did you find out?"

"It was a suicide. I have my investigator tracking it down right now."

"A suicide? How the hell can anyone link a suicide and a murder like this one?"

"Well, I guess it's enough that both victims spoke to the same priest, and both were gay. The vics, I mean. Not the priest."

"Yeah. I guess that's enough. In some minds. Not in mine, though. Why the hell would someone from the chancery pass along that garbage?"

"Maybe because they don't know the real story. Or maybe because they don't like Father Brendan. Hell, Matt, don't ask *me* to explain human behavior. How many cases have you had where there was no good motivation?"

"Too many. It would be nice if people were rational."

"Hah."

"Exactly."

As expected, he ordered a stack of pancakes and an extra side of sausage. Managing not to shudder, Chloe ordered coffee.

"You know," Matt remarked, "we could never live together."

"Why should we want to?"

"That's not the issue. The issue is whether we could. And we couldn't. You shudder every time I eat."

"I shudder because what you're eating isn't healthy. It'll shorten your life expectancy."

"I'm touched," he said after a moment.

"Touched?"

"You care." He looked at her and smiled. "Gotcha."

"It's only the general kind of caring I have for humanity at large."

"Yeah. Right."

She didn't dignify that with an answer.

"Say, have you heard the joke? Some college professor . . ." He trailed off as the waitress set his breakfast before him and refilled Chloe's coffee cup.

"Anyway," he continued, pouring on enough maple syrup to support the entire state of Vermont, "this professor was teaching his class about double negatives. You know, like 'I'm not gonna not do that,' and how the double negative makes a positive."

"So?"

"So, he goes on that we use double negatives all the time to express the positive, but that nowhere in the English language is there a double positive that means a negative. And this kid in the back pipes up, 'Yeah, right.'"

Chloe laughed. "That's cute."

"I don't know if it's a true story, but I like it anyway."

Matt had always liked wordplay, Chloe remembered. In the past he'd driven her almost nuts with his constant punning. Sitting in the car with him for hours on end sometimes left her feeling frustrated beyond words because everything she said drew a pun out of him. But it had also been funny. The thing was, back then he wouldn't ever let anyone get serious around him. It was as if the wordplay was a way to divert everyone.

She thought about that while he dug into his meal, and tried not to think about those pancakes clogging his arteries.

"Okay," he said, swallowing. "We've got a suicide and a

murder that someone is trying to link. Ergo, we have someone with a huge grudge against your Father Brendan. It might be really interesting if we could figure out who's involved in this little vendetta."

"Good luck. The silence from the Church can sometimes be thunder."

"I know. But whoever's doing this has prior knowledge of Father Brendan because the information isn't in his file at the chancery."

"Right. So I'm thinking it's someone he knew back in the navy."

"Exactly. How many thousands would that be?"

"Quite a few, according to him. He told me this morning that he got transferred five times." But then she cocked her head. "However, it's likely that this person knew him at his last station. Otherwise, he or she wouldn't know about the suicide."

"Bingo." He smiled at her. "I always thought you should've stayed on the force. You'd make a hell of a detective."

"Well, it became a little difficult."

"Yeah." He frowned. "It's too damn bad you were married to a cop. Any other Joe, and they'd all have been on your side."

Chloe was glad she hadn't ordered anything to eat, even dry toast. Something she'd put firmly behind her had come up twice in less than twelve hours, and she was beginning to feel as taut as a bowstring. "Matt . . ."

"I know. You don't like to think about it. But you know what? I can't *help* thinking about it. I remember how you were back then. Well, before you married that jerk, anyway.

And I see what all that did to you, and it's just not something I can ignore."

"I'm okay."

He shook his head and pushed aside the calories, reaching instead for the black coffee. "You're not okay. Any jerk who knew you then can see that. I've noticed it every time we've run across each other for the last eight years. You're getting by, sweetie, but you ain't living."

"Please don't call me sweetie."

He shrugged. "Whatever. Fact is, you've gone so far away inside yourself that it'd take an ice pick to get to you."

She didn't answer. She couldn't answer. For the first time in a long, long time, she was feeling something, something so strong that it filled her throat with a painful lump and wouldn't let words come. She almost hated him for causing her to react.

"I'm still working on it, you know." He spoke as if oblivious of her reaction, but Chloe had a feeling he wasn't. Even with her features frozen, she feared something was showing in her eyes. And Matt missed very little.

"On the murder," he explained when she didn't speak. "I'm going to find that son of a bitch and clear your name completely."

She managed to clear her throat. "It's been a long time. It's a cold, dead trail."

"Maybe. But that doesn't mean I have to stop trying. And I'm not going to."

Chloe had absolutely no hope that Matt would find her husband's murderer after all this time. She'd learned to live with that, and she refused to accept any other possibility at this late date. Matt had managed to clear her enough that she'd been able to get on with her life. That was sufficient.

"Anyway," he said, "I shouldn't have brought it up. But sometimes . . . sometimes, Chloe, it just plain hurts to look at you."

She had to fight to keep the ice around her heart from cracking, a crack that would allow her feelings to pour through. "Then don't look at me."

He surprised her by laughing. "It's kinda hard not to. But okay, back to bidness. These rumors are coming up at the same time as a terrible murder. I don't think it's a coincidence. Either we've got someone taking advantage of the current situation, or we've got someone who is in some way involved. You get my drift?"

"Absolutely."

"And we have a chancery that wouldn't talk if we put hot needles under their fingernails, so we're not going to get any answers there."

"I can virtually guarantee that."

He reached for his plate again and ate another mouthful of pancake. "So we gotta find this suicide, and see what links we might be able to make."

"I agree."

He looked at her, his eyes sparkling. "So what do you say, Chloe? Maybe it's time we started working together, as partners. Two heads are always better than one."

"Your bosses—"

"Screw my bosses. They don't have to know."

"Matt, you could get into serious trouble. Sharing an official investigation with a civilian is not a minor peccadillo."

"Again, they don't have to know you're anything except a source in the parish. But I'll tell you something, Chloe. Something I haven't told anyone else. There's an odor to this that's really bugging me. You know I'm not a religious man, and I know that's always wound your crank, but even so, the thought of crucifying somebody in a church really sets my hackles up. It's more than a nasty murder."

"Yes," she agreed quietly, "it is."

"And I'd really like to be able to sleep again. This damn case is waking me up in the middle of the night, and I'm tired of it. So instead of quid pro quo, let's just put our heads together and solve this damn thing."

Her agreement was simple. "I hope this doesn't cost you your job."

CHAPTER 13

The call came late at night. It was there on his voice mail when Brendan returned to the rectory around ten, having attended a somewhat uncomfortable meeting of the pastoral council, which seemed to be looking at him through a changed lens.

Dominic was still out, tending to a hospital emergency. Sister Phil, who was his guard dog this evening, had stationed herself downstairs until Dominic returned.

This was the first time Brendan had been alone since seven that morning, and he didn't even want to reach for the telephone. He needed time to pray and reflect, and sort through his thoughts and feelings. But first, duty called. He settled at his personal desk with a notepad and reluctantly reached for the phone, bracing himself for the litany of grief, anger, and problems that were invariably waiting on his voice mail. Ordinarily these calls reminded him he could be useful. Tonight they felt like an intolerable burden.

He punched in his code, and the litany began. He scrawled down names and phone numbers, and made small notes of the problems mentioned and how urgent they were. Some of these calls could be answered tomorrow or the day after when time permitted. Some might well need to be answered tonight. Some he couldn't tell; all they said was, "I need to talk to you. Please call me." Those he marked for answering that evening or tomorrow morning, just in case.

And then came the one that froze his blood. A whispery, raspy voice filled his ear. "It's your turn. Say your last prayers, priest."

Quickly, Brendan punched the number to save the message. Then he put down the receiver with a trembling hand.

A moment later, shock fled, replaced by anger. Enough was enough.

The group gathered again in the rectory parlor: Phil, Dominic—who had just returned—Matt, Chloe, and Brendan. They sat on the uncomfortable armchairs and listened as Brendan described the call.

"I need a recording of it," Matt said.

"I can do that," Brendan agreed. "I'll punch it up for you, but I don't have a tape recorder."

Matt reached into his suit jacket pocket and held up a minicassette recorder. "I do. It balances the cell phone in the other pocket."

No one smiled.

"Is the call time-stamped?" Matt asked.

"Yes, time and date."

"Where were you when it was placed?"

"At a meeting of the pastoral council." He shook his head a little as if the memory wasn't a particularly good one.

"People can testify to that?"

"Seven of them, at least."

"Okay." Matt stuffed the recorder back into his pocket. "That's good enough for me."

"But that doesn't solve the problem," Dominic remarked. "If someone wants to kill Brendan, we've got to find this maniac."

"Obviously," Matt said acerbically.

Dominic spread his hands apologetically. "Sorry, I wasn't questioning you, just wondering what we can do to help Brendan."

"Well, first," said Matt, "I need to put a trace on all incoming calls to that line."

"No." Brendan's voice was firm.

"No?" Matt raised his eyebrows. "Father, forgive me, but are you *nuts*?"

"Maybe so," Brendan said, annoyance creasing his brow, "but the fact remains that I don't want you checking up on every parishioner who calls me with a personal problem. Or worse, questioning them."

"But—"

"No buts," he said. "People have a right to call a priest without having to fear that the cops are going to get their phone numbers."

Matt then did something very unusual for him. He dropped his forehead into his hand. "I can't believe this," he said. "Most people are willing to do damn near anything to save their lives."

"I'm not most people," Brendan said quietly. "And there are many things more important than my own life."

"Yeah?" Matt raised his head. "Then why'd you bother to call the cops, Father? Why don't you just ignore this caller until he puts a bullet in your brain like he did to Steve King? Maybe you'd *like* to be crucified?"

"Matt!" Chloe said his name warningly, but before she could go on, Brendan spoke.

"No, Matt, I don't *want* to be killed, and I certainly don't *want* to be crucified. But whether I am or not is in God's hands more than yours. Whether you like it or not. Now, I'm willing to cooperate in any way that I can without sacrificing my priestly duties and responsibilities in the process. But I *do* have that limit, and I will *not* cross it."

Dominic was nodding his full agreement. Phil looked worried. And Chloe . . . Chloe suddenly had an idea.

"Is there some way calls could be traced, but only Father Brendan sees the numbers? So he can sort out which ones don't belong to parishioners?"

"Maybe," Matt said, looking relieved to have another idea.

"It still doesn't work," Brendan said. "Plenty of people call me who aren't members of the parish. People who are thinking about coming back to the Church, people who are just having a problem and need to talk to someone. I don't want to subject them to harassment either."

Matt expelled a heavy, loud sigh. "Let me tell you something, Father. This guy, assuming he means what he just said, wants to tell you something. There's something eating at his gut so bad that he wants a face-off with you. That's the only reason he's making these calls. So you gotta figure that when he acts, maybe he won't just come up behind you and kill you unawares. He'll want to spew whatever it is he has to spew. So that means you gotta be careful about where you go, and make sure you're not alone."

"To a point I can do that."

"But," said Chloe, "if he spills the story on the phone, then there's going to be no face-off. He could do to you what he did to Steve."

"Maybe if I could talk to him—"

Matt interrupted, looking at Chloe. "Tell me I didn't just hear that."

Chloe turned to Brendan. "Father, you've got to be realistic about this. If this is the same guy who hurt Steve, and if this guy really wants to hurt you, you're not going to talk him out of it. Something has happened in his head, something he's not going to be talked out of."

"In short," Matt said, "he's a sick twist, and ten years of counseling probably wouldn't be enough."

Brendan rubbed the back of his neck, but didn't say anything.

"I think," Dominic said after a moment, "that for a while everyone in this parish is going to get used to having two priests answer every call."

Brendan turned toward him. "There's no way."

Matt spoke. "Get real, Fathers. Get real. Father Dominic, you wouldn't be any more protection for Father Brendan than no one at all. All it means is the killer uses two bullets instead of one."

"But Chloe is protection?" Brendan asked.

"She's a trained cop," Matt said firmly. "She knows what to be on the lookout for, and she knows what to do about it."

"Well, she can't be with me every moment of the day, and if you'll pardon me for saying so, she's as vulnerable to an unexpected bullet as anyone else."

"All right, all right," Chloe said, holding up her hands. "Maybe we can compromise."

"How so?" Matt asked.

"Father Brendan goes on visits only when he knows the person who calls. He knows the person, and he knows the address is legit. Otherwise, he stays put on parish property. And we put guards on the property."

Matt frowned. "Chloe, I don't think I can get enough cops to guard this whole place. It's a big property, with what, five buildings? Athletic fields. A cemetery."

"The church can hire some off-duty cops. We do it all the time."

"They're expensive," Brendan said. "We can't really afford—"

Chloe cut him off. "We can't afford to lose *you*."

Silence greeted her words. For a minute or two, no one spoke. Finally, Brendan broke the silence.

"Okay, I'll admit I'm scared. But I'm even more angry than scared. And I can't function as a priest with a perpetual bodyguard."

"He *is* nuts," Matt said to Chloe. "Really and truly nuts."

"Well, it's a holy kind of nuts," she answered.

"Yeah. Holey. Full of holes."

"Cut it out, Matt. Don't be insulting."

"Maybe if I insult the man enough, he'll develop a sudden case of common sense." He turned back to the priest. "Listen, Father. Please, just listen. If the same guy is after you that killed Steve, you've got a real problem on your hands. A life-and-death problem. Now I'm not a religious man, but I *have* read the Bible. Once upon a time, I even went to church every week. And I don't remember one damn thing where it says you ought to throw your life away carelessly."

"I'm not being careless."

"Maybe you don't think so, but from where I sit, you look about as careless as it gets. This isn't martyrdom we're talking about here. This isn't dying for the faith, or being eaten by the lions in the Roman Circus. This is about some sick son of a bitch who wants to kill you, and you won't prove a damn thing by getting yourself killed."

Brendan was looking straight at Matt, and now he waited, as if wanting to be sure Matt had finished. When he spoke, his voice was gentle.

"Matt, it *is* about proving something. It's about proving that nothing and no one will prevent me from carrying out the duties to God and His faithful that I undertook at my ordination. It's about keeping my word to God, and fulfilling the mission He gave me when He put me in this world. I can't make it any clearer than that."

"Don't tell me you want to be a martyr!"

"Nobody wants to be a martyr, Matt. But sometimes . . . sometimes it can't be avoided."

Chloe and Matt left a little while later, after Matt made a recording of the phone message. Dominic said he was going to call Merv Haskell about getting off-duty policemen to patrol the parish property. Out in front of the rectory, a squad car, summoned by Matt before he left, pulled up silently and parked. Phil excused herself to go back to her apartment. She had a full day of teaching ahead of her.

Brendan went to his room, leaving Dominic alone.

The first thing Dominic did was call Merv as he'd promised. Merv sounded groggy, but he promised to rattle the bars of the Finance Council members the next morning, and get permission for some kind of security. By the time he hung up, Merv sounded wide-awake, and Dominic suspected the man wasn't going to wait for morning, but was going to hound the Finance Council immediately.

All well and good. But there was one not so well and good, and Dom sat for a long time on the edge of his bed, debating whether to call Monsignor Crowell. The excuse of reporting "everything that went on" would cover his butt, but what he wanted to say to the monsignor was something else altogether.

For a priest who'd spent most of his career at the chancery, buried in an office, he'd managed to avoid the almost unavoidable politics. Unfortunately, he had somehow become considered a friend of Crowell's. At least from Crowell's perspective. And fool that he was, he'd been flattered.

So when Crowell had told him he needed someone he could trust to come down to St. Simeon's and find out what the problems were that parishioners were complaining about, Dominic had assumed the monsignor had the best interests of the parish at heart and simply wanted to know if there were real problems or merely the inevitable complaints of a small number of people who wouldn't have been happy if Christ himself had pastored the parish.

He'd never guessed what he was stepping into. But after his last call to Crowell, he'd realized that Crowell was biased against Brendan, and this mission was designed to force Dominic to give Crowell what he wanted. Thus the outcome would appear to be completely free of political taint.

Dominic hated to be used. But even less did he like the feeling he had now that Crowell's machinations might be putting Brendan in grave danger. Calling Crowell just to vent would be a foolish thing to do, though. Especially so late at night.

He rubbed his eyes, continuing to stare at the phone. Throughout most of his priestly life, doing the right thing had been easy. After all, he'd been dealing with people who were stories on paper and listening to the recommendations of their priests. It had been ugly, yes, but it had been morally easy. Never, not once in all those years, had he been called upon to stand up for his beliefs in a way that might harm him.

Brendan's devotion to the priesthood was beginning to shame Dominic. And it was shame that drove him to reach for the phone.

Outside the rectory, away from the squad car parked out front, walking across the rear parking lot toward their cars, Chloe and Matt said little at first. When they reached their cars, however, neither of them started to get in. Instead they leaned back against their own vehicles and faced each other across six feet of grass.

Finally, Chloe spoke. "He's a truly holy man, Matt."

"Yeah." He made a sound of disgust. "I believe in evil, Chloe. I've seen enough of it to make a snake vomit. It's everywhere, in every dark corner of people's lives. Even in nice people who all of a sudden do something so totally out of character that everyone who knows them reels. I believe in evil. It lives, it breathes, and it slinks into people's lives to steal every good thing."

"But you don't believe in God."

"It's kinda hard, since evil seems to be running the place."

"That's a cop's warped perspective, Matt. You ought to try hanging out with some of the good people. The really good people."

"Like churchgoers?" The words were almost scornful.

"Not necessarily. But I'll tell you something. It was the good people in this church who saved me, back then."

"Hell, I saved you, too, Chloe. Me and my stubborn streak."

"True." She sighed. "Maybe I never said thank you. Thank you, Matt."

"Just doing my job."

"No, just being a good man."

He looked away, then looked back at her. "You know, if this priest of yours keeps on this way, he's going to have me believing in God."

"Heaven forbid!" She laughed quietly.

"Yeah. I don't need that."

"Or maybe you do."

It was his turn to sigh. "Just . . . let it be, Chloe."

"Okay," she said indifferently. "So . . . wanna come to my place for a drink?"

Crowell was almost jovial when he answered the phone. Either he was well into his brandy for the evening, or he was really pleased with the way things were going. Dominic hoped he wasn't pleased because of having dirt on Brendan.

"Dominic," Crowell said warmly, "how are you doing, my son?"

Since they were of an age, Dominic wasn't exactly taken in by being called "my son." It was one of Crowell's affectations, one better suited to the Church of another age than the modern U.S. Church. "I'm doing fine, Monsignor." Dominic resisted the urge to call him Freddy.

"So, you have something to report?"

"Yes, actually, I do."

"Good, good, I was beginning to wonder if you were up to the job. And I have such faith in you."

Dominic was surprised to discover that he was developing a bullshit meter, and just then it was about to pop off the scale. He'd never needed one before, but latent abilities were beginning to stir within him.

"Well, Monsignor, what I have is this. Someone wants to murder Father Brendan."

For once Crowell was silent. Dominic guessed he was imagining the headlines if a parish priest were found brutally murdered. They'd be worse, even, than the ones about Steve King.

Presently, Crowell cleared his voice. "Surely not."

"Surely yes," Dominic said firmly. "Someone is making threatening calls, and the police are very concerned."

"Police?" There was no mistaking the distaste in Crowell's voice. "Well, perhaps they should look at a friend or family member of that poor young man who was crucified. If the two of them were having an affair—"

Dominic had had enough. "Monsignor, you sent me down here to find out what was going on, did you not?"

"Well, yes, of course. Didn't I say so?"

"Did you want me to find out what's *really* going on, or did you expect me to find what you *wanted?*"

Thus cornered, Crowell had only one possible answer. "I wanted you to find out the truth, of course." But he didn't sound jovial anymore.

"As I thought. I was sure you were honest in your concern." That was an uncharitable twisting of the knife, but Dominic figured God would understand. "Well, I have found out what's going on down here."

"Yes?" Crowell's interest returned.

"What's going on, Monsignor, is that St. Simeon's is blessed with the saintliest pastor in the diocese."

"You can't know that so soon."

"Yes, actually, I can. Brendan Quinlan is a priest who is willing to risk his life in order to carry out his pastoral responsibilities. How many of us can say that, Monsignor?"

"You—"

Dominic interrupted him. "It's not an act. He has twice refused to allow the police to protect him in ways that he feels would adversely affect his ability to serve this parish in spiritual ways."

"Maybe," said Crowell tightly, "he's hiding something."

"No." Dominic said the word firmly, and felt a wave of peace flow through him, uplifting him. For once he was putting himself on the line for what he believed was right. It was a fantastic feeling.

"You can't be sure," Crowell said.

"Oh, I can be sure, Monsignor. I've been living with the man, working with him. I've been listening to him."

"Well, then," the monsignor said, his voice drawn taut, "perhaps it's time to return to your duties here at the chancery."

"No," Dominic said again, just as firmly. "I'm not leaving until this matter is settled."

Silence conveyed the depth of Crowell's annoyance.

"I am not going to leave Brendan alone with this mess. Moreover, Monsignor, I'd like to know why the chancery is spreading ugly tales to the police about Father Brendan."

"What?" But Crowell's astonishment seemed feigned to Dominic. He had lost whatever trust he had once foolishly felt for this man.

"Yes, it seems someone at the chancery said they've been getting calls linking Brendan with the mysterious death of a young man just before he left the navy. Only it seems no one at the chancery bothered to investigate. The supposed mys-

terious death was a suicide, hardly the kind of thing that
happened to Steve King."

"Well, it could be that . . ." But the monsignor trailed off,
as if fearing he might reveal too much.

"I'll tell you something, Monsignor," Dominic continued, fully enjoying his moment of speaking out, conse-
quences be damned. "If someone at the chancery is trying to
direct the police investigation toward Brendan, then they're
aiding and abetting the real killer by distracting the police. I
don't know about you, but I wouldn't care to have that sin
on my soul."

"No," Crowell answered, sounding more thoughtful and
subdued than Dominic had ever heard him. "No, indeed I
wouldn't. I'll look into this, Father. I will definitely look
into this."

When Dominic hung up the phone, he felt better about
himself than he had in a long, long time.

CHAPTER 14

Matt told himself that if he'd had an ounce of common sense, he would have gone straight home to his own bed. He was weary, as he usually was when working a case. In his life, regular hours existed only in lulls between murder investigations.

But instead, he followed Chloe to her house, wondering why he was being an ass. She didn't want to get laid; he knew her better than that. Despite the inevitable whispers in the squad room when she'd been on the force—she was, after all, a beautiful woman—he knew damn well she wasn't easy. He'd made a kind of play for her, once upon a time, and discovered that Chloe didn't give her body unless she gave her heart, and these days he wasn't sure she had any heart left.

So why had she invited him over? Well, he supposed he was going to find out.

Cozy little house, not what he'd expected for a big shot lawyer. Near the church, which somehow didn't surprise him. Inside, however, the coziness was shortchanged by the decor, which was cool and nearly colorless, almost a reflection of Chloe herself.

But he knew that colorlessness was a lie. He could still remember a different Chloe. One who had passionately committed herself when she chose to commit. At least until that son of a bitch husband of hers had started beating on her.

"Have a seat," she said, waving him to a couch upholstered in pastels so light they were almost invisible. He obediently plopped down. "What's your poison?" she asked.

"Anything nonalcoholic."

She looked at him a moment, as if considering what he'd just said, her eyes reflecting nothing of what she thought. He realized that he'd love to make that face of hers express something. Anger. Passion. Hate. Anything but ice.

"Tea, soda, or coffee?" she asked.

"Soda. Please. Any kind."

She brought them each a can of cola, then sat facing him in a Boston rocker.

"So," he said finally, wondering what this was about.

"So," she answered, smiling faintly.

Impatience prickled him. "Did you want to talk about something specific? The case?"

"Actually," she said, her gaze fluttering away, "I wanted to talk about us. You and me."

He barely restrained himself from expressing shock. "What about us?"

"We go back a long way, Matt."

"I guess you could say that, even though I've hardly seen you in five years."

"I know. I sort of ditched you right after . . . you proved I was innocent."

"Understandable. Unpleasant associations and all of that." But his hand was so tight around the can of cola that it ached, and he began to fear he would crush it. Carefully, he put it down on a coaster.

"Well, I feel bad about it, and I wanted you to know that."

"No big deal." Although at times over the years, it had felt like a very big deal.

"And I want you know that I'm glad you're on this case."

"Sure." Now he felt awkward. It was the luck of the draw, and all that. Someone else could just as easily have been assigned to Steve's homicide. It wasn't as if he'd done anything to wind up here.

"Well," she said, "I just thought maybe it was time we mended some fences."

"Your conscience getting the better of you?" He regretted the question as soon as it popped out. It was spoken in self-defense, but it didn't do a damn thing to "mend fences."

"Yeah, I guess," she said, some of the edge coming back to her voice.

"Good." He managed that much, even if he couldn't quite summon an apology. After all, years ago there'd been a spark between them, a spark he'd never quite forgotten, but as soon as she got what she needed, namely getting cleared of the murder, she'd turned him off like a faucet.

"I'm sorry, Matt. I treated you badly."

"Some might say that."

She simply looked at him, waiting for whatever else he wanted to say, and that made him feel like a shit.

"Okay," he said finally, "so we start fresh, here and now. What kind of fresh do you have in mind?"

She gave a little shrug. "Friends, maybe."

"Sure, friends." Once he had wanted far more than that. Now he wasn't sure he wanted even that much.

"You ever marry?" she asked.

He looked down at his naked hands. No rings. "Who'd want to marry a cop who doesn't keep regular hours? A cop who might as well be on another planet when he's involved in an investigation."

"You always were intense."

"So were you."

"Yeah."

He wondered if that was a faint blush in her cheeks, but he couldn't be sure because the lamplight was so yellow and dim. "Well, seeing as how we're both so intense, friendship is apt to be rocky."

"I guess so." Again that faint smile. But at least some of the tension went out of the air, as if they'd reached some kind of agreement.

"So," she said, "how are we going to get this killer?"

"Damned if I know." He reached for his cola again, feeling relaxed enough that he didn't think he would crush the can. He wasn't exactly certain what had been settled between them, but it seemed something had. "The evidence we have is so muddied it's hopeless. The techs are pretty sure the fibers came from the floor mat in a car, but that probably includes ten thousand cars. You know how that goes. A check showed there were nearly twenty places in this town alone that had been oil-and-graveled in the past few months, most of them alleys. The grass is your typical parking-lot sod. It matches the sod at the church."

"So he might have been killed at the church."

"My guess is he was."

"Then why was he carried away and brought back?"

"That's the question, isn't it? Maybe it was a deliberate attempt to muddy the scene."

She shook her head. "But think of the risks involved. If

you kill somebody at the church, and your intention is to crucify the body at the church, why take it away and dump it in an alley?"

"Well, we don't *know* it was dumped in an alley. The vic might have picked up the gravel from the trunk of the car."

"Yeah, right. How much gravel was there?"

He sighed. "Too much," he admitted.

"So, okay, Matt. Face facts. Steve was murdered, moved, dumped, picked up, and crucified. Does that sound even remotely rational?"

"Hell, I've been convinced from the outset that this isn't a rational crime."

Chloe looked down at the can she held, as if thinking. When she looked up, her face was completely without expression. "Have you considered, Matt, that we have multiple operators here?"

"Well, obviously. One man couldn't have gotten the vic up on that cross."

"But what," she said slowly, "if they weren't working *together*?"

It took him a split second to absorb what she was saying but when it hit him, all he could say was, "Whoa!"

She didn't speak, just let him think about it. He turned the idea around in his mind—he *did*, after all, have a lot of respect for her instincts, learned years ago when they'd worked together—but this was boggling his mind.

And yet, as he considered it, pieces began to fall into place, and the whole thing didn't look as crazy as it had looked ever since they found the body. Separate actors with different purposes. That would explain a lot.

"The only problem," he said finally, "is why you'd have two different perps involved."

"I know. It's been driving me nuts, Matt."

"Well, now it's going to drive me nuts. Because, damn it, it fits."

He drained his cola in one long swallow and slapped the can down on the coaster. Then he rose to his feet. "Thanks a bunch, Chloe. I won't get a wink of sleep now."

"Sorry."

He headed for the door, and she followed him. Once there, he stopped to face her. "You get any wild ideas at all, let me know."

"I will."

Then he did the stupidest thing of all. He bent and kissed her lightly on the lips. And he knew as he drove away that he wasn't going to sleep at all, because of what she'd said, and because of what he'd felt when he kissed her.

Just the slightest quiver of response from soft lips. No, he wasn't going to be able to forget that.

The question was whether he wanted to walk into the Chloe Ryder buzz saw once again.

Across town, in a run-down motel room, a man turned into a monster by grief, anger, and hate, stared at the telephone and considered calling the priest again. He hadn't been satisfied by the message he'd left on voice mail. He'd wanted to hear the priest's voice. He'd wanted to hear the man's response.

But he didn't let himself make the call. He had too little time to waste it on indulging his hunger for the man's fear and distress. He had to figure out a way to get his quarry alone, and he had to do it soon. Time was running out.

* * *

In another, equally seedy hotel room, the watcher sat before the television, drinking scotch, his eyes glued to a TV show he wasn't watching.

The cannon was in town. The ball was rolling. His superiors were happy with him.

But he wasn't happy himself. For some strange reason, he was having qualms. Not just about the priest, but about the whole plan.

He kept trying to shake himself out of it. He'd devoted years to this plan, figuring it was the most patriotic thing he could do. The biggest and best thing he could do for his country.

But now he was wondering about that. And he didn't like it one little bit.

Chloe couldn't sleep. She'd tried to read herself into drowsiness, but the latest thriller she'd bought had proved too entertaining, so she'd picked up one of her bar journals and started reading about appellate practice, guaranteed to be soporific. Only her mind wouldn't focus on the articles. She thought about picking up the tattered Bible on her bedside table, then refrained. She doubted she would find comfort there, but comfort wasn't what she needed at the moment.

What she needed was to stop thinking, but her mind seemed determined to wander down the byways of the past and remind her of every one of her shortcomings. Inviting Matt over had apparently been a stupid thing to do.

Because she found herself remembering other times they'd shared a drink, usually after finishing a shift together. She remembered how Jules, her husband, had grown increasingly annoyed by that until she stopped seeing Matt at all, except when they had to work together. She remembered how Jules had continued to grow in jealousy and possessiveness until he was demanding she quit her job.

Jules had been a cop, too. He should have understood the hours and the strain. Or maybe he'd been reacting to his own stresses. All she knew was, as time went by, he hit her more and more often.

He'd always apologized, and she'd always made excuses for him, and anyway, when you were a devoted Catholic, divorce wasn't an option.

But since his murder, she'd emerged from that strange netherworld he'd gradually driven her into, that place where she didn't seem able to defend herself or even find the gumption to leave. That place where he had somehow convinced her that she deserved every bit of the abuse he heaped on her.

And she'd vowed never to let anyone hurt her again. She'd also vowed she'd never again do anything of which she had to be ashamed, and she was ashamed of her entire relationship with Jules. It stood in her mind like a flashing neon sign, reminding her always of her weakness and folly.

No, the Bible wouldn't offer her any comfort. It would just remind her that she had locked herself up so tightly that she felt almost nothing, and any way she looked at it, that was a sin. It was a sin not to care about your neighbor. It was a sin to perform acts of charity only at a safe distance. It was a sin to avoid involvement.

And maybe her greatest sin of all was despair. She talked the talk, but she didn't walk the walk. She had told Matt he needed some exposure to good people, like those in the church who had stood by her during that difficult time, but she didn't believe it in her heart of hearts. No, in her heart of hearts she no longer trusted any human being on the face of the earth.

There, in the dark of the night, in the privacy of her own bed, she finally admitted she didn't like the person she'd become.

Across town, the watcher was staring blearily at the TV in his seedy motel room, watching one of the three local channels it offered. In his hand was a glass of scotch, and beside him on the rickety table was a half-empty bottle of the same.

His conscience was killing him. From the minute he'd had to take care of Steve King's body, he'd begun to have doubts about what he was doing. At first he'd been able to pretend they weren't there, but tonight they reared up in all their ugly glory.

Innocent people were going to die. Somehow, taking care of King's body, the body of a young man who hadn't done a damn thing to deserve a bullet in the back of the head, had rattled him out of his comfortable detachment with the *reality* of what they were about to do. In his mind, tonight, King's body multiplied by the dozens. By the hundreds.

And he wasn't at all sure that what he was doing was justified by love of his country and a desire for all people to live free of fear of terrorism.

Tonight had been the night when he'd sent the coded go-ahead message to the point man, giving him the date and the tail number of the plane that the watcher had rented. And somewhere out there, a misled man was making his final preparations to kill.

It didn't ease the watcher's conscience any that they were striking at a military target. It didn't ease his conscience that he was just a cog in a convoluted machine. He might as well have been the trigger man.

Finally, sodden with scotch, he staggered over to his laptop and re-sent the coded e-mail, a fudged photograph, this time to the cannon. He knew what the cannon would do with it. The man, for the most part, was pathetically predictable.

And the watcher would have deniability if it ever came out. Would be able to claim he'd only been pushing the cannon.

Then, feeling his conscience ease a bit, he let the scotch take him down. He dozed fitfully on his bed, propped against pillows, the TV still running. He'd been having trouble sleeping for a long time, and finally the mixture of scotch and fatigue caught up with him.

Beneath the sound of the TV—some World War II documentary—he didn't hear the sound of someone picking the lock. He wouldn't have heard it even if he had been awake, and the scotch had taken him to deeper realms of unconsciousness than mere sleep.

A few seconds later, something disturbed him. He opened his eyes and started to sit up. And looked into the last human face he would ever see.

CHAPTER 15

"T he maid discovered the body at around two-thirty this afternoon," Mort Phelan told Matt.

The two detectives stood at the doorway of the motel room, looking in. The criminologists were already busy, dusting, photographing, vacuuming, checking every surface and drawer. The victim lay on the bed, covered by a white sheet.

A large section of the exterior passageway was cordoned off, and down at one end some guests were complaining loudly that they wanted to get to their rooms and their belongings. A manager was assuring them that he'd move them and their possessions to other rooms just as soon as the police allowed it, but not one minute before.

This was a cheap motel in a bad part of town, the kind of place that catered to a combination of transients and skinflint tourists. The kind of place where it wasn't exactly astonishing to find a murder victim. Although to hear the manager tell it, he had never had any trouble.

Matt Diel knew better. He remembered having to roust drug dealers and prostitutes from the place during his days in uniform. Things probably hadn't improved all that much.

"The lock was picked," Phelan went on. He was a stubby, heavy man with a comb-over that did little to conceal his baldness and a fondness for brown linen suits that always looked as if they'd been slept in. "The chain and dead bolt weren't set. The vic's throat was cut, probably while he was sleeping. No sign of struggle. No wallet, no ID, no watch."

"So it was a robbery."

"It looks that way."

Matt nodded, debating whether to follow the carefully taped path, laid out by the criminologists, over for a look at the corpse. Probably not. The blood spray all over the room and floor opposite the corpse said all that needed to be said about the fatal injury. From where he stood, he could see a half-empty bottle of premium scotch on the night table.

He pointed it out to Phelan. "That's expensive stuff."

"Well, the anomalies don't end there, I'm afraid."

Matt looked at him. "No?"

"No. The clothes are decent. Better quality."

"How much better?"

"Well, he shopped at Penney's and men's stores. It's all casual stuff, but definitely middle class."

"Maybe he was down on his luck."

"Maybe. All of it's in good condition, not worn or stained. Even his underwear looks relatively new. The suitcase is a middle-quality wheeled carry-on, looks like it's done a lot of flying. The manager says this guy checked in about two weeks ago."

"From where?"

"Baltimore."

"Hmm."

"Anyway, we've got his name, address, and credit card number."

"But no perp."

"Hell," said Phelan, "we're never going to find the perp unless he was kind enough to leave a batch of prints that are already on file. Or unless somebody squeals."

"Somebody will squeal."

"I hope." Phelan pointed across the parking lot. "That's his car."

"Keys?"

"Yeah," said Phelan, holding up a key ring. "Rental car. Budget."

"Well, he must have been on an interesting budget himself. Rental car, decent clothes, and staying in a fleabag motel." Matt sighed and edged into the room, realizing he was going to have to make his own assessment. Mort was okay as a detective, but he tended to see only the obvious. And nothing about this case was obvious.

Slashing a throat was a stupid way to kill someone. It was a bloodbath that usually left a trail of evidence from footprints to . . . aha! There on the wall beside the closet was a partial silhouette outlined in dry blood. The perp. The guy had left the crime scene covered in blood.

And footprints on the blood on the carpet near the door. Ridged soles. It appeared the perp had wiped his feet repeatedly just inside the door, not wanting to leave a blood trail outside.

So he hadn't been hurrying away in terror. Whoever had committed this robbery hadn't been in a panic, at least not after he'd killed the victim.

Stepping carefully to one side, Matt peered into the bathroom. Bloody towels. Cripes, the guy had stopped to wash up. Okay, so the perp hadn't been insanely stoned. Didn't mean much. The guy could simply have felt safe once the vic was dead.

"Did the maid come into the room?" he asked, looking at the footprints by the door.

"No," Phelan answered from outside. "She unlocked the door, pushed it open, then ran."

"Okay. Can we look at the car yet?" Since Phelan was lead on this case, he needed to be careful not to tread on his touchy toes.

"I dunno. Max?" he called to one of the techs.

A tall woman with short black hair straightened and looked around.

"Car?" Phelan asked.

"We haven't done that yet," she answered. "Why? You need to look?"

Phelan shrugged. "I doubt it's involved. Not from the way the scene looks." He looked at Matt. "You got a reason for wanting to look?"

"Just that I like to scan everything, and I've got an appointment to get to another case."

Max shrugged. "No problem. Use your gloves and be careful. You don't want to ruin prints. Lew, log it, will you? Phelan and Diel are going to open the car."

The car, like most rentals, was in fairly pristine condition. The vic, whoever he was, apparently didn't stash papers and notes in the car. The only giveaway that the car had ever been used was a bag from a fast-food restaurant, indicating the guy had eaten a burger, fries, and large drink recently. The glove box held only an owner's manual. Matt found the rental agreement tucked behind one of the visors.

He opened it carefully, hating the way the latex gloves felt on hands. The victim was apparently named Lance Brucon, he'd paid by credit card, had skipped the deductible waiver and . . .

Matt's head snapped up, and he looked across the top of the car at Phelan, who appeared to feel they were wasting their time.

"The vic got a government discount on this car."

Phelan's eyebrows mounted his forehead. "Which government?"

"Federal."

"Oh, holy shit."

Matt looked at the papers again. "That's what it says."

"So what's a federal employee doing in a fleabag like this?"

"Maybe saving on his per diem," Matt suggested. "I hear they get a cash advance for travel. If they don't use it all, some of them keep it."

"Yeah. Makes sense. Okay, let's look at the trunk. Maybe there's something useful in there."

But there wasn't. It was empty.

But it wasn't spotless. A rusty stain, about four centimeters square, marked one side of it. Maybe nothing. Matt leaned in and sniffed it. The odor was faint, very faint, but he knew what it was. "Blood," he said. His scalp began to prickle.

"Oh, Jesus, Mary, and Joseph," Phelan said. Then he turned. "Max!" he yelled.

"I've got to go," Matt said abruptly. "Listen, I want this blood run against the DNA database. It might be tied into a case of mine. And I want carpet samples from the trunk."

Phelan looked at him. "Talk about grasping at straws."

But Matt was already leaning into the trunk again, peering around very carefully. No oily gravel. Shit. But his scalp wouldn't stop prickling. "Just do it, Phelan. Do it for me, okay?"

Phelan shrugged. "You should only be so lucky. But yeah, I'll ask 'em to run it."

"ASAP," Matt said. "I need it ASAP. Priority. As fast as they can frigging do it, okay?"

Phelan just shook his head. "You know the FDLE lab. They're in their own world. They hate to be pressured. Makes 'em dig in their heels. They're *scientists.*"

"Just do what you can." Then Matt left, headed for his meeting with Chloe.

"We've got to stop meeting like this," Chloe said as she faced Matt across another table in another diner, with chipped mugs of coffee.

"You want I should find someplace with tablecloths?"

"How about the zoo? We could walk while we talk."

"Hell, I need to sit down sometimes. This is a good excuse."

She almost laughed. He loved it when those icy eyes of hers actually held humor.

"I got a problem," he said. "You know anybody at the FDLE lab?"

"Are you kidding? Those people refuse to hang out with cops and lawyers. It might affect their impartiality."

He hadn't really expected to hear anything else. And he told himself it didn't really make any difference. If the bloodstain was linked with the murder of Steve King, then King's killer was probably dead, and Father Brendan should be safe.

But he wasn't buying it.

"Matt, what's going on?"

He sighed, stirred some creamer into his coffee. "You know you might be right. At a better restaurant, at least I could get Half & Half."

"Matt?"

She wasn't going to let it go. And for some reason he didn't want to tell her, because he didn't want her to say, "Matt, you're crazy." He didn't want to hear that from *her.*

"Matt?"

He sighed again. "Oh, what the hell. Tell me I'm nuts. I was out on a case earlier this afternoon. Fleabag motel. The guy's throat was slashed."

"Ugly."

"Messy. Anyway, we were checking out his car, and in his trunk we found a bloodstain. Just a small one, but . . ."

Her eyes once again looked like glaciers. He hated when she hid like this.

"Who was the victim?"

"Apparently he was a federal employee."

Her gaze drifted away toward the window at her elbow. He let her be, because he'd known her long enough to recognize when she was thinking. He would let her think as long as she needed, because regardless of whatever other problems he might have with her, he respected her instincts.

Finally, she spoke. "You know what a reach that is."

"I know."

Her eyes came back to his. "However, when you said federal employee, I thought of Father Brendan being in the navy."

"So maybe I'm not nuts."

"Or maybe we both are."

"Maybe." She rolled her head as if trying to ease tension. "Well, okay. We know there had to be a couple of people in-

volved, or Steve never could have been put on that cross. So
if the victim in your other case was one of the killers, there
are still others out there."

"True."

"Which means maybe Father Brendan isn't safe." She
shook her head. "Matt, just don't say the 'c' word."

"The 'c' word?"

"Conspiracy."

Which finally brought into clear light the ugly little thing
that had been running up and down his back since he'd seen
the car trunk. "I didn't say that," he pointed out. But now he
was sure as hell thinking it.

"Do you know how insane that sounds? We don't want to
go off the deep end."

"Trust me, I have no desire to do a Mel Gibson." And
truly he didn't, but that ugly little word kept looking him
right in the eye.

"However," Chloe said, "we have this little problem."

"To say the least."

She fell into thought again, this time for a minute or two.
"I know an expert witness. She used to be with the FDLE
crime lab."

His interest perked. "Really?"

"Yeah. Five years is about all any of them can take of the
job. Burnout comes fast. Anyway, she works for me and
other defense attorneys as a forensics expert. Paid witness.
I'll talk to her. Maybe she still has a friend or two at the lab."

"Thanks, Chloe."

"Give me the case info in case she agrees to help."

He scrawled it all down for her, tore the page from his
memo book, and passed it across to her. "Now, what about
the zoo?"

She looked at him, a smile lurking in her eyes. "The zoo closed hours ago, Matt."

"Hell, in this town, the *real* zoo never closes." She laughed, and he allowed himself to enjoy the moment. "Why'd you mention the zoo if you knew it was closed already?"

"I just wanted to see how you'd react."

That was interesting, he thought. Very interesting. However ... "We've got a headache here, Chloe. A big headache."

She rested her elbows on the table and folded her hands together beneath her chin. "I know," she said. "But let's not jump our fences before we come to them. I'm going to go call Agnes."

"Agnes?"

"The expert witness."

An hour later, they were sitting in Agnes Lucci's living room. Matt guessed that expert witnesses made a lot more money than crime lab grunts. Either that, or Agnes had married money.

Agnes herself was a quiet-looking woman, pretty enough, but no standout. Maybe thirtysomething, on the early side of the decade. She wore a tasteful beige linen dress and a strand of pearls. Rather dressy for an evening at home.

"Okay," Agnes said, after she'd offered them refreshment, which they had declined. "What is it you need?" She looked at Chloe as she spoke, apparently considering the cop in the room to be a mere appendage.

"I need your influence," Chloe said bluntly. "There was a murder today that might be tied in with a murder a week ago. What I'd like to know is if you think you can get someone to do a match with the blood of last week's victim and the blood found in the car trunk today."

"That can be requested through channels."

"We don't have time," Chloe said. "Whoever killed the guy last week is making threats against someone else. We need to know as soon as possible if these two crimes are linked in any way."

"It takes about a week to process blood for the database."

"I know that. But if you knew someone who could prioritize this, so it could be run against the last vic's blood, it would be a great help."

Agnes sighed. "Chloe, you know how they are about interference over there. They don't want their objectivity to be compromised, and I can't say I blame them. I feel the same way."

"I know you do, and that's admirable, and I'm not asking anyone to compromise anything. What I need is speed. I don't want them to hear my theory of the case or anything else. I just want some speed. Lots of speed. Before someone else gets killed."

Agnes pursed her lips a moment before speaking. "Let me tell you something else. If that blood was in that trunk for a week, in this climate, then the likelihood they can get a specific match is about nil."

Matt felt his stomach sink. "Why?"

Finally, she favored him with a look. "Because DNA deteriorates rapidly in the heat. I seriously doubt you could get a specific match at this late date."

"Oh, hell."

Chloe leaned forward. "But they could get *something*?"

"Well, they might come up with a phone book. Maybe. Dozens, if not hundreds or thousands of names."

"Then I want the phone book," Chloe said firmly. "Because if the right name even pops up in it, we might be on to something."

Agnes was silent for a few moments. Then she said, "All right. I still have a friend over there. I'll see what I can do."

"I'm gonna kiss your feet," Matt said, as they stood outside beside their cars.

"You never would have said that to a man," Chloe remarked.

"No," he said, "I probably wouldn't have. But what does that have to do with the price of peas in Polatka? Cripes, Chloe, do you always have to be such a ball-buster? Where the hell did that come from?"

She turned to face him, and her expression was almost sad. "I don't know," she said.

"Well, maybe it's time you stood down from high alert status. I'm not trying to start World War III with you."

On that grouchy, irritable note, he turned on his heel, climbed into his car, and drove away.

And Chloe stood there alone, staring at his departing taillights.

Victor bought the clock because it ticked. He'd been using a digital clock in his room because digital clocks seemed to be the only kind cheap enough to be affordable. But then he came across an old-fashioned-looking windup clock that actually ticked. He bought it and put it right beside his bed, close to his head.

Lying down, he closed his eyes and listened to the tick-

tick-tick. He'd always loved the sound of a ticking clock. The sound of time's passage soothed him with its promise. He knew most people were afraid of time, afraid of its gradual erosion of life. Victor loved it, and it wasn't only because he was so young.

All his life he'd loved the sound of time marching audibly past, *tick, tick, tick*. It reassured him with its steady progression no matter what else might be happening, no matter how horrible or unendurable it might seem. He even enjoyed it in happy moments, enjoyed its measure.

He listened to it now and tried to curb the excitement that fluttered in the pit of his stomach. He had his date and his plane was waiting for him. He'd fabricated the smudge pot that would burn the tire mulch, and the canister that would feed the chemical payload into the smoke, and the nozzle and control mechanisms to dispense the deadly gaseous cocktail.

Tick, tick, tick. It was the most beautiful sound in the world.

CHAPTER 16

B rendan had a headache. It was pounding and throbbing in his temples, and he knew it was tension, pure and simple. Being watched all the time by off-duty cops, at considerable expense to the church, and being limited in his duties was making him about as happy as a caged tiger.

He eyed the bottle of bourbon on the cart in the rectory parlor. It was Dominic's bottle, used only occasionally in the evening, just a sip or two of whiskey. Brendan never joined him.

But that bottle was looking awfully good right now, and he had to tear his gaze from it. Booze had become his crutch toward the end of his navy days. Never interfering with his duties, but becoming too important eventually to be denied. He'd managed to shake it during his time in the monastery, and hadn't touched the stuff again.

But Jack Daniel's was looking like an old friend right now, and that wasn't good. He couldn't afford to fall into that pit again. He'd managed to catch himself before the stuff had taken over his life, and he wasn't going to give it another run at him.

But oh, God, his head hurt. And his heart hurt. And his

soul hurt. He needed to get moving, but he had this awful gap in his afternoon, a gap caused by the limitations Matt and Chloe had put on him. Dominic was out dealing with things Brendan should have been dealing with.

He hated this.

Just then a cry reached him. It sounded like Lucy, the secretary, and he was out of his chair in an instant, headed toward the front office.

When he stepped through the doorway, he saw her. She glanced toward him, her face almost white, then swiveled back to her computer, clicking her mouse.

"Lucy? What's wrong?"

She shook her head, her attention fixed on her screen. "Nothing, Father. Nothing. You know how we sometimes get that obscene junk e-mail from those porn websites."

"Sure." But he didn't believe her. They'd gotten those messages before, and she hadn't cried out. "It must have been a bad one."

"It was. I can't believe the filth of some minds."

She was shaking, he realized. Shaking and looking ready to shatter. He stepped farther into the room. "Lucy?"

She looked at him finally. "Yes, Father?" Her eyes were pinched.

"Lucy, it was more than that."

"No, it wasn't, Father. It was just worse than usual. Don't you worry about me. I'll be fine."

But he still wasn't buying it. "Show it to me, Lucy."

"No!" Then she looked a little embarrassed. "I'm sorry, but there's really no need for you to see it."

"You don't need to protect me. But I *do* want to know what upset you. Maybe I can do something about it."

"You know you can't do anything about the mailing lists we get on to. There's no way to stop this stuff."

He stood beside her and put his hand on her shoulder. "Don't lie to me, Lucy."

She gasped quietly.

"It was worse than that, and I want to see it."

"Father . . ."

"Lucy."

After a moment, she reached a trembling hand toward her mouse and clicked it a couple of times.

Then, filling Brendan with horror and numbing shock, he saw a photo of himself. A photo of him standing over a body sprawled in the grass.

Matt was ready to beat his head against a brick wall, but one wasn't handy. He absolutely hated it when all his cases were stuck and every single one of them, from the murder of Steve King, to the throat-cutting, to the attempted murder of a prostitute, was mired. No leads, and going nowhere.

Nobody was putting a priority on the prostitute case, except him. He gave all his cases top priority, and there was little that frustrated him as much as having no solid leads to pursue.

So he sat at his desk and worked his way through the files, trying to find something, anything, that he might have overlooked. Something that when viewed from a different angle, might give him the break he needed.

Most murderers knew their victims. Those cases could usually be solved in a few days, or a few weeks. But when there was no link between victim and slayer, and nothing but inconsistent or nonexistent physical evidence left by the perp, it was like heading down a blind alley.

So back to Steve King. Why would a stranger kill the

kid? Unless the stranger wanted to scare the priest, which was where this case pointed. Still . . .

Chloe was right. He didn't even want to think that "c" word, at least until they had some reason to link the two murders.

So far they'd worked on interviewing parishioners and parish employees, but nobody had an unkind word to say about Brendan. Which didn't mean a damn thing. But as far as he was concerned, any possibility that the father had committed the murder had gone out the window after the call from the diocese, linking the King case to something that had happened in Brendan's past. That was just too damn convenient.

Which reminded him. He needed to call Chloe and find out if she'd learned anything about the suicide at Brendan's last naval station. His own request for information still hadn't yielded anything—which was hardly surprising. Cops digging into suicides from several years ago were hardly going to be top priority at a distant M.E.'s office. Chloe's investigator was apt to get a faster response.

He reached for his phone to call her, just as it rang. "Detective Diel," he said automatically, his mind still roaming the St. Simeon's case.

"Detective, this is Father Abernathy with the Diocese of Tampa. I believe you're working on the murder of one of our parishioners, a Steve King?"

"Yes, I am."

"Well." The priest's voice seemed to quaver. "I think you should come to the chancery office as soon as you possibly can. We've received . . . something. It might shed light on the case for you."

Matt's interest revved to top speed. "I'm on my way." He

glanced at his watch. "Allowing for traffic, I'll be there in thirty minutes."

"I'll be awaiting you. Just ask for me, Father Abernathy."

A minute later, Matt was out the door. Behind him on his desk, his phone started ringing, but he ignored it. His voice mail could pick it up.

"I'm calling Chloe, Father," Lucy said, her voice still shaking. "I'm calling her right now."

Brendan had sunk onto one of the reception chairs, his elbows on his knees, his head in his hands. "Call the police," he said, his voice muffled.

"No!"

He lifted his head. It was still throbbing, but now it felt as if every muscle in his face were trying to drop to the floor. "They need to see this, Lucy."

"No. No. They'll jump to conclusions. I'm not going to see you arrested, Father."

He managed a faint, wan smile. "You don't believe the evidence of your eyes?"

"Absolutely not." She was still shaking, but her voice was growing stronger.

"That's a lot of faith." Faith that he wasn't exactly feeling himself right now. What if he'd had some kind of psychotic break? What if that really *was* him, and he hadn't been safely in his bed as he believed. What if—?

"Father," Lucy said sternly, "it's not faith. I know you. Besides . . . people can fool around with photos on computers these days. Nearly anyone can do it. What's more, are you going to try to convince me that someone was out there taking pictures of you committing a murder? Oh, please!" Then she rattled off a string of Spanish words so rapidly that he couldn't follow it. Nor did she particularly seem to want him to. He was fairly certain she used a few words that he had never before heard pass Lucy's lips, in either Spanish or English.

She reached for the phone, making her own decision, and punched in numbers. Moments later she was telling Chloe to come to the rectory immediately.

When she hung up, she turned back to Brendan. "She'll be here in a few minutes."

"I need a drink." His weakness. And he was about to give in to it because he couldn't make that obscene picture go away, not from his mind, not from that computer. Because he was suddenly filled with a self-doubt that wanted to push him to the edge of madness.

"No, you don't, Father," Lucy said firmly. "You know you never drink, and it will only make you feel worse."

Right. At the moment, getting thoroughly sloshed actually sounded attractive. Then he despised himself for the weakness. "You're right," he said.

"Whoever made up that picture is sick," Lucy said, anger overcoming her initial shock. "Very sick. I hope they can find him."

Brendan managed a nod, even though he feared the only person they might find was *him*. But why, at this stage of his life, would he go crazy like that? Maybe he'd had a mild stroke or something?

How could that be *him*? He'd felt so much affection for Steve, so blessed to know a young man with such a pure, generous heart. A saintly young man. Yet not perfect. A young man with plenty of demons to wrestle, yet one who wrestled them well, from the strength of his faith.

It was cruel, so cruel that his life had been cut so short,

before his soul and heart had fully blossomed, before he had been able to bless the lives of the many who would now never know him.

That obscenity of a picture. A shudder passed through him, but he forced himself to sit upright. Whatever was coming, he had to face it. And whoever this evil person was, even if it should prove to be himself, he needed to be brought to justice.

Just then, Chloe hurried into the office, dressed in a polo shirt and khaki chinos. She paused on the threshold, looking at the two of them. "My God," she said, "don't tell me there's been another murder."

Matt made good time to the diocesan offices. His cell phone rang insistently a couple of times, but he ignored it, leaving voice mail to take it. When he asked for Father Abernathy, he was taken immediately to an office on the second floor, where he found not one priest, but two awaiting him.

"Detective Diel?" said the younger of the two, coming around his desk. "I'm Father Abernathy. And this is Monsignor Crowell."

Matt shook the hands of both men. "I believe we spoke on the phone once, Monsignor."

"Yes, I believe so." Crowell didn't look pleased. "I would appreciate it if you would keep this meeting private. I'd much prefer if we didn't have to show you this."

"It might be evidence," Father Abernathy said. "We can't withhold evidence."

"I don't know why not," Matt said, looking at Crowell. Something wasn't adding up here. As he understood it, Crowell outranked Abernathy. Therefore, if Crowell wanted to conceal whatever this was behind the silent stone façade of the Catholic Church, then it would be hidden, the way so many things involving priests had been hidden in the past. "You guys will even hold a murder confession in confidence."

"Only under seal of confessional." Crowell sighed, then waved his hand. "This is no confession."

"No? What is it?"

"An . . . accusation, I suppose."

"What is it?"

"In a moment." Crowell waved Matt to a seat. "I want to tell you something first."

Matt sat and waited attentively, wondering what kind of bullshit was about to be shoveled. Something about Crowell was seriously bugging him.

"It is with the greatest trepidation," Crowell said, "that I'm sharing this with you. However, in light of the questions I have about things at St. Simeon's, I suppose I must. Sometimes the line between the Church's province and the province of secular authorities is quite clear. This is one of those occasions. This falls clearly into both our domains, and we will have to deal with it each in his own way."

"I understand." Not that he did. Matt wondered why he suddenly thought of Pilate washing his hands.

Crowell sighed. "I can't bear this. Father, you take care of this matter. I need to go pray on this."

"Yes, Monsignor."

Matt watched Crowell take his leave, and was absolutely convinced that the man wasn't nearly as distressed as he was pretending. Why? What the hell was going on? Chloe had said something about the diocese riding Brendan's ass, and he himself remembered the call he'd gotten about how something of this nature had happened in the priest's past. That call had been anonymous, but he had a strong feeling it had been generated by Crowell.

Now the gloves were off. Crowell was showing his hand. No more anonymous calls.

"I suppose," said Abernathy, when Crowell had closed the door behind him, "that I might as well just show you. You'll make of it what you will. But I *will* tell you privately that I'm sure this is some kind of hoax."

"Monsignor Crowell doesn't seem as certain."

"No. I noticed." Abernathy made a face. "Well, that's Monsignor, and I am I, and we have differing opinions on some things. The point is, we received an e-mail this morning, and it's some kind of evidence, I'm sure, although I do *not* feel it's the kind of evidence Monsignor thinks it is."

"I'll keep that it mind."

"Please do."

Matt was getting impatient. "What did you get?"

Abernathy turned the monitor on his desk toward Matt. "This arrived a short while ago."

Matt looked at the picture, and one thought, one thought only, came into his head: *Fuck.*

"Okay," Chloe said, once she had absorbed what she was seeing. "It's a fake."

Brendan's eyes looked haunted. "How can you be sure?"

"Because nobody, but nobody, was out there taking a picture of you committing a murder."

"Well, I'd like to think I had more sense than that at least," Brendan said in a poor attempt at humor.

"You not only have more sense, you're not a murderer. Okay. Somebody really wants to screw you."

Brendan cleared his throat. "I thought they wanted to kill me."

"They seem to. But first they want to take you down. Lucy, can I sit at your desk?"

"Sure."

Chloe took the secretary's seat and looked at the e-mail header. "This was copied to the diocese."

"Wonderful," said Brendan.

"The sender address is meaningless. But we've got a computer nerd or two around here. Maybe they can trace it back to an origin."

"I hope so," said Lucy. "You know Father didn't do that."

"Of course I know Father didn't do that." Chloe sat back a little in the chair and stared at the photo. "Look at that. It could be anyone lying on the ground. No face. Just a white shirt, jeans, and blond hair."

"That's what Steve was wearing," Brendan pointed out.

"Sure. But a lot of people would have known that. Then there's you. That picture of you could be from anywhere."

"But it *is* me."

"Oh, yes, of course." She leaned forward and looked closer. "I don't know. It's so easy to fudge these things nowadays. Heck, I even do it with my photos at home. Software right off the shelf at most office and computer stores lets you erase things from pictures, combine pictures. . . . We need an expert to look at this."

Brendan rubbed his eyes and gave a heavy sigh. "Lucy, do we have any aspirin down here?"

Lucy leaned over, around Chloe's legs, and pulled out her purse. "I have ibuprofen. Two?"

"Please."

He swallowed them dry, hoping they would ease the pounding in his head. "No Matt?"

"I'll try him again." Chloe reached for the phone and dialed Matt's cell. Still no answer. "Not yet. It won't be long though."

"I don't understand," Lucy said, "why we have to bring it to the police. It's a fake."

Chloe swiveled the chair to look at her. "That's exactly why we have to bring it to the police. This might be from the murderer."

Matt left the chancery with a hard copy of the e-mail and a list of those who had seen it. The list was short. Monsignor Abernathy vetted the e-mail that came into that particular office, and Monsignor Crowell was the only other person he had shown it to.

Matt would have liked nothing better than to tell Abernathy to delete the damn thing, but he couldn't do that. He was no computer wizard, but he realized that a trained person might be able to glean a great deal of information from the original e-mail that couldn't be found in a mere printout.

Back at his car, he decided to pick up his voice mail on his cell. There were three messages, all from Chloe, and all saying the same thing.

He punched in the rectory number. Chloe answered.

"I'm on my way," he said. "And I've already seen it."

"The chancery?"

"The chancery."

"Yes, I see from the header it went there, too. What do they think?"

"Let's just say that there is a division of opinion."

"Anybody can see it's a fake."

"Well, of course." Matt sighed. "How's Father Brendan holding up?"

"Okay, I guess. Just get here, soon. Please."

Matt didn't like the sound of that. Brendan struck him as a strong man, strong of heart as well as of body. But he had suffered a severe blow, and was enduring great stress thanks to the threats against him. Matt supposed it would hardly be surprising if the man was near breaking.

But near breaking was not what he found when he arrived at the rectory. The Father looked fatigued and worn, but he didn't look anywhere near breaking. He and Chloe were sitting in the parlor. Lucy had gone back to her job, for now holding the world at bay.

Matt closed the parlor door behind him and nodded to Brendan. "How are you holding up?"

"I'm fine. It's a bit shocking, however, to realize that someone hates me so much."

"Anyone would be shocked by that. Tell me the e-mail is still on the computer it was opened on."

"Yes," Chloe said. "I had Lucy save it to a locked file."

"Good. I want to get an expert to look at it." Matt laid the hard copy of the photo on the end table between Brendan and Chloe. "What's wrong with this picture?"

Chloe gave him a faint, wry smile. "Other than that it's a fake?"

"No, I'm not talking about that. Take a good look at it. It tells us something about the person who sent it."

She and Brendan both looked down at it.

"Father," Matt said to Brendan, "do you know where King was killed?"

Brendan paused thoughtfully. "I assumed . . . I guess I assumed he was killed in the church until I saw this photo."

"That's it," Chloe said. "That's it. Whoever sent this photo knows that Steve died facedown on grass."

"Exactly." Matt reached for a chair and pulled it close, sitting with them. "Nothing's been out in the press except that King was found nailed to the cross after being shot in the back of the head. Absolutely *nothing* has been said about where he was murdered. So whoever sent this knew the real story. This is from our murderer."

Brendan bowed his head a moment, and it seemed to Matt he was saying a silent prayer.

"That's the first thing that leapt out at me when I saw it," Matt said. "I'm going to get one of our computer experts on this immediately and see if we can find out the source of this e-mail. I didn't figure the diocese was going to let my guys paw around in their computers, so I'm glad you saved the e-mail. I'm going to have one of my men come over here and work on it, okay?"

Brendan nodded slowly. "As long as that's *all* he looks at. A great deal of the information on our computers is private."

"That's all he'll be looking at. What else do you notice about this picture?"

Chloe spoke. "You mean aside from the fact that it's highly unlikely anyone was out there taking pictures when this happened?".

"Apart from that, yes."

"Well, there's no real discernible background. It's a dark picture, so you don't notice that at first, but there's really nothing there."

"It's been smudged so it's not recognizable. That means wherever the base picture was taken, the sender tried to conceal it."

Brendan's eyes widened a bit. "It's so dark I didn't notice that."

"Well, you and the body come out clearly enough. Which is another thing. Whoever did this picture took clear photos and combined them, then darkened them so they looked to be taken at night. Because there's absolutely no evidence of a flash, and it's not taken through a night-vision lens. That's obvious."

"I'm feeling better by the minute," Brendan said.

"Good. The other thing is, you can't see the face of the supposed victim. It could be anyone. Anyone at all. I wouldn't be surprised if our killer posed for that part of it."

"And the picture of Father Brendan," Chloe said. "Do you see? The first thing you notice is that he's holding something in both hands. It could be a gun. But that's smeared out, too, and his hands are too far apart."

"Bingo," Matt said. "It's an obvious fake. Painfully obvious."

"I could do better myself," Chloe admitted.

Matt sat back in his chair, nearly grinning. "This is our break. We find this guy, and that's it."

Brendan seemed to sag a little in the chair, as if releasing a great tension. "You're sure I didn't do it?"

"I'm more convinced than ever that you didn't do it."

Brendan nodded. "Thank you."

"Now." Matt leaned toward him. "I want you to think about any link you can come up with between this murder and the death of that young man when you were in the navy."

"Other than that they were close in age?"

"Other than that."

"I don't know. I mean . . ." Brendan looked away

thoughtfully. "They were nothing alike, these two young men, other than that both were wrestling with their homosexuality. Steve was thoroughly dedicated to the Church; Tom was just finding his way into it. There really aren't very many parallels."

Just then Matt's cell phone rang. He pulled it out of his pocket and flipped it open, punching the talk button. "Diel," he said.

It was Phelan. "We got a rat," Phelan said. "He says he saw the guy who came out of the motel on the slashing case. We've got good ID."

"Who was it?"

"Some addict. I'm having him picked up now."

"Great."

"Well, I'd agree, except for one thing."

"What's that?" Matt asked.

"Our vic doesn't exist."

CHAPTER 17

Matt and Chloe left the rectory together. Behind them Brendan sat thoughtfully slumped in a chair, and Lucy answered the incessantly ringing phones.

"You know that 'c' word we didn't want to use?" Matt asked, as they stood beside their cars. A hundred yards away, children were starting to spill out of the church's school, toward buses and waiting cars.

"Yeah?" Chloe faced him. "What happened?"

"I'm not sure. That was Phelan on the phone. They think they've got the killer of that guy I told you about."

"The one with the blood in his trunk?"

"The same. Problem is, he doesn't exist."

"Who? The killer?"

"Sorry. The victim. I'm heading back to the station to find out what the scoop is."

"Let me know, will you?" Chloe's eyes suddenly looked pinched. "I'm getting a horrible feeling about this, Matt. A horrible feeling."

"Me too. I don't like shadowboxing."

* * *

In the Burglary-Homicide squad room, except for a couple of secretaries, no one was present but Phelan. And Phelan was looking like a man with major indigestion.

Not that that was an unusual expression in this room. Antacids populated every drawer, it sometimes seemed. Between stress and diet, every person who worked in the squad room was a candidate for an ulcer or a coronary.

"Okay," said Phelan, when Matt had pulled up a seat, "it's like I told you. I've got two uniforms hunting for the perp, an addict known as Jerry 'Squeaky' Schurtz."

"I know him. I never thought he'd go that far. His usual is burglary of an unoccupied dwelling."

"Yeah, and a string of car break-ins. Well, this time the judge isn't going to send him to rehab."

"Not likely. What about the victim?"

"That's where life gets interesting. No such social security number, no such address. No such name. I have NCIC running his prints, but that'll take days. In the meantime, the guy doesn't exist."

"What about his credit cards?" Matt drummed his fingers on the desktop.

"Both accounts were opened in the last couple of months. No credit history."

"Now wait. How do you get a credit card with no credit history?"

Phelan gave him a significant look. "I checked with the car rental company. They rattled around a bit, then somebody remembered that he'd shown them travel orders with the proper discount code on them. So he got a government discount. But nobody remembers who issued his travel orders. So we have no idea if he was military or civil service, or what agency he was claiming to be with."

"Well, if he doesn't exist, I seriously doubt he was with the EPA."

"Yeah." Phelan sighed and leaned back in his chair until it squeaked. "I suppose at any minute I'll get a call telling me to back the hell off. But it's kind of weird to prosecute a murder when you don't know who your victim is."

"You know it's not impossible. You go to court for the murder of John Doe. It's not like we don't have the body."

But Matt was imagining other ramifications, things like the body being claimed, the records being taken, a nameless faceless person with a squirrelly government ID telling them to drop the entire thing.

"I'm getting paranoid," Phelan said after a moment. "Nobody's gonna call. It would make too big a deal out of it. The guy was probably some kind of dealer with a false ID. Nothing more than that."

"Let's hope so." But Matt knew it was more than that. Government travel orders could be faked, but why would some dealer or crook bother to do so? "The car rental company was sure the guy had travel orders?"

"They wouldn't have given him the discount otherwise."

Then they were probably real. But he didn't say that to Phelan. He didn't want the other detective to find reasons to stop working the case.

That uncomfortable feeling was crawling up and down his spine again when Phelan's phone rang. There was a short conversation, then Phelan hung up and looked at him.

"They're booking Squeaky downstairs right now. They'll have him in interrogation in about thirty minutes."

"Good. Let's have a shot at him."

* * *

Squeaky Schurtz was a waste of humanity. At least that's how Matt always thought of him. At one time he'd been smart, a high school salutatorian, a college student with high grades, headed for success in engineering. He'd also had a solid family, until they'd given up on him.

That was why judges kept trying to rehabilitate him. Until cocaine had gotten its hooks into him, Squeaky had showed great promise and had never been in trouble.

After ten years on drugs, though, he was a pathetic figure, too thin, too dirty, and willing to do anything to get his fix.

Right now he was sullen and trembling. Needing another fix.

"Okay, Squeaky," Phelan said, as he and Matt faced the no-longer-young man across the table in the interrogation room, "we know you slashed the guy's throat. Someone saw you come out of the motel room."

"Yeah? Who?"

"Come on," Matt said. "You know it'll stand up. You left your prints all over the place."

Squeaky rubbed his face, and a shudder passed through him. "I gotta get out of here, man."

"You're never going to get out of here again."

"I'm gonna be sick."

"Then we'll take you to the hospital."

Phelan looked at Matt. "Why bother? He's just going to get the death penalty anyway."

Squeaky's head jerked. A wild look came to his bloodshot eyes. "I'll go back to rehab. I swear."

Matt shook his head and leaned forward. "Squeaky," he said almost kindly, "why'd you do it? Why'd you cut the guy's throat?"

"He started to wake up, man!" Then, realizing what he'd admitted, Squeaky began to cry.

Matt waited until the man was reduced to sniveling. "Why'd you pick him?"

"Cuz he had money, man. Not like everybody else down there. He had money."

"How'd you know that?"

"I saw it when he was paying for something at the store up the block from the motel. He had a thick wad in his wallet. So I followed him back and found out where he was staying."

"Did you take his wallet?"

Squeaky wiped his eyes with his hands and nodded.

"What else was in it?"

"Papers. Credit card. I don't touch that stuff."

"What'd you do with it?"

"I ditched it. In a Dumpster."

Matt felt Phelan look at him, and knew what he was thinking: Oh, no, not a trash search.

Phelan asked, "Did you take anything else?"

"A laptop computer."

"Where'd you pawn that?"

Squeaky told them. He even told them where he'd ditched the wallet.

"Too damn easy," Phelan remarked, as he and Matt left the interrogation room. "Well, that's one mystery solved."

But only one, Matt thought. Only one. He lucked out, though. Phelan sent him to hunt up the laptop. Maybe the guy was hoping that once they found that, they wouldn't need to look for the wallet.

Yeah.

*   *   *

The pawnbroker was expecting him. "I figured it was stolen," the guy said. "So I only loaned him a fiver for it." Without waiting to be asked, he pulled out the computer and the contract that Squeaky had signed.

"So why didn't you call us?" Matt asked.

The pawnbroker shrugged. "If I called you guys about everything, I'd never do anything else. I knew you'd show up eventually. People always report these things to the cops."

"Yeah, well this time the guy was murdered for it."

The pawnbroker leaned an elbow on his display case and looked fully at Matt for the first time. "No shit? I wouldn't have thought that asshole capable of murder."

"Me neither."

"Don't that beat all." The pawnbroker looked bemused.

"If you thought it was stolen, why'd you take it?" Matt asked, picking up the laptop and contract.

"Simple. I figured some yuppie stockbroker would want it back. If I didn't take it, Squeaky mighta sold it somewhere else. To somebody who'd want to keep it."

"A good citizen, huh?"

The broker shook his head. "A better one than you guys seem to think."

Phelan was right, Matt thought as he walked out to his car. It was too easy.

Thus far.

Back at the station, he cracked open the laptop and powered it up. Phelan was out somewhere, which would at least give him time to explore the hard drive without interference. Maybe find out something useful. Something that tied in with the crucifixion.

Did covert operatives actually carry computers? He tried to shake the question away, reminding himself that they had no evidence of conspiracy and he was grasping at straws.

But the straws wouldn't go away, and he kept trying to grab them.

Of course, the very first thing that popped up as he was waiting for Windows to boot was a demand for a password. Hell.

He called for the computer expert. He used the things, but he hadn't even a vague idea how to hack them.

"Where's Lance?" the man with the cigar asked.

"Dead." The other man dropped into one of the chairs and reached for the bottle of scotch, pouring himself two fingers into a hotel glass, no ice. "Maybe we should call off this operation."

"Dead? Wait a minute. What happened?"

"All I know is, I couldn't get him on the phone, so I went to that fleabag motel and his room is closed off with police tape. I thought about going in to question the manager, but decided not to. I did, however, see a cop pull up, so I acted like a gawker and asked what happened. He was murdered."

"Who? How?"

"What do I look like? The oracle at Delphi? How many questions do you want me to ask? I didn't want the cop to think we might be connected."

The man with the cigar dropped his stogie into the ashtray and joined the other man at the table. "There's no reason to call the operation off. Nobody can connect Lance with us."

"Maybe not." But the second man didn't look terribly

convinced. "The thing is, nobody knows where the cannon is right now. Or how to push him, if he lags."

"Lance said the cannon was moving. That's all we need. If nothing happens to the priest in the next couple of days, we'll consider halting the operation."

"Fair enough." The second man took a huge swallow of his scotch. "But I don't mind telling you, I've got the worst feeling about this."

"Don't get spooky on me. We've been planning this for years. And nobody, but nobody, can connect *us* with it."

The other man sighed. "I don't like that crucifixion. I don't like it at all."

"Neither did I . . . but Lance is dead now. So whoever pulled that stunt can't get any further. We're not linked to anybody. Now will you just relax?"

But relaxing was going to be the hardest thing in the world for a while to come. And they both knew it.

That damn priest was never alone, the killer thought in disgust. Everywhere he went, there was someone dogging his steps, half the time a cop. A good sniper rifle would have solved the problem, but that wasn't what the killer wanted.

He wanted to see the look in the priest's eyes when he knew he was going to die. He wanted the satisfaction of making sure the man knew exactly *why* he was going to die. Anything less would leave him feeling unsatisfied.

Well, there was one way to cut a priest out of the herd.

He had spent all day watching, waiting, fighting down his own nerves. It would have been so much nicer if he could get the priest away from everyone, to a quiet place somewhere. But that didn't look possible.

And he had to get the guy before he left town. That was

what his friend had said. The priest was going to be leaving town in a couple of days. Hardly any time left. Hardly any at all.

He was getting so he could identify a lot of the people who were in and out of the rectory. The cute blonde who hung around too much. The man he was almost positive was a police detective. The secretary. The other priest. A few other people.

But mostly his quarry spent the afternoon locked away behind those rectory doors. So when the detective and the blond woman left, he waited a half hour or so, then walked casually over, and entered.

He was greeted by the secretary, a pleasantly smiling woman who asked if she could help him.

"I need to make confession," he said, knowing that was one way to get a priest alone. Knowing that the other priest was away at the moment.

She should have said yes immediately. A priest, he had read, should drop everything to hear a confession. Nothing should stop him.

Except a secretary with salt-and-pepper hair and a warm smile.

"I'm sorry," she said. "No priest is available at the moment. But if you'd like to wait in the church, Father Dominic should be back soon. I'll send him over."

"I was hoping to see Father Brendan."

"I'm sorry," she said firmly, "but he's not available."

The hard knot of anger inside him tightened, and he struggled for a minute as his vision nearly turned red. But he caught himself, finally saying, "Thanks. I'll come back another time."

Then, feeling as if every muscle in his body had turned rigid, he about-faced and walked out.

He knew Brendan was there. He *knew* it. But if he tried to get past that secretary, the cops would be there in a minute. He had to find another way.

"Lucy," Brendan said, "did I just hear you tell someone I couldn't listen to his confession?"

Lucy looked up at him, her lips tight. "You did, Father. I don't know who he was."

"That doesn't make any difference. I'll go after him."

"Father!" Lucy snapped the word. "If you set one foot toward that door, I'm going to scream my head off and get every policeman on the property here to stop you."

Brendan looked surprised, but also a little wounded. "Lucy—"

"No," she said. "I'm telling you, Father, you're not going to hear that man's confession. I don't know who he is. And if he really wants to make a confession, he could wait a couple of minutes for Father Dominic. Now you go back to whatever you were doing."

"Do I sign your paycheck?"

Lucy looked disgusted. "Don't even try that with me. If you want to fire me, go ahead. But you're not going out there."

Brendan had the grace to look ashamed. "I'm sorry."

"You ought to be. I know this is hard on you, Father, but it's nowhere near as hard as it will be if you get killed. So park your hard head at your desk and take care of the paperwork."

Brendan suddenly smiled. "I would never guess you've raised six children."

"Eleven, if you count my priests. And that's what all of you are, Father. You're children."

"Children?"

"Most definitely. The Church spoils you all rotten. Your job is to keep your head in the spiritual clouds. My job is to take care of the practicalities. Now go do your job and let me do mine."

Suitably chastened, Brendan returned to his office, where he was working on a pastoral letter.

But it wasn't the pastoral letter he thought about. It had been a long while since he'd really thought about the suicide of that young man Tom just before he resigned from the navy. But for the past few days, ever since Crowell had leveled that accusation at him, he'd been thinking about the young man more and more often.

He still couldn't remember his last name. That sorely troubled him, because for some time he had felt that he'd failed in his counseling of Tom. The young man was wrestling with his homosexuality, wrestling with the fear that he might have been discovered by some of his fellow sailors, fearing he was about to be thrown out of the navy. Fearing that his father and mother would disown him if they found out.

But there had been something else, too. Something else that had been referred to upon occasion. The main thing he remembered was the genuine fear that would come into Tom's eyes when he alluded to something he'd stumbled into.

At the time, the bits and pieces had seemed jumbled and paranoid, and Brendan had thought the young man was mixing his fears in his mind, viewing some classified operation in light of his other fears.

Now he wasn't so sure.

* * *

"The weather's beautiful up here in Norfolk," Dianna told Chloe over the phone. "Springtime in Virginia. Wonderful," the part-time investigator added.

"I'm glad you're having such a great time," Chloe said drily.

"Fabulous. I've looked at enough microfiche to blind me. But I found your guy."

Chloe's heart quickened. "And?"

"You ready to write?"

Chloe was already pulling a pad and pen from her purse. "Go ahead."

"Petty Officer First Class Thomas Wayne Humboldt. Died of a self-inflicted gunshot wound on November 5, two and a half years ago. Body discovered early morning November 6 in his off-base apartment by a roommate who'd been out late. Roommate had an unimpeachable alibi, and the wound was consistent with insertion of the barrel of a pistol in the mouth by the victim. The weapon was a twenty-two caliber pistol owned by the victim."

"Twenty-two?"

"Yup. Seems like an odd gun for a sailor to have, but that's what it was."

Chloe felt her heart skip a beat. Steve King had been killed by a twenty-two also. A connection? "Can you get the ballistic analysis for me?"

"Why? It's an open-and-shut case."

"Get me the ballistics, Dianna. Okay?"

She sighed. "So much for my nice drive through the country. Okay. Will do. Now, do you want me to interview the roommate? Assuming I can find him?"

"Yes. And I want you to talk to the family."

"Oh, man, you know how I *love* to do that."

"It's been a while. They'll be calmer now."

"Sure. Right. And just what is it you expect me to find out from these people?"

"Anything they think they know about their son's state of mind. And what happened to that pistol."

"You got it."

"Thanks, Dianna. How soon can you get me the ballistics?"

"How do you want them? By fax?"

"For a start. My home fax. I may need you to have the M.E. send copies to the Tampa PD."

"Why don't I just do that at the same time? I'll see if I can get them to express a copy. Detective Diel, right?"

"Right."

When she hung up the phone, Chloe realized her heart was racing like a trip-hammer. Two deaths, linked by an anonymous caller. Two cases of young men meeting their deaths by a shot from a twenty-two. Such pistols weren't uncommon, but they were rarely a weapon of choice except for women and children. The coincidence was just too great.

Reaching for the phone again, she called Matt.

CHAPTER 18

Stuart Wheelwright, the head of the Burglary-Homicide squad, looked over his glasses at Matt. "Run that by me again. You *think* there's a connection between a two-year-old suicide and the crucifixion at St. Simeon's?"

"There's a connection of some sort. Start with the phone calls the diocese has been receiving, claiming that the two cases are linked. Add the threat against the pastor at St. Simeon's. And finally, account for the fact that both the suicide and the murder were committed with a twenty-two caliber pistol."

"Fine. You still don't need to go to Virginia."

"I want to interview the family of the suicide. Find out what they know."

"About what, for God's sake? The guy killed himself. He was despondent. The case here was a murder. How do you think the parents of the suicide are going to know anything? And if you think it's the same weapon, then use the telephone, call the family, and find out what the hell happened to the gun. That's all you need to know."

"I think they might know something more."

"About what?" Wheelwright's impatience was palpable.

"Look, we've got our hands full right now. I can't afford to have you chasing a wild goose. You use the telephone if you need to talk to those people, and you keep your eye on the main ball, which is finding out who's threatening that priest. At this point, I don't care how long it takes to catch whoever crucified that victim as long as we keep it from happening to the priest. My God, the headlines! It's already bad enough. You can't do the job in Virginia."

"I *will* be doing the job."

Wheelwright shook his head. "Nothing you can't do from here by phone. We need the ballistics anyway. Without the ballistics, it doesn't matter what happened to the suicide's gun."

"I'm working on that."

"So fine. You give me a match on ballistics, and we'll talk about going to Virginia. But not before."

Frustrated, Matt left Wheelwright's office. He knew his boss was right, but that didn't make him any less frustrated. For the love of mike, working this case was like trying to swim through spaghetti. Too many strands, and all of them seemed to loop around in crazy directions, never quite bringing him to a terminus.

Back at his desk, he pulled out a stack of index cards on which he'd written every fact and every suspicion he had in this case. He spread them out, and began to try to order them in some way that made sense without having to invoke some faceless, nameless government conspiracy, because if he so much as breathed a word of such a thing around here, they were going to call the men in the white coats.

And just as important as what he knew was what he

didn't know. Sighing, he took out another stack of cards, blank ones, and began to write questions on them.

How were Humboldt and King linked? Through Brendan, of course. Dumb question. But *why* were they being linked?

Someone was working very hard to establish that connection. Possibly for no reason other than to frighten Brendan. Or possibly it was . . .

REVENGE.

He wrote the word in large capital letters on one of the cards and stared at it. Of course. He'd suspected that for some time. But it didn't answer the questions about the crucifixion and the body being moved. Or the blood in the trunk of that rental car, assuming it proved to be King's.

Something else was going on here. Chloe was right. They had two sets of perps, and the perps had different motives. The two sets came together at the crucifixion of Steve King. That had been the nexus.

But why. Dammit, why?

He picked up his phone and called Chloe. "You busy?"

"Other than beating my head on a wall, not at the moment. I'm heading over to the rectory to make sure Father Brendan is tucked in for the evening. I want to check before Lucy leaves. If you ask me, the horse is getting ready to bolt the barn."

"Yeah. I can't say I blame him. I just wish he'd be a little more frightened."

"Me too. But you have to remember, for him death is merely the promise of something a whole hell of a lot better."

"I'll meet you afterward then. We need to have a brainstorming session."

"Sure. Come about six. Bring your own refreshments. All I have is rabbit food."

"You're on."

When he arrived at Chloe's at six, he was carrying a pizza and a six-pack of cola, and his pockets were full of index cards.

"Oh, God," said Chloe when she opened the door, "you didn't!"

"Didn't what?"

"Bring a pizza. I can't resist pizza."

"No reason you should. And there's plenty here." He found himself distracted from his purpose, as he took in her tousled blond hair and her barely there gray T-shirt and shorts. If she was wearing a bra, it was invisible to him. He gave himself a stern mental shake and marched into her house, bearing the pizza. "Got any paper plates?"

"No, but I have regular plates. Sorry, you'll just have to suffer." Turning, she headed for her kitchen.

"Napkins?" he called after her.

"Sure."

He plopped the pizza on the coffee table, next to the icy six-pack, and told himself that it wasn't healthy to have spent all these years wondering what one woman's breasts looked like. There were plenty of great breasts in the world, and he'd eyeballed his share. He didn't need to be wondering about the set adorning the ice queen.

She returned with plates, napkins, and two glasses filled with ice on a tray. That touch of organization and homeyness reminded him they were miles apart. At his place, he'd have eaten out of the box and drunk out of the cans.

Why was it women didn't do those things? Or was it only

some women? And how did men and women ever live together when they were so different?

Stupid question. He supposed the men gave in and started
using glasses and plates. After all, he knew the steel most
women called a backbone.

Chloe's phone began ringing just as she was about to join
him on the couch. She turned at once and answered it.

"Hi, Agnes," he heard her say. "Did you get something?
Yes? I want the whole list. Unless you can scan it quickly for
me. Okay, will do. Thanks a bunch. I owe you."

She hung up and faced Matt. "That was my expert. She
got news out of the lab. The blood sample was in bad condition, as she warned us."

"Shit."

"The markers that are still identifiable brought up about
two thousand matches. She asked for a printout and should
be bringing it by in an hour or so."

Matt nodded, feeling a ray of hope. Or possibly fear. If
the two cases were related . . . "I just wish linking these two
murders would actually get us somewhere."

"Yeah." She sat beside him on the couch. "I'm not really
hungry, Matt. You go ahead and eat."

But his own appetite had waned. He didn't even open the
pizza box. "The slashing victim used government travel orders to rent his car."

Chloe stiffened. "No."

"Oh, yes." He leaned back on the couch and rubbed his
eyes briefly. "The car rental company saw them. However,
no person by the name of Lance Brucon exists. No such
name, social security, etc. Credit cards are new, only a couple of months old."

"You're giving me chills."

"Yeah, it didn't make me feel too good either."

Chloe suddenly popped up off the couch and picked up the phone.

"What are you doing?" he asked.

"Calling Father Brendan."

"Why?"

"Because this is just too damn much of a coincidence. My instincts are shrieking."

"Go for it. Maybe a good jogging of his memory will shake something out. Except that we don't yet know these two cases are linked."

"True." She put the receiver back. "Okay, let's wait until Agnes drops off the list."

"That woman must have lit a fire under somebody's butt at the lab."

"She used to be somebody over there, I'll tell you. Considering how nervous it makes them when she shows up to testify against them, I'm kind of surprised she could shake anything out of that tree."

"I'm just grateful. All I want is an acorn I can actually gnaw on."

"Try gnawing on your pizza." She settled onto the couch beside him again and twined her fingers restlessly. "If these two cases are linked, we've got something bigger than a couple of murders on our hands."

"You don't have to tell me that. The 'c' word could actually become part of my vocabulary. Except . . . Damn it, Chloe, what would a chaplain have to do with anything like this?"

"Maybe it wasn't the chaplain who was involved."

"You mean the kid who killed himself?" Matt shook his

head as if trying to dislodge an insect. "This is crazy. Absolutely crazy."

"It would be, if someone weren't so hell-bent on linking the two deaths with Father Brendan."

"Maybe it's just some weirdo who hates him for some reason."

"Sure. And he transported Steve King's body not once, but twice. And managed to nail it to a cross single-handedly."

He was rebelling, and he knew it. The vaguely formed suspicions that kept creeping into his brain were driving him nuts. He didn't have a single solid peg to hang any of them on; but at the same time, nothing else added up unless he mixed in this disquieting notion of some conspiracy. Why else had he been so ready to assume that the bloodstain in the trunk of a murder victim's car had anything at all to do with the murder of Steve King?

"Relax, Matt. If we're crazy, we'll know soon enough."

"Yeah? How?"

"The list Agnes is bringing over won't have Steve King's name on it."

"Yeah. And we'll be no closer to solving this case."

"We may not be anyway, since the slasher victim doesn't exist."

Again that chilly feeling ran along his spine. "Fact is, that alone has me as jumpy as a cat."

She nodded, her eyes now opaque, revealing nothing at all.

Giving in to the demands of his body, if not his appetite, he opened the pizza box, pulled out a slice, and for form's sake passed it over one of her plates before biting into it.

"If the slashing victim really works for the government, they'd have his prints on file at the FBI, wouldn't they?"

"Yeah. If he does, if he needed a security clearance. I don't know about people who don't need clearances. If he's military, they'll be there. And maybe our guys can get into his computer and we'll learn something there."

"You have his computer?" Her brows lifted.

"I think so. The perp told us where he'd pawned it, and I picked it up. Password protected, of course."

"Of course. But that doesn't really mean anything by itself. My computers are password protected. Do you have any idea when your specialist is going to look at the e-mail?"

"In the morning. First thing. He's also going to hack the laptop."

"Good." She poured herself a glass of cola and sipped it. "Maybe it's a good thing I left the force."

He twisted to look at her, pizza in hand. "Why?"

"Because I just realized how fortunate I was in all my cases on the beat. The perp was always as obvious as the wart on the end of a hag's nose."

"Usually. But it's the same in homicide, babe. It's almost always writ large on the scene. But occasionally . . ."

"Yeah. Occasionally. I remember those cases, too. I don't like dealing with the absence of information when homicide is involved."

"None of us do. But in your case it's worse. You might want to remember that."

"Worse how?"

"You're involved with the victim. And the potential victim."

"True. And don't call me babe."

He looked down at the pizza he held. "So . . . when this is all over, you wanna go out for dinner?"

It was as if everything inside him stopped, frozen in that instant of terrible anticipation. It didn't help to realize that he cared a helluva lot more than he'd thought he should. Slowly, uneasily, he looked at her.

Her eyes had taken on the color of glacial ice again, blue upon blue, with depths that seemed to hold no warmth.

But after a moment, she tilted her head. "Ask me when it's over."

That, he thought, could either be a reprieve or a delayed execution. But at least the question was still open, which was more than he'd hoped for.

The doorbell rang, saving him. Chloe answered it, returning with Agnes Lucci, who carried a briefcase.

"Detective," Agnes said, shaking his hand when he rose to greet her.

"Ms. Lucci. Care for some pizza?"

"Actually, yes. I'm starved. I haven't eaten since this morning."

Chloe promptly got her a plate, napkin, and glass. But before she helped herself to food, Agnes opened her briefcase. "I wish you two joy of this," she said, pulling out a ream of computer printout. "This is a list of all possible matches, along with their rap sheets, if they have any."

"Is it alphabetized?" Matt asked hopefully.

Agnes shook her head. "Sorted by probability of match. My contact says the sample from the car was badly deteriorated from the heat. She also added that the matches aren't good enough to stand up in court. Any of them." She placed the stack of paper on the coffee table and helped herself to pizza.

"Well," said Matt, "I don't need it to stand up in court. I just need to know if there's a possible link."

"With this list, you've probably got a possible link to twenty-two hundred people."

"All that matters is if one name shows up."

Agnes looked wry. "Good luck."

Chloe spoke. "Thanks, Agnes. I can't tell you how much I appreciate this."

"Well, I *did* have to do some arm twisting." But Agnes smiled. "It's a worthless list. My contact didn't like giving it to me. And she said to warn you that if you try to pull her in court to testify on anything in here, you're not going to like what she says."

"I have no intention of doing that," Matt assured her. "The thing is, Ms. Lucci, *I* need to know if there's a link. But it won't turn up in court, because the guy who owned the car is dead. I'm certainly not going to charge him with murder now."

Agnes laughed. "Okay. I realize you guys get frustrated with the lab, but you have to remember—they work based on evidence only. Not on theories of the case. And the care they need to exercise usually takes time. They're not out to prove or disprove, but only to discover the *facts*. And they're very proud of that."

Matt nodded. "I see their point. But they need to remember our point."

Agnes shrugged. "Theories are just theories, and we can't allow them to affect our impartiality."

She left a half hour later, and Matt looked at the stack of printouts.

"Let's move to the kitchen table," Chloe said. "We'll have more room."

He helped her carry the dinner things into the kitchen, load the dishwasher and dump the pizza box. Then they sat at the table and divided the printout in two. Another hour passed, then Chloe looked up.

"I've got it."

Matt's heart jumped. "Yeah?"

"Yeah. Steve King's name is on the list."

Brendan served Mass that morning with a heavy heart. Seventy faces looked back at him from the pews, and they seemed to reflect his sorrow.

He felt cut off from them. All the strictures on his movements were slowly taking him away from his flock, from people he had come to know and love over the last six months. He couldn't allow this to go on much longer. He simply couldn't. There was a fine line between protecting himself and failing as a pastor.

But the reality was that there was an officer standing in the doorway of the sacristy, keeping an eye on him every moment. The reality was that after he removed his vestments, he would be escorted across the small courtyard right back into the rectory.

Somehow he had to find a way to continue his duties within these boundaries, or despite them.

During the moment of quiet after the prayers of the faithful, he asked God to show him a way. Any way.

After Mass, despite his guard, he went to the back of the church to talk to his parishioners. They seemed glad that he was reaching out to them again, and shared their worries, their hopes, even a few jokes. Brendan believed that laughter was a good thing, but aware as he was of the gaping hole where the crucifix used to be, it was almost painful to him.

At last, he allowed himself to be escorted back to his temporary prison.

There he found activity at a high peak. Lucy's desk had been taken over by a young man in civilian clothes with a badge on his pocket. Chloe and Matt were both there, watching him work.

He considered waving to them and heading to his office to return phone calls, but instead he found himself drawn into the room, taking a chair near Chloe.

"What's going on?" he asked.

Matt answered. "Jim here is trying to find out more about that e-mail."

"Ah." He folded his hands together and squeezed tight, wondering if he should say anything about the memories that had been plaguing him. The weird things that poor young sailor had been hinting at before his suicide. It would probably sound as crazy to them as it had sounded to him.

"You know," Lucy said, turning suddenly to Matt, "there was . . . A man came by asking Father to hear his confession yesterday."

Brendan sighed. "Lucy, people ask for that all the time."

"I know, but . . ." She glanced at Brendan, then returned her attention to Matt. "The more I think about it, the more it bothers me. Maybe I'm overreacting, but . . . it bothered me. He was insistent on seeing Father, even when I told him that Father Dominic would be back shortly. Then he left and said he'd come back another time."

"Well," said Brendan, "he *should* have been able to see me."

"No," said Matt. He turned back to Lucy. "What did this guy look like? Did he leave a name?"

"No name. I'd say he was fifty or fifty-five. He was thin,

maybe a little too thin, not too tall. Average, I guess. Nothing about him stood out."

"Coloring?"

Lucy thought about that. "Nothing that stood out to me. I don't remember his eyes except they looked tight. And his hair was mostly gray. He was just ordinary."

Matt pulled a pad out of his pocket and scribbled the description down. "Thanks," he said. "That could wind up being useful. Which reminds me." He turned to Chloe. "Do you have a phone number for the family of Thomas Humboldt?"

"Humboldt?" Brendan sat up straighter. "That was his name. Tom Humboldt. Why do you want to call his family?"

"To find out something about his state of mind. And to find out what happened to the suicide weapon."

Brendan, his heart thudding, managed a nod.

"I don't have a number," Chloe said. "But my investigator will. Let me call him." She pulled a cell phone out of her pocket and left the office to make the call from the hallway.

Brendan spoke to Matt. "You think there really *is* a connection?"

"Let me put it to you this way, Father. Somebody's trying to *make* that connection. If nothing else, that makes a link, namely a person who wants to harm you in some way."

"I can see that. So you want to know Tom Humboldt's state of mind?"

"Yes, I do."

"Well, I can tell you. He was scared to death."

"Of what?"

"Of being forced out of the closet. Of losing his navy career."

Matt nodded. "You've already shared that with me."

"Well, there's something more. I didn't think too much of it at the time. It sounded too wild, as if he was imagining things. When he killed himself, it occurred to me that he'd been far more over the edge than I'd thought at the time. That he was truly psychotic, not just a little disturbed and wild. I even began to think that he might have been schizophrenic."

Matt leaned forward. "But something's changed your mind?"

Brendan hesitated. None of this had been revealed under the seal, and if Tom hadn't been imagining things, it might well have something to do with what was going on now. Especially considering that e-mail. "Yes," he said finally. "That e-mail."

"Why?"

"Because before he died, Tom gave me a fractured account of some kind of conspiracy he was involved in. And I don't exaggerate when I say it was fractured. Some black ops group was planning some terrible event, and they were apparently sending messages hidden in e-mail. Pictures, he said, that contained messages. Something like stega . . . stego . . ."

The computer expert at Lucy's desk looked up. "Stegnography," he said.

"That's it."

"Holy shit," said Matt. Rising, he looked at the expert. "Jim, see if you can find anything embedded in that photo." Then he left the room, apparently to go hunt up Chloe.

Jim, the computer expert, looked at Brendan. "Like I can figure out something like that without studying it. I've only just heard about it."

The bemused priest spread his hands. "I didn't understand a thing about it, when he told me."

"Well, Father," Jim said, "basically the idea is that a few pixels are changed in a digital photo, not enough to alert anyone to the fact the photo's been altered in any way. It looks perfectly innocent. But the altered pixels contain information. So . . ." He looked at the computer screen. "I guess I can look for something suspicious. Other than the fact that this is one of worst photo-doctoring jobs I've ever seen." He looked over the monitor at Brendan and smiled. "There's one thing I can tell you for sure, Father."

"What's that?"

"The priest didn't do it."

CHAPTER 19

With the phone number that Chloe had gotten from her investigator, Matt slipped into the rectory parlor and called the Humboldt household. A woman answered.

"Mrs. Humboldt?"

"Yes?"

"This is Detective Matt Diel of the Tampa Police Department."

From the other end of the line came a gasp, and a moment of silence. Then, "Was Wayne hurt? How bad?"

The question surprised him. He hadn't expected to upset her, because he hadn't thought . . . "Is Wayne in Tampa, Mrs. Humboldt?" He almost held his breath, awaiting her answer.

"Yes, I think so. Tell me he hasn't been hurt!"

Matt felt his scalp tense. "No, ma'am, he hasn't been hurt. I wasn't calling about your husband."

"Thank God!"

Matt waited a few moments, waited for her ragged breathing to ease, waited for her to be ready to speak again. "I'm sorry, I didn't mean to distress you. I had no idea Mr. Humboldt was in town."

"It's all right. I guess, as long as he isn't hurt, you wouldn't know. But . . . why are you calling me?"

"I'm calling about your son's suicide, ma'am."

She caught her breath audibly. "That was a long time ago. What do you want? Why are you asking about it?"

"There's a case I'm working on down here that may be related. Or at least, someone is claiming it is. So I need to ask you a few questions if you wouldn't mind."

"It's that priest, isn't it."

Matt was a little surprised that she drew the connection so quickly. Or maybe not. "What about the priest?"

"Well, you know or you wouldn't be calling. This man who used to know Tommy, that's my son, said that the priest drove him to suicide."

"What man was this?"

"Some guy named Lance."

Matt's grip on his cell phone tightened. "How was the priest involved?"

"Well, he seduced Tommy. I mean, our boy wasn't a fag. He was a good boy. But that priest seduced him."

"Which priest?"

"I don't remember his name. Wayne probably would, though. He's been stewing about it something fierce. Too late to do anything now, I tell him, but he's still angry."

"Do you know where I could get in touch with Mr. Humboldt?"

"No, he calls me when he's traveling. He moves too much. He's in sales, you know. Are you after that priest again?"

"Not exactly. Mrs. Humboldt, do you happen to know what became of the gun Tommy used to kill himself?"

There was a sigh from her end of the line. "I wanted to

trash it, but Wayne kept it. He said he had given it to Tommy when he was fifteen, and he wanted to keep it. Why? What does the gun have to do with anything?"

"I'm not sure, Mrs. Humboldt. Thank you for all your help."

"You let me know if you get that priest. That man should rot in hell."

"I'll let you know, ma'am."

Matt disconnected and turned to Chloe, who was waiting expectantly. "Bingo."

"We need to get a photo of him," Chloe said. "Of Wayne Humboldt. I'll get Dianna to try to get one from the wife."

"And I'm going to have my people start calling all the hotels in town. Maybe we can track him down. Check the incoming flight passenger manifests over the past week."

"That'll take a lot of time." Chloe frowned. "It sounds like he's our man, though, especially that mention of Lance. It's got to be Lance Brucon."

"But who the hell is *he*?" Matt started to pace the parlor. "And who the hell is he connected with . . . if anyone."

"That stegnography thing . . ."

Their eyes met, and each of them knew what the other was thinking.

"Let me make some calls," Matt said. "Get the ball rolling."

"Yeah, me too. I'll call Dianna."

Dianna was on her way to the Humboldt residence when Chloe reached her. "We need a photo of Wayne Humboldt, the father. I need it faxed to me PDQ."

"Yeah, yeah, okay."

"And find out if the wife knows when he left town on his current business trip. Also, see if she can find the gun."

"If she talks to me, sure. By the way, I faxed the ballistics report to you early this morning and overnighted a copy to your detective friend. He'll have it in the morning."

"Thanks, Dianna. I have a feeling time is running very short."

"I hear you." She sighed. "I shoulda been a cop."

"I pay you better. Which fax did you send the stuff to?"

"Your office. The machine is better, remember? It was the best way to send the ballistics photos."

"Thanks, Dianna. When do you think you're going to reach the Humboldt place?"

"I'm in town already. It's just a matter of finding their street. Say twenty minutes."

"Call me after you talk to her."

"On your cell?"

"Yes."

"You got it."

When Chloe disconnected she found Matt waiting. "She's almost at the Humboldt house. And the faxed ballistics report is at my office."

"Can we get it?"

"Sure. You wanna pick it up, or have it messengered to the station?"

"I'll pick it up."

"Let's go then."

They stopped in the office on their way out to remind Brendan to stay put in the rectory.

"It seems," Matt told him, "that the guy who wants you dead is in town."

Brendan nodded slowly. "Okay. I'll stay."

"Good," said Lucy. "Because if you don't, I'm going to nail your shoes to the floor."

Matt looked past them to the computer tech. "Anything?"

"Yeah. The e-mail originated in Virginia, but it was a forward of an e-mail sent from a dot-gov address."

"Dot gov?"

"Government."

"Shit," Chloe murmured.

"Which part of the government?" Matt asked.

"Damned if I know. I don't recognize the domain. But I'm working on it. Oh . . . and Kyle Birdsong called. He hacked the password on that laptop you gave him."

"And?"

"The files are encrypted—256-bit encryption."

"Which means?"

"It could be a long time before we break the code."

"Hell." Matt hesitated, then turned to Chloe. "Let's go. Jim? Call me on my cell if you find anything else."

"Sure thing."

At Matt's suggestion, they went in his car. That was probably a good thing, because the usually impervious Chloe was feeling rattled.

"I don't believe this," she said, more than once. "I can't believe . . . Matt, I'm getting really uneasy about this."

"So am I. Black ops is something I only enjoy in novels and movies. Real life is another matter altogether."

"But why would they be after Father Brendan? He doesn't know anything."

"That," Matt said heavily, "is where I think you might be wrong."

"How so?"

"I think he knows more than he remembers, and the right key might jog his memory."

"Maybe."

"Or it may just be that someone fears he knows more than he really does. And is afraid his memory might be jogged."

"But what could they be up to that would have them worried about one parish priest?"

"Damned if I know. But considering the amount of effort that's going into this, it must be something worth killing to keep secret."

"How does Humboldt fit into that? Is he part of the conspiracy?"

"I don't know. From what his wife said, it would be my guess that he's being used."

She looked at him. "Used to do what?"

"Remove Father Brendan in a way that can't be traced back to them."

Chloe looked out the window, but she barely saw the passing houses and businesses. "That's ugly, Matt. That's very, very ugly, to play on someone's grief that way."

"I agree. And it makes me *very* worried about what these invisible people are up to."

"I don't like to think my government does such things."

"Maybe it's not the government at all."

She twisted on her seat to look straight at him. "Meaning?"

"Well," he hedged uncomfortably. "Oh, hell, in for a penny and all that. If I'm going to dive headlong into conspiracy theories, I might as well go all the way. This might not be the government, per se. It might be some kind of cabal."

"Uglier and uglier."

"It was pretty ugly from the outset, babe," Matt reminded her. "Crucifixions aren't pretty."

"But why would they do that? Why not just leave the body?"

"It beats the hell out of me."

"And why would they kill Steve to begin with, if it's Brendan they want?"

"I think," Matt said slowly, "that Humboldt has his own agenda. I don't think Steve was supposed to be on the hit list. And maybe they moved the body to cover his tracks."

"Well, it seems insane, if you want to keep a secret, to crucify the victim."

"I agree. But something's out of sync here. Maybe things aren't going the way they're supposed to. I can't tell how exactly, because I don't know what the plan is. But my feeling is—and this worries me—that the cabal is not in full control."

"So anything could happen."

He glanced her way as he braked at a stoplight. "Yeah. And I don't like that one tiny bit."

Brendan went into the church to pray. He didn't have the solitude he wanted, because Lucy made sure one of the off-duty cops followed him, but at least the man was respectful enough to stand a few pews away.

Brendan loved the silence of an empty church. The faint odor of incense still clung from Easter, a scent that reminded him of his childhood, when being in church had filled him with such awe.

Some of that awe still lingered. It sometimes seemed to

him that in the absolute silence of an empty church, he could feel the touch of God.

Looking up at the red sanctuary light, the reminder of Christ's presence in the tabernacle, Brendan had not the least doubt that his Savior was here in the silence with him. Here they could have an uninterrupted conversation, and if he could still his own hammering thoughts enough, sometimes he could even hear the answers. Or feel them in his heart.

Right now, he had a lot of questions and petitions. He prayed for the repose of Steve's soul, prayed that the young man was safely in God's arms. He prayed for those around them, that none of them would be harmed as they tried to protect him from the man who wanted to kill him.

And he prayed for his own weakness in accepting the strictures placed on him. Asked Christ to forgive him. Thought about all the apostles and other martyrs who had faced ugly deaths bravely rather than sacrifice their beliefs, rather than stop preaching and practicing their faith.

So what was he doing, hiding out like this? Was he being wise, or was he being cowardly? He had to admit, though, that he had little desire to worry Lucy or the others. Nor did it seem right to make it harder for others to do their jobs by refusing to cooperate.

But he thought about that man who had been denied confession the day before, and he felt sick at heart. Sometimes it wasn't enough for people that another priest was available. Sometimes it was essential to them that it be the *right* priest, a particular priest whom they felt they could trust.

Despite Lucy's attitude, not everyone would have been comfortable speaking to Dominic rather than him, or vice versa. He saw it all the time. People would approach him to hear their confessions, and wait until he was available. Others would approach Dominic.

Nothing wrong with that.

That man might have a soul in mortal peril, and Lucy had stood between him and absolution. Worse, he himself had not run after the man when Lucy forbade him to.

He was failing in his duty. And he vowed he would not continue to do so. No matter what the cost. He'd allowed himself to be browbeaten into submission, but he couldn't allow that any longer.

When he walked out of here, he was going to resume his duties. *All* of them.

With that decision, a deep peace filled him.

Wayne Humboldt was long past caring what happened to him, as long as he got rid of that priest. So he sat in an expensive hotel room, under an assumed name, and considered the possible ways he could cut the priest out from the herd.

The man was evil and needed to die. Of that he had not the least doubt. He'd read enough about the Catholic Church and the way it covered up the misdeeds of priests to know that he couldn't really expect help from anywhere else. He could make that priest's life uncomfortable for a brief while, but already they were planning to move him someplace where no one would know about his past. Where Wayne couldn't find him. Where he might ruin the life of another young man.

Of course, even as he told himself these things, he knew they were a thin veneer of an excuse for what he really wanted: vengeance. Vengeance was the reason he'd killed that young man. Vengeance pure and simple. He'd wanted the priest to feel some of the pain that he had felt himself over his son's death.

Now he wanted to confront the man, to make him realize that at least one person knew of his perfidy, and that someone was willing to see that he paid for it.

But he still had to find a way to get the man alone. A way to confront him before killing him. Only then would his own grief ease enough. Only then would he feel satisfied.

Tomorrow. He had to do it tomorrow.

Somehow. Some way.

"Well, well, well," said Naomi, when she saw Chloe enter the law office with Matt. "You *didn't* fall off the edge of the planet."

"No, I'm still around. Naomi, this is Detective Matt Diel. Matt, my law partner, Naomi."

The two shook hands, and Naomi eyed him from head to foot. "I guess you're as good a reason as any for her to abandon our law practice."

Matt felt a flush creep into his cheeks. "She's helping me on a case."

"Right," said Naomi.

"Oh, cut it out," Chloe said impatiently. "I told you what I'm doing, Naomi. I think a fax came for me this morning?"

"It's on your desk. And don't forget to buy me those cruise tickets."

"Cruise tickets?" Matt asked, when they were alone in Chloe's office. The room was well-appointed, looking prosperous and long-established, the way a law office should. Only the computer and printer suggested that the room hadn't been decorated eighty years ago. One wall was lined with law books, everything from the US Code to Florida Statutes.

"You guys still read books?" Matt asked.

"That's for appearance. All my case law I get on-line. It's faster."

"I thought so."

Chloe picked up the papers on her desk and flipped through them quickly. "This is it." She passed them to Matt.

He flipped through them too, and was relieved to see that the photos of the scores on the bullet casing were probably clear enough to do a comparison immediately.

He looked up. "Wanna call your friend Agnes again?"

Chloe almost smiled, an expression that made her eyes seem suddenly warm. "You have no idea just how many favors I'm going to owe people."

"I'll help buy Naomi's cruise tickets."

"How about you just pay for Agnes's two weeks in Nepal?"

Matt shook his head. "You know the weirdest people."

"You among them. Well . . . *you* can take *me* to Hawaii."

For once in his life, Matt Diel didn't have a word to say.

In the end, though, they didn't call Agnes. Matt called the lab himself, explained the situation and asked if he could bring the fax over immediately. Much to his amazement and relief, they agreed.

"Well," said Chloe as they sped across town again, "ballistics are different from DNA. All somebody needs to do is compare two photos. Why wouldn't they be willing to take a quick look at it?"

"It's the phase of the moon," he explained mock-seriously.

"So today they howl?"

"I guess." But after a moment, he said, "I need to be fair about this. These folks work their butts off, and they're not uncooperative. They just don't like to be hurried."

"They especially don't want to hear a theory of the case."

"Well, I didn't ask them that. I just asked them to look at the ballistics and compare them."

When they arrived at the lab, they were ushered immediately to the ballistics section, an area that consisted of one man and his office.

"Today's your lucky day," Brett Hallwood said as he greeted them and shook their hands.

"How so?" Matt asked.

"You didn't get my assistant. He prefers dithering to decision. Now what have you got?"

Matt passed over the fax. "I know it's just a fax, but I honestly can't afford to wait. This casing could be the clue to a murder, and to the person who is now stalking a second victim."

"Now that's exciting," Hallwood said. "Most of my job consists of proving that a particular bullet came out of a particular gun."

"This time you could save a life."

Hallwood smiled. "I already agreed, Detective. You don't need to butter me up any more. And I recall the recent case. We all do. Crucifixion doesn't happen every day. But odd, very odd. We're all still wondering."

"About what?" Matt asked, realizing that he was being prodded for information, and willing to share a little to get what he needed.

"Well . . . why shoot the man, then crucify him? There's

something very . . . personal about that choice, don't you think?"

Matt hesitated, but before he could speak, Hallwood forestalled him.

"I'm an amateur profiler," he explained apologetically. "Don't mind me. But the two things only add up one way."

"And that is?"

"Everyone around here is suspecting some kind of ritual, some kind of serial killer who's just expanding his repertoire. But it doesn't strike me that way."

"No?" Matt leaned forward.

"No, I see at least two different sets of perps here. I don't think the shooter crucified the young man. The killing was execution style. The crucifix . . . that was something more. Something that doesn't fit."

"Apart from the fact that a single man couldn't have put the victim on that cross."

"That, too." Brett nodded slowly. "It's a very tangled case. But that crucifixion . . ." He drew the word out and looked at Matt over his glasses. "That was something *personal.* Take my word for it. Something *very* personal. And I'm not sure that it was intended to be a profanity."

"Because?"

"Because, from what I read of the M.E.'s report, not a bone in that boy's body was broken. That required great care. Loving care. But"—he slapped his palms on the desk—"you wanted me to compare the ballistics. Wait here a moment while I go get the file."

Chloe looked at Matt. "Are the hairs on the back of your neck prickling?"

He nodded reluctantly. "I never thought of that as a loving act."

"Me neither." She looked away a moment. "I belong to a faith that believes in miracles."

Now his neck was *really* prickling. "What are you saying?"

"I'm saying I believe in miracles. I believe the miraculous is all around me, in every leaf and blade of grass. But by the same token, I don't believe major miracles happen in my church, in my life."

He wanted to scold her for going off the deep end, but something held him back.

She looked at him again. "We're never going to find out who put him on that cross."

"Maybe not."

"And that may be the most significant thing about this entire case."

"Don't go nutso on me."

"I'm not. But do *you* really think that a bunch of guys who had nothing to do with the murder went into the church and did that?"

"I'm choking on the 'bunch of guys.'"

"Exactly."

"But it's possible."

"That's just the point, Matt. *Anything* is possible."

"Hallwood is right. This case is tangled. We've got an execution-style slaying with a twenty-two. A body that was then moved to an alley, then moved again back to a church to be crucified."

"That's the point, Matt. Why take the body away, then bring it back? I can understand removing it, but bringing it back? Unless someone was sending a warning . . ."

"We knew it was a message from the start."

"I'm not talking message here. I'm talking warning. I'm talking trying to *save* Father Brendan's life."

"The phone calls were a warning."

"Would any of us really have worried about those phone calls if Steve King's body hadn't been found? Or if it had been found in an alley in a bad part of town? Would we have made any connection? I doubt it. But putting the body on the cross signaled the threat was against the Church. Even before the calls came, we suspected we needed to protect Father Brendan."

He nodded, tight-lipped. "Just don't tell me God put that boy on the cross."

"I'm not saying that. I have no way of knowing that."

"Good. As long as you're not losing touch with reality."

She shook her head, smiling almost sadly. "The thing is, Matt, the miraculous *is* reality. The greatest reality of all."

Hallwood returned then, bearing a file. He opened it on his desk and pulled out a couple of photos of a scored bullet casing. Beside it, he placed the fax photos.

"Okay," he said. "I couldn't say it in court, because I need a clearer photo, but off the cuff I'll tell you . . . it's the same gun. Get me a better photo from the Virginia ballistics, and I can swear to it."

Matt rose. "The photo will be here tomorrow, Mr. Hallwood. I'll see that you get it. And thanks so much for your time."

"Just one thing," Hallwood said.

"Yes?"

"If you find out who crucified that man and why, I want to know."

"That's a promise."

CHAPTER 20

And just what do you think *you're* doing?" Lucy's voice reached Brendan from the office and cut across the hallway, where he was trying to slip past unnoticed.

"When did you become Irish?" he asked her, pausing in the doorway with a sheepish grin. He was sure he hadn't felt like this since he was seventeen and his mother had caught him trying to slip out with Sean Kilkenny to go to a midnight showing of *The Rocky Horror Picture Show*.

"Irish? What does that have to do with anything?" Lucy was proudly Hispanic.

"Then maybe it's a mother thing. But I swear you sounded just like my mother just now. 'Brendan Quinlan, where in the devil do you think you're going?'"

Lucy didn't smile. "You haven't answered my question."

"Her other favorite line was, 'Brendan Quinlan, just who the *hell* do you think you are?' I used to chide her for swearing, but she always said 'hell' wasn't a swear word. What do you think?"

"Do you think you're pulling that Irish wool over my eyes?"

In spite of himself, he had to laugh. "I'm going to the hospital. Merv's wife called. He's had a mild heart attack."

Lucy's faced saddened. Everyone loved Merv Haskell, the facilities manager. But she didn't bend an inch. "I'm sure Merv doesn't want you risking your life to give him an anointing that Father Dom could give him just as well."

"Dominic is saying Mass and taking the Interfaith Council meeting this morning. That leaves me."

"I'll call another parish and see—"

"Lucy, I'm going."

"No, you're not."

"Yes, I am."

"You could get killed!"

"Then so be it. But our Lord didn't stop His ministry because it was dangerous, and it's His example I promised to follow."

That appeared to stump her. Her dark eyes flickered with annoyance, and finally she muttered something under her breath that he imagined probably translated to "stupid, idiotic, pigheaded Irishman."

He had to admit he felt a bit guilty, though. He didn't want Lucy worrying. "I'll be safe in my car and at the hospital, Lucy. Nothing will happen. The killer, if he's really after me, prefers the cover of darkness and the isolation of a sleeping world."

She shook her head, then pulled open a desk drawer. Out of it she drew a rosary, the glass beads clattering against one another. "I'm going to say a rosary for you," she said.

"That's always welcome."

"I'm going to pray that Our Lady knocks some sense into your head."

"Now you're sounding like my mother again. She must

have prayed ten thousand rosaries for me when I was a child."

"I'm sure she did, because I can see what a mule you are. So go. But be careful."

"Always."

He stepped into the office, gave her shoulder a squeeze, then walked out of the front door of the rectory. It was like emerging from prison. He hadn't been on the street alone in so long. . . .

Nor was he right now. One of the off-duty policemen the parish had hired rounded the corner of the church, saw him, and said, "Now what the hell do you think you're doing, Father?" There was no mistaking the brogue.

An Irish cop and an Irish priest. Brendan almost sighed. Where many others in the parish wouldn't dream of telling him what to do, an Irishman wouldn't hesitate. And a police officer even less.

"I'm going to the hospital." He held up his leather visitation case. "An anointing."

"Well, then, I'll just be riding shotgun, Father."

"It's not necessary. I'm sure I'll be safe at the hospital."

"Maybe so, Father, maybe so. My car or yours?"

Which was how he came to be riding to the hospital in a police cruiser. A police cruiser with a riot gun bolted upright against the dash. Ugly thing.

Behind him, unbeknownst to him, a desperate man watched him drive away, and grew more desperate and angry.

"Jesus," Matt said the word, but it somehow didn't sound profane the way he said it.

Chloe glanced at him. "What?"

"I don't like where this case is heading. I don't like the feeling that it's going to leave cosmically unanswered questions."

"Sometimes life is that way."

"I know, but I don't have to like it."

"I particularly dislike the idea that someone who works with the government may be involved. Or that Tom Humboldt was terrified of some conspiracy he'd tumbled into that involved encoded messages in photos. I don't like it that Father Brendan knows about it because that could mean he's a target because of his knowledge. Which could make you a target."

"Or you."

"I'm not worried about myself."

"Well, I am."

He glanced her way and felt something so warm, so electric, pass between them that for a moment he was rendered breathless. Then, quickly, he snapped his eyes back to the road and told himself he'd imagined it.

"Where are we going now?" she asked.

"The station. I want to find out if Jim's learned anything."

"He's not working at the church?"

"He took a copy of the e-mail with him. Said he had more tools on his own system."

What they found, waiting on Matt's desk, was a note from Jim, typed and printed out.

"I found it. I was up all night, but I got it. There *is* an embedded message in the photo. At first I thought it was encoded, but after banging my head on the damn thing until five this morning, I realized it's not coded at all. It's a date, time, and a number: 4 23 2030 N14713. I read this as 8:30

P.M. on 4/23, tomorrow. I have no clue what N14713 is. I thought it might be coordinates, but it doesn't make sense. I'll keep working on it, after I get a nap."

"Eight-thirty tomorrow," Matt said heavily. "Well, now we know when it's going to happen. Whatever it is."

Chloe was still staring at the typed sheet. "That number looks familiar somehow."

"The one Jim couldn't figure out?"

"Yes. I keep feeling like I ought to know what it is."

"Well, if you get a glimmer, let me know."

He went through the rest of his messages and made a couple of calls. "No luck on finding a Wayne Humboldt registered in a local hotel," he told her. "They're branching out wider and looking for any Humboldts at all."

"He's probably using a fake name."

"At this point, I'd believe almost anything. Including the fact that the nonexistent Lance Brucon gave Humboldt a false identity and a credit card in another name."

"Can we get Humboldt's credit records?"

"I'll need a warrant."

"And time's already tight. But you've got enough to get a warrant."

"Yeah, probably. Might as well, I suppose. Every damn trail seems to lead nowhere."

Just then Chloe's cell phone rang. She answered it, and Matt watched her face change, going completely blank. Which, he was learning, meant Chloe was feeling too much. That ice wasn't her, it was a façade.

She ended the conversation and collapsed her antenna. "Well, guess what? As if things weren't good enough, the horse bolted the barn."

"What?"

"Father Brendan's out. On his way to the hospital. Lucy's worried to death." She rose. "Call me a cab, will you? I know you have work to do. And I'm going to lasso a priest and give him a piece of my mind."

Chloe found Brendan at Tampa General Hospital, on Davis Island, to the south of the downtown area. He was with Merv and Margaret Haskell, sitting with them and praying a rosary. His visitation kit sat open on the tray table, with the cross upright. She guessed they hadn't gotten to the Anointing for the Sick yet.

So quietly, and a bit irritably, she stayed outside the room. Across the way was a cop, leaning against the wall with folded arms. "Who are you?" he asked.

"Chloe Ryder. Why?"

"What's your business in there?"

She turned to face him fully. "Why is it *your* business?"

"Because I brought the priest down here. You could say I'm his bodyguard."

A wave of relief went through Chloe. "Thank God. I thought he'd come down here all alone."

"No. I caught him, you might say. So who are you?"

"A parishioner. I came down here to give him a piece of my mind about bolting the barn."

The cop smiled. "Yeah, I said a thing or two. I'm Sean Duggan, by the way."

"Nice to meet you, Sean." They shook hands. "You're not from St. Simeon's, are you?"

"No, I'm from Sacred Heart. If you're going to wait, it'll be a while. We just got here."

"I *am* going to wait. I can't believe he did this."

Duggan laughed. "Well, I got a wee bit of a lecture on

how Christ wouldn't shirk His duties, whatever the risk. Leaves your jaws kinda flappin' in the breeze."

"He's good at that."

"Typical bullheaded Irishman." Duggan shrugged. "Well, so am I."

"I'm glad to hear it."

Another half hour passed before Brendan emerged from the hospital room. The first thing Chloe noticed was that he looked more at peace than he had in a while.

He caught sight of her and smiled. "Save it," he said.

"No way. And Officer Duggan is going to keep you right here so I can talk to you after I say hi to Merv and Margaret."

"Chloe, I don't need the lecture."

"I'm not going to lecture you. I have some information you need to know."

He looked dubious but nodded. Then he looked at Duggan. "Why don't we go down to the cafeteria and have some coffee. Chloe can meet us there."

"That's a good idea," Chloe said. "I'll be there in a few minutes."

Then she stepped into the hospital room, where she was warmly greeted by Margaret. Merv's welcome was weaker, but he was smiling.

"How are you doing?" Chloe asked Merv.

"I'm going to be fine," he answered. "Tired for a little while, but I'm going to be okay."

"I'm so glad to hear that."

"He's going to be quitting as facilities manager, though," Margaret said firmly. "That's just too much work for someone who ought to be retired."

Merv raised a brow. "You want to kill me? I need to feel useful."

"Well, you can cut back your hours then. Get an assistant."

Merv opened his mouth as if to argue, then looked embarrassed. "Chloe doesn't want to hear this."

"It's okay. I just wanted to see how you were doing, and let you know I'll keep you both in my prayers."

She remained another few minutes chatting with them, but she could see Merv was rapidly tiring, so she excused herself and headed to the cafeteria. Brendan and Sean Duggan were there as promised.

She picked up a coffee and joined them.

Brendan cocked his head and looked at her. "So what's the lecture?"

"No lecture. Just that we've found out there's a deadline tomorrow at eight-thirty P.M. Do you think you can behave yourself until then?"

He looked startled. "How did you find that out?"

"There was a message coded in that ugly e-mail. Date and time. And since they used the kind of coding you mentioned, and you know that Tom Humboldt was worried about a conspiracy of some kind, it may just be they want you out of the way because of what you might remember."

He started to shake his head, then paused. "Okay. It's possible."

"Father"—she leaned toward him, keeping her voice low—"we suspect there's something really big going on here. Something worse than Steve's murder."

"It's hard to imagine anything worse than that." Then he

caught himself. "No, it isn't. I just don't want to imagine such things."

"So will you behave?"

He gave her a rueful look. "I'll try."

She sighed, figuring she wasn't going to get any more out of him than that, but knowing it didn't mean much. So she turned to Duggan. "You keep your eye on this guy."

Duggan grinned. "Believe it. No priest is going to get killed on my watch. My mother would never forgive me."

Brendan cracked a smile. "With the Irish, it always comes back to Mother."

Duggan laughed. "It sure does."

Chloe smiled, too, but laid her hand on Brendan's arm. "Listen to me, Father. Please. Just until tomorrow night."

"I will. Insofar as I can."

So she let it go. And decided that he was going to have to be watched like a hawk. But it was so good to see him almost his old self again, happy in his priesthood. Happy to be doing all those things that only a priest could do.

Duggan drove Brendan back to the church. Chloe took a longer route, driving around the edge of the island, taking in the water, passing the private airport.

It was as she was passing Peter O. Knight Airport that something caught her eye. She jammed on the brakes and pulled over to the side, unsure what had brought her to attention. Her gaze ran over the flat acreage, over the runway and the few planes parked near it.

Nothing. She couldn't imagine why she had felt compelled to stop.

Then she saw it: a number painted on the tail of a plane. And she knew.

* * *

"Still no ID on the victim," Phelan told Matt. "I've sent out a description in case he matches any missing person report, but since he died only a couple of days ago, that may not yield anything for a while."

"Fingerprints?" Matt asked.

"No response yet."

"You may not get any."

Phelan arched his brows. "What do you mean?"

"I'm not sure. Let's just say something strange is going on here. Something bigger than a murder by a crack addict."

Phelan took a swig of coffee from his foam cup. "Well, it's weirder than shit that everything on his laptop was encrypted. Not many people do that."

"Not unless they have something important to hide. So let me draw some connections for you."

"Okay. I'm all ears."

Matt sat forward, resting his elbows on his knees. "Okay. The bloodstain in the trunk of Lance Brucon's car may be the blood of the crucifixion victim, Steve King. The lab listed it as a possible match, and we know King was moved from the place he was murdered, not once but twice. So a car trunk was probably involved."

"Fair enough. I'll buy that." He sipped more coffee.

"Now, since the crucifixion, a number of threats have been made against the parish priest, saying that he's next. And someone has been trying to link this priest with a suicide that occurred a couple of years ago in Norfolk."

Phelan nodded. "Okay."

"But it got really squirrelly in the last couple of days. First, we found out that both the crucifixion vic and the suicide died from a shot from a twenty-two. And the bullets matched on the ballistics."

Phelan straightened in his chair. "Shit."

"Wait, it gets better. An e-mail with a doctored photo was sent to the parish and to the diocese, making it look like this priest was standing over the body of the crucifixion vic. So badly doctored, though, it doesn't really fool you. But"—he raised a finger—"there was an embedded message coded in the photograph."

Now Phelan was leaning forward, coffee forgotten. "What message?"

"Wait a sec. It seems the guy who killed himself a couple years ago complained to the priest—the same priest who's being threatened now—that he had stumbled onto some kind of conspiracy within the military that involved sending coded messages in e-mail photo files."

Phelan's jaw dropped open.

"Now, we have this e-mail photo, which Jim was able to trace back to a federal government e-mail address, and he found a coded message in it. Are you beginning to see connections here?"

Phelan nodded slowly. "And the slasher victim can't be identified."

"But he was almost certainly involved."

"We gotta crack into that laptop."

"It's not likely we can do it in time."

"In time?"

"The embedded message was a time and a date. Tomorrow, eight-thirty in the evening. But we don't know what's going to happen."

"I don't like this." Phelan leaned back in his chair and

shook his head. "I don't like this at all. Haven't you got *any-thing*?"

"Yeah, one thing only. The gun involved has been in the hands of the suicide's father since the death. The father is missing, but he's supposed to be here in Tampa, according to his wife. We haven't been able to find out where."

"Shit, shit, shit. So the suicide's father probably whacked Steve King, and the Brucon guy probably carried the body all over hell and gone, and Brucon used government travel orders to rent a car, and now we got a government e-mail address on a coded message. . . ."

"You're getting the picture," Matt agreed.

"Loud and clear, and I don't like it at all. This would have to involve some kind of black ops. You know how danger-ous that could be?"

"It's already dangerous, and we have to keep it from be-coming more so. And we've only got until tomorrow evening."

"But we don't even know what we're looking for! How can you stop it when you don't know what it is? And maybe it's nothing important at all."

"Oh, it's important," Matt said. "At least two people have been killed to protect it, and one more may die."

"But the first was a suicide."

"At this point," Matt said heavily, "I'd almost bet my badge that it was nothing of the sort."

"That still doesn't help us stop whatever it is. We need more information."

Matt's phone rang. He picked it up, spoke briefly, then turned back to Phelan. "Well, we know what to look for now."

"What do you mean?"

"There was another number embedded in the photo. A friend of mine just figured out what it is."

"Well?"

"It's the tail number of an airplane."

CHAPTER 21

E verything stays on schedule," the man with the cigar insisted. "Everything."

The other man stared him down. "You don't get it, do you? Somebody else knows what's going on. Somebody followed Lance when he dumped that body in an alley, then they put it on the cross at the church. Then Lance turns up dead. I don't like it. We can reschedule."

"No, we can't. Lance already sent the order."

"What if somebody followed Lance to *us*?"

The man with the cigar shook his head. "No way. But even if they did, we have a legitimate connection. We can always explain the contact away. Lance was working on his own."

The other man sighed. "Okay."

"If you're that worried, I can send you abroad. Attach you to some embassy in intelligence."

The other man hesitated. "I just don't want this to fail. To send the wrong message. If anyone finds out this wasn't precipitated by a terrorist group . . ."

The smoker shook his head impatiently. "Believe me, we made sure that the action can't be traced to us. It'll look like foreign terrorism, and there won't be any reason for *anyone* to think otherwise."

"Maybe."

"And they can think what they want anyway. There's no evidence. The point is, if we don't broaden this war on terrorism, to include every radical fundamentalist nation, this country will never be secure. We need to clean out that entire nest of vipers."

"I know that."

"So it's a clean operation. When's our flight?"

"We need to leave in an hour for the airport."

"Good. I'll be glad to get back to Washington."

The other man sat thoughtfully for a few minutes. "You know, I always wanted to go to England."

"Consider it done. I'll post you to the embassy there."

The other man nodded and smiled. "Ruth, my wife, will like that."

"I'm sure she will."

The seated man never guessed that he'd just signed his own death warrant.

The man with the cigar turned back to the window, puffing thoughtfully. Why was it they all turned weak on him? Sooner or later, every one of them started to screw up. Started to get scared.

And as soon as they got uneasy, they became liabilities. You couldn't trust a man who began to worry about his own hide. It was as simple as that. Lance's death was merely serendipitous, saving him the trouble of staging it. But this man, his closest associate of many years . . .

Well, a plane accident ought to do it. Or an auto accident. After they got back to Washington. The police were nosing around too much in Tampa.

* * *

"The FAA is checking the tail number against their registry," Matt told Chloe that evening. "Did our wayward priest agree to behave until tomorrow night?"

"Yes, he did."

"Thank God for small favors." He shifted uneasily against his car. Once again they were standing in the parking lot at St. Simeon's. It was crowded since religious education classes were meeting and the choir was practicing.

Brendan had waved at them a few minutes ago as he passed on his way to the parish hall. Chloe almost smiled when she saw Officer Duggan glued to his side. "Duggan will keep him in line," she said to Matt.

"As long as Duggan is on duty here." He ran a hand impatiently through his hair. "How long can it take for them to trace a tail number?"

"There are a lot of planes registered in this country."

"There are also computers. It would have been helpful if they hadn't closed their web registry access after nine-eleven." He threw up a hand. "Of course, I can understand why they don't want just any Tom, Dick, or Harry to be able to look at that stuff."

She understood his impatience and moved to stand beside him, taking his hand. He started a little, then looked down at her. She squeezed his fingers in what she hoped was a comforting gesture. And she was utterly astonished when she realized that she had also comforted herself.

"Dinner, when this is over," he said. "We're definitely going out to dinner."

"Yes, Matt."

"Why'd you shove me away back then?"

"Because it hurt too much. Everything hurt too much."

She sighed and studied the ground. "It wasn't just my marriage and the things he did to me. It was everybody—friends, colleagues, everybody—thinking I'd killed him. Not one of them gave me the benefit of the doubt."

"Except me."

"Except you."

"You can't live forever without caring," he said.

"I know. I'm beginning to figure that out. I cared when Steve was killed. I care that Father Brendan's at risk. I might as well start caring about other things, too."

"Sounds like a plan."

She lifted her head then and smiled at him. It was a dazzling smile, free of shadows and ice. But only for a moment. Reality could never go away that long.

Matt's phone rang and he answered it. "Yeah. Yeah? How do I contact him?" He pulled out his pad, turning as he did so to set it on the hood of his car. Then he tugged a pen out of his breast pocket. "Give it to me again. Yeah. Yeah . . . Okay, I got it."

He disconnected and looked at Chloe. "That tail number belongs to a plane owned by a company in Maryland. Vreeland Aviation."

He was already punching numbers into his phone. A few seconds later, he swore. "They're closed until tomorrow morning at seven."

"We could be up there by then."

"Yeah, but could we get back here in time?"

"In time for what? We don't even know what's supposed to happen, let alone where."

"True." He ran his fingers through his hair again. "Okay, let's go."

They headed straight for the airport.

*   *   *

Tomorrow, Wayne Humboldt promised himself. It was the last day that damn priest would be at the parish. The last day before the church sent him somewhere else.

It had been impossible for him to get anywhere near the man all day, thanks to that damn cop who seemed glued to his side. But at some point that cop was going to leave, and at some point he'd be able to get to Brendan. Some way.

God, he had to think of a way.

The man missed his cigar and hated that they wouldn't let you smoke on commercial flights anymore. It made him edgy, and he didn't like to feel edgy. Beside him sat his associate, all unaware that his fate had been sealed.

Funny how the priest had turned up in Tampa at just the right time. He knew Lance had been worried about that, worried that the man knew enough to interfere, but he was of a completely different opinion.

When you were doing the right thing, the universe cooperated. The priest had been put there just so all the loose ends could be tied up. So the operation couldn't be traced back to the Group.

God was good.

Chloe and Matt landed at Baltimore-Washington International at four-thirty in the morning. It was one of the delights of modern air travel that unless you departed from a hub, you had to, as Matt put it "fly around your ass to get to your elbow." They arrived at BWI by way of Chicago. And they were going home by way of Miami.

Finding Vreeland Aviation proved not to be difficult. The community airport was about twenty minutes out of Baltimore, in an area near wealthy homes. Planes of all types were neatly lined up and tied down on the apron. They arrived there by six and waited for someone to show up at Vreeland's hangar.

They'd both managed to catch some shut-eye in the air, but it hadn't been enough, and Chloe found herself wanting to doze off as they waited. Her head kept nodding, but as soon as it drooped, it woke her back up.

"We'll catch some more sleep on the way back," Matt told her.

"Maybe. Or maybe not." She had a feeling that whatever they learned here, it wasn't going to make them happy. They weren't talking much, and she figured it was because they were both exhausted and tense. This day, she thought, couldn't be over soon enough.

At five minutes before the hour, a car pulled up in front of Vreeland Aviation, and a man in jeans and a bomber jacket climbed out, heading for the door.

"Let's go," Matt said.

The man at the door turned to face them as they approached. Keys dangled from his hand, and he looked a bit wary. Chloe supposed most general aviation companies were probably feeling a bit wary since September 11.

"What can I do for you folks?"

Matt showed his badge. "I'm Detective Diel from the Tampa Police Department. My associate and I would like to ask you a few questions about a plane that's registered to you."

The man hesitated only briefly. "I'm Bob Waterson, owner of this joint. Come on in. I'll make us some coffee while we talk. You two look like you could use it."

"Thanks," Matt said. "We've been flying all night."

Waterson cracked a grin. "It shows."

The office was pleasant, well-appointed, in keeping with the wealth of the surrounding suburbs. Waterson immediately started making coffee in a commercial drip machine.

"What exactly does Vreeland Aviation do?" Matt asked him.

"Oh, a little of this and that, basically. The company belonged to my granddad Elmer Vreeland. He started it way back, just after the First World War. The family's been running it ever since. He started it as a crop-dusting outfit and flight-training school. We still train pilots, but we're out of crop-dusting. We also have our own group of pilots who fly charters, and we rent planes to qualified pilots. We fly organ donations as a public service. That's about it."

"That's quite a bit," Chloe remarked. "You must be proud of your history."

"We are." The coffee started brewing, and Waterson sat down so that he faced them across what was probably the reception desk. "The whole family is pretty much involved to one degree or another. We were one of the few general aviation firms to survive the flight ban after the World Trade Center attack."

"I bet you fly a lot of famous people."

Waterson grinned. "My lips are sealed."

Chloe laughed.

Matt pulled out a piece of paper and passed it to Waterson. "Do you recognize this tail number?"

"Hell, yes. That's one of my twin-engine Cessnas. Rented it to a guy . . . Lessee . . ." He rose and went to a file cabinet, opening a drawer to pull out a folder. Back at the desk, he opened the file. "Okay, I rented it to a Lance Brucon eighteen days ago."

Chloe and Matt exchanged looks. She felt ice water running down her spine.

Matt spoke. "Did he say why he wanted it?"

"Family vacation, it says here. He was supposed to fly to Kentucky, Texas, Louisiana, and finally to Orlando. Wife and two kids with him."

"When's it due back?"

Waterson looked up. "Day after tomorrow."

Chloe leaned forward. "Did he leave a home address?"

Waterson hesitated. "I don't know if I should. . . . This stuff is supposed to be private. My customers wouldn't like it if I was telling folks where they lived."

"Would it help," Matt asked, "if I told you Lance Brucon was killed in Tampa four days ago?"

Fifteen minutes later, they were pulling up in front of a large house situated on the golf course in a gated community. Matt's badge had gotten them in.

The lights were on, a car sat in the driveway. Shadows could be seen moving behind some of the curtains.

Together they climbed out and went to the door. A sleepy woman answered the door. "Yes?"

Matt flashed his badge. "Is this the Lance Brucon residence?"

She looked confused. "I'm sorry. You have the wrong address. This is the Mayer residence."

"Do you happen to know a Lance Brucon? Or anyone named Brucon?"

She shook her head. "I'm sorry, I've never heard of him."

"Sorry to have bothered you, ma'am. I guess we have bad information."

She gave them a wan smile and closed the door. Somewhere inside a small child wailed.

They climbed into the car together, then Matt pulled out his phone and placed a call. "Phelan? Yeah, I know it's early. Listen, I need you to get a team on something PDQ. I need you to start hunting all the airports within a couple of hours flying time of Tampa for that number I showed you yesterday. Yeah, it's a plane tail number. And it was rented by Lance Brucon."

Then he placed another call. "This is Detective Matt Diel of the Tampa PD. I need to speak to your terrorism desk."

While he waited, he glanced at Chloe. "I'm calling the FBI in on this." Moments later, he relayed the sketchy information they had.

"Okey-dokey," Matt said as he disconnected. "Let's get our asses back to Tampa and see if we can hunt down this damn plane."

Dominic paused by Brendan's office door and knocked. "Come in."

He entered the small room, and took the only other available chair. "How are you doing?" he asked.

Brendan shrugged. "All right. My keepers assure me I'll be free as of this evening. I hope they're not wrong."

"It's been driving you nuts, hasn't it, being confined this way?"

Brendan leaned back in his chair. It creaked as it tipped. "It's not easy."

"No." Dominic folded his hands and sighed. "I have to make a confession."

Brendan nodded. "Go ahead."

"Monsignor Crowell sent me down here to spy on you."

Brendan arched a brow, then chuckled. "Man, he must be disappointed. How can I get into any trouble when I'm not even allowed out the front door?"

Dominic returned a smile, but it wasn't a happy one. "I wanted you to know that. I also want you to know I told him he was all wrong about you. I haven't spoken to him since."

"I'm sorry. You just made a powerful enemy on my behalf."

"No, I did it on my own behalf. I told the truth and did the right thing. And I'm not sorry."

Brendan's smile became almost sad. "I guess you won't be going back to your office at the chancery."

Dominic shrugged. "Maybe not. Actually, I hope not. I'm beginning to love it here."

"And the parish is beginning to love you."

"So anyway, I wanted to ask your forgiveness and absolution."

"Well, there's really nothing to forgive, Dom. Nothing at all. You didn't do anything wrong. The chancery sent you on a mission, and you came down here to perform it faithfully. And it seems to me that you've done exactly that."

"I still feel guilty. I wasn't honest with you."

Brendan leaned forward and gave Dom a quick squeeze on his forearm. "Read any Bible lately?"

Dominic looked confused. "All the time."

"Then maybe you can refresh my memory about where it says that we have to tell everyone everything."

Dominic cracked a smile. "It was still devious."

"No, Crowell is the devious one. You, on the other hand, were performing a legitimate task. What if you'd gotten down here and found out I was some kind of pedophile?

Would you have felt guilty for not telling me your mission then?"

"No." Dominic nodded. "So okay. But I still feel guilty."

"That's a waste of emotional energy. You confessed, I absolve you—although you don't need absolution—now give it a rest. Remember that saying? Once you confess, God throws your sins into the deepest part of the pond and puts up a *no fishing* sign."

Dominic laughed. "Of course I remember."

Brendan gave him a crooked smile. "I use it all the time in confession. The thing is, Dom, guilt is only useful insofar as it makes us aware that we need to do things differently. After that, it's a waste. The parish would benefit far more if you saved the energy for something else."

Dominic nodded. "Thanks, Brendan. I hope they let me stay here."

"Me too. Do you know how hard it is to find another priest to comfortably share a rectory with? I hear horror stories all the time."

"I've heard them, too. Well, I won't take any more of your time. Just know you can trust me now."

Brendan smiled. "I knew I could trust you all along."

But just as Dominic reached the door, Brendan stopped him.

"Dom? I don't know why, but I'm feeling uneasy. Could you hear my confession?"

Dominic turned to face him, concern creasing his brow. "What's wrong?"

"I don't know. Just a feeling. So if you wouldn't mind . . ."

"It would be my *honor.*" Then he hesitated. "Brendan?"

"Yes?"

"Maybe, given the things that have been happening lately . . . maybe I ought to give you the anointing."

Brendan lifted a brow. "I'm not sick."

"But . . ." Dominic stepped closer. "But you might be near death."

Brendan looked down at his hands, hiding whatever emotions flitted across his face. When he looked up, his face was serene.

"Thanks, Dom. I'd like that."

CHAPTER 22

Matt dropped Chloe off at home. She wanted to shower and change, and he promised to let her know when they located the plane. She had a bad feeling about this, a really bad feeling. Of course, since the terrorist attacks in New York and Washington, it was easy to feel concern when somebody who didn't exist rented an airplane.

It was probably innocent, she told herself. After all, the guy had been traveling on government orders. Even if he was some kind of spook, he was dead. So how could he do anything deadly with that plane?

But, like Matt, she couldn't forget the coded message. It might not have been intended for Lance Brucon, whoever he was. It might have been intended for someone else.

And there was that sketchy, garbled story Brendan had heard from Tom Humboldt about a conspiracy of some kind.

No, she wasn't going to assume it was innocuous.

But she was equally worried about Brendan. Maybe more so. That date and time might also be a deadline directed at him. Someone out there might even now be stalking him, prepared to kill him before the witching hour.

Frustration and fatigue combined to make her scrub herself ruthlessly with a loofah, until her skin glowed red. She didn't want the fatigue to overwhelm her, but she needed a rest. She'd be useless to anyone if she couldn't think clearly.

Wrapped in a towel, she padded into her bedroom and glanced at the clock. Amazing. It was already four-thirty. She called the rectory to make sure that Brendan was planning to behave himself.

"I promised," he said, when Lucy put her through. "I'm sitting here like a good boy."

"Good. Answer your phone tonight, will you? I'll be over later, but in the meantime, I want to be able to check up on you. And I want to keep you posted if Matt learns anything."

"Okay," he said, agreeably enough. "But this is the last night."

Sighing, Chloe hung up, then collapsed on her bed for a couple of hours of sleep. She had to sleep, or she wasn't going to be any good to anyone.

Matt was sitting at his desk, restlessly shaking one leg, trying to be sure that nothing had been overlooked. Not that it was his case anymore. The feebs, of course, had thrown him a bone and allowed his team to keep hunting for the tail number, but they were in on little else. How many calls had he made just since returning to the office an hour ago? He'd lost count. And he'd gotten tired of hearing from every airport, "Yeah, we got the alert. We've got an eye out."

Apparently the FBI had gotten the FAA to put the plane on an alert watch list, and apparently the notice had gone out to all airports by midafternoon.

So he was nothing but a fifth wheel. That hadn't kept him from calling local airports personally, though. This was his town and *his* case. And pardon him, but he just didn't trust the FBI to care as much about the Tampa Bay area as he did.

But nobody local had seen the plane. So, what the hell. He'd probably made a huge mountain out of a molehill . . . even if the FBI had practically shit their pants when they heard the message had been sent by stegnography. It seemed the Al Qaeda had used stegnography to communicate.

Interesting. So how did someone on government travel orders fit in with Al Qaeda? A new twist?

Phelan came up and dropped a fax on his desk. "Take a look at that."

It was from NCIC, in response to the Lance Brucon fingerprints. The message was pointedly brief.

This information is classified. Cease inquiries immediately.

Phelan dropped into the chair beside him. "Case closed," he said. "Bing, bang, boom. No lookie, no talkie. What do you think? CIA? NSA?"

"Black ops of some kind."

"Yeah, that's my read. So this guy is linked to that plane, which no one has found yet, and the government says butt out. I love it. I guess I'll go home and spend the evening with my family for a change. I wonder if they still recognize me."

"I'm sure they do."

Phelan rose. "You might as well get out of here, too. The feds aren't going to tell you anything, even if they find that damn plane."

"I'm not so sure about that."

Phelan laughed bitterly. "We probably stumbled into

some covert operation trying to locate a terrorist cell. You know they were all over us after nine-eleven."

Tampa had a large Islamic community, which *had* made the feds poke around quite a bit. But that was a long time ago. Things had quieted since then. Maybe.

"Go home," Phelan said again. "You look dead beat."

"Yeah. In a bit." He watched Phelan walk away. Matt's phone rang, and he picked it up. "Diel."

"Detective, this is Special Agent Bruster, FBI."

"Yeah, hi. What's up?"

"Well, we got a call from a small airport outside Miami. The plane we're looking for flew out of there around three-thirty, headed for Jacksonville."

"Oh? You find it?"

"That's the problem. The plane got caught in a thunderstorm just north of Miami. The pilot radioed in that he'd been hit by lightning and lost his avionics. His transponder even went out. Then he dropped off radar and never reappeared. We've been checking, but it seems he went down in the water."

"Thanks for letting me know. Keep me updated?"

"Of course. We're not through investigating. We've got a good description of the pilot. Maybe we can find out more about him."

"I hope so."

"I do, too, Detective. I do, too."

Bruster sounded like he really meant it, but as he hung up the phone, Matt found himself wondering whether the FBI was in on this "classified" thing, too, or whether they were as blind as he.

Down in the water. How very fucking convenient. He

tipped his chair back and closed his eyes, and waited. Because as sure as he was sitting here, this wasn't over.

The plane landed at Albert Whitted Airport in St. Petersburg at six that evening. The alert had been canceled by the FAA at five, so the tower didn't even bother checking the alert against the tail number. The lack of a transponder didn't bother them either. Lots of private pilots didn't have one, or if they did, didn't bother to check it out to make sure it was working as often as they should. The tower called to a mechanic to have him go tell the pilot if he had a transponder, it wasn't working.

The pilot set the Cessna down gently and and taxied over to refuel. He climbed out and spoke to the mechanic, laughing when the guy told him his transponder was out.

"Sorry," he said. "Maybe something's loose."

"Want me to check it out for you?" the mechanic offered.

"Nah, I'll check the wiring first. If I can't figure out what's wrong, I'll ask you for some help."

"Sure." The mechanic was accustomed to pilots who didn't want to pay for help with their planes if they could do the work themselves. "Nice plane," the mechanic said, patting the side of the Cessna.

"Yeah, I like it. I rented it."

Which explained why the guy didn't want to pay to have the transponder fixed.

"Thinking about buying one?" the mechanic asked.

"I wish. No, I'm just puddle-jumping on vacation."

"You gonna be here long?"

"Nah. A couple of hours. I've gotta get to Jacksonville tonight."

The mechanic nodded and walked away. As he did so, he

glanced at the tail number and wondered why it looked so familiar.

Back in his office, he put his feet up, thinking about the dinner that Judy was going to have waiting for him when he got home. She'd promised him roast turkey and all the trimmings for his birthday dinner, and he could hardly wait.

But amid his visions of stuffing and gravy, the tail number of that Cessna kept floating. Finally, he pulled out the alert that had come earlier and felt his heart jump when he saw that the numbers were the same. He reached at once for his phone and called the tower.

"The alert was canceled at five P.M." the tower told him.

"Oh. Okay. Thanks." The mechanic went back to daydreaming about cranberry sauce and heaping mounds of breast meat.

But the controller supervisor who had answered his call was troubled. He looked out at the Cessna on the tarmac getting refueled. Why would they put out an alert like that, then cancel it?

And he remembered that detective from Tampa had called him and seemed quite concerned. He hesitated, then picked up the phone and dialed the number the detective had left. It couldn't hurt anything to pass the information along. If someone had made a mistake of some kind, they'd just tell him so.

Down below, the pilot of the Cessna was filing a flight plan for Jacksonville, departure time 8:15 P.M.

The sound of the ringing phone jerked Matt out of his doze so suddenly that he nearly tipped back his chair. Funny, he thought groggily. Phones must have been ringing all around him while he dozed, but only his own had disturbed him.

The squad room was nearly empty, though. And quiet. It was dinner hour, and even detectives ate. And went home to families. Unless, of course, they were called out on something fresh.

Rubbing his eyes, he reached for the phone. "Diel."

"Detective Diel? This is Carl Kessler over at Albert Whitted Airport. You called earlier about a Cessna with a particular tail number."

"That's right."

"I see the alert's been canceled. Was it a mistake?"

"No. It appears that the plane crashed into the Atlantic north of Miami."

"Well," said Kessler, "that can't be, because I think it's sitting on our apron right now."

Matt's hand tightened on the phone. "Are you sure?"

"Well, I can't exactly see the number from here, but one of the mechanics out here said it was the same."

"Thanks, Mr. Kessler. I'm on my way over."

As soon as he hung up, Matt started to call the local FBI field office. But before he had punched in more than a couple of numbers, he stopped and hung up the phone.

It was possible Whitted had made a mistake about the tail number. After all, according to the feds, Miami said the plane had gone down in the ocean.

On the other hand . . . He stopped the thought, not wanting to have it at all. But it finished anyway. *What if the feds had lied to him?*

He rubbed his eyes again, impatiently, then decided what he'd do. He'd go over to Whitted and check it out. If it was the same plane, he'd alert everybody from the FBI to the

National Guard. But until he knew for sure that plane was on the apron at Whitted, he had nothing to tell anyone.

Chloe pried one eye open and looked at the digital clock on her night table. Seven-ten. Morning or night? Then panic hit her like a tsunami. What if she'd slept all night?

She sat up immediately, looking around in confusion. The little light was illuminated on the clock. That meant it was P.M. Didn't it?

Yes, yes it did. Relieved, she picked up the phone to call Brendan, and make sure he was still behaving himself.

There was no answer. His voice mail, provided by the phone company, picked up after four rings, a sure indicator that he wasn't on the phone, that he simply hadn't answered it.

She waited five minutes, in case he was in the bathroom or something, and called again. No answer.

She jumped up and started dressing.

There were times when Matt was absolutely convinced that the area was nothing but one great conglomeration of parking lots passing for roads. I-275, which ran directly to St. Petersburg across the bay, was choked on the Howard Frankland Bridge. Traffic was moving, but not nearly fast enough to suit him.

Drumming his fingers impatiently on the steering wheel, he wondered what the hell he was doing. After all, if this was all tied up in some classified operation that the entire federal government was determined to hide from him, what the hell good would it do him to find that airplane at Whitted?

If he tried to prevent it from taking off, they'd merely remove him. The pilot wouldn't tell him a damn thing. He might even find himself without a job.

On the other hand, Lance Brucon had had something to do with the death of an innocent young man, and someone was linking that death—and an earlier death—to Brendan, and by God, Matt had had enough. Whatever was going on, he was getting to the bottom of it, even if it did cost him his job.

Dominic went out just before seven to pay some home visits. He said he should be back by eleven. Brendan, who'd done as much paperwork as he could stand for the day, decided to settle in front of the television in the back parlor, the one the public never saw, and watch some mind-numbing sitcoms, or maybe some animal shows on one of the cable channels.

Animals, he decided. There was a show on about wolves, and he punched in the channel. He liked animals. People might think they didn't have souls, but he felt quite differently. He hadn't the least doubt that he was going to get to heaven and find all kinds of animals, particularly dogs. Cats he wasn't so sure about.

But the thought held amusement, born of the time he'd had a cat named Bandy, because its legs were so bowed. Bandy had been the most independent cuss ever to walk the planet, and simply trying to pet her would get him clawed until he bled.

Bandy had come and gone as she pleased, until one day she had never come home again.

Brendan's mother had told him that cats were like that: they up and moved whenever the whim took them. Bandy, she said, had probably moved a few blocks away to another family.

The explanation had been a happier one for a seven-year-old than the likely truth, which was that Bandy had probably been hit by a car. But ever since, he had not quite trusted cats.

He wondered if Dom would have a problem with getting a dog for the rectory. After all, he was the pastor at St. Simeon's, which meant he was pretty much settled here as long as he wanted to be.

As long as Monsignor Crowell didn't find a good reason to get rid of him. But Brendan forced that thought away and focused on the program about wolves. They were actually shy animals, and he liked that about them. Yes, they had to kill to survive, but, unlike human beings, they *only* killed to survive.

Suddenly he heard a sound behind him, but before he could move, something icy pressed against the side of his neck.

"Don't move, priest," said a rough voice. "Or you'll wind up dead."

Once past the bridge and the Fourth Street exit, traffic began to speed up. Matt relaxed. A glance at the clock on his dashboard told him he had plenty of time before eight-thirty. Time to see if the plane was really the same tail number, time to try to locate the pilot. Time, even, to call for help from the St. Petersburg police, if he needed it.

Screw the feds. They were going to hear about this once it was all over.

CHAPTER 23

The man moved around the chair, keeping the gun pointed at Brendan. He looked to be nearing sixty, but not a healthy sixty. His hair was thinning and white, and his skin had an unpleasant sallowness to it. The hand holding the gun trembled.

It was a small gun, something that could be easily tucked in a pocket. To Brendan, however, it seemed plenty menacing. Once the man was standing in front of him, facing him, Brendan managed to speak. "What is this about?"

"Oh, you'll find out," the man said bitterly. "I have every intention of making sure you know what this is about."

"Good. Now, would you like to sit? Can I offer you some coffee?"

The man looked confused. This was not at all the response he'd expected to get. "Aren't you afraid?"

"Well, of course I am," Brendan admitted. "I imagine it hurts to be shot."

"It hurts to die, too."

"Well, I'm not afraid of that."

The man was startled. "Not afraid of what?"

"Of dying. Dying is a beautiful thing. It's being born into

a better life, a life with God. Have you ever spent much time with the dying? I have."

The man, looking absolutely stumped now, eased down onto a chair facing Brendan, keeping the gun aimed at the priest.

"It can be a painful process letting go of the body," Brendan continued. "Medical science, unfortunately, has helped with that, drawing it out beyond belief in some cases. But in the moments near death . . . well, those who are blessed to be conscious seem to see the most beautiful world awaiting them. If they can talk at all, they sometimes say things about it. About seeing Jesus, about the light, about seeing deceased family members awaiting them. And they grow incredibly peaceful."

"Bull."

Brendan shrugged. "I don't expect to convince you. But I know what I've seen and heard. And even if I hadn't seen and heard those things, I would still not be afraid of death."

"Why?"

"Because I believe in our Savior Jesus Christ. And He told me I would have eternal life."

The man with the gun stared at him in disbelief.

"Would you mind if I turned off the television?" Brendan asked. "I'd be able to hear you better. But I'll need to reach for the remote."

The gun waved, telling him to go ahead. An instant later, silence filled the rectory. The phone rang sharply, causing the man to jerk. Brendan didn't move a muscle. "Don't worry about the phone," he told the gunman. "My voice mail will take care of it. And people are used to getting my voice mail when they call here."

The man was sweating now, but nothing in his face revealed wavering determination. Brendan sent silent prayers winging heavenward as he waited. He didn't ask God to spare him, but to forgive this poor, troubled man. At some level he was feeling surprised at the calm with which he was facing this threat. But the calm remained with him, the same calm that had come over him when he had made the decision to continue his pastoral duties whatever the threat, the same calm that had filled him when Dominic had given him the anointing earlier.

The man with the gun didn't say anything. The silence grew protracted. Apparently the man wasn't finding this as easy as he had anticipated.

"Would you like to pray with me?" Brendan asked.

That seemed to jolt the man back to his intention. "No! You're evil! Why would I want to pray with *you?*"

At that moment, Brendan felt a twist of sharp fear, and realized he was not going to be allowed to die in saintly spiritual peace. The will to survive was still alive in him.

"Okay," he said after a moment, forcing his fear down. "Why don't you tell me what it is you want to tell me?"

Once his plane was refueled, Victor paid with a credit card, then left the airport in a taxi to find someplace to eat.

It wasn't that he was really hungry. In fact, he was almost positive he wouldn't be able to swallow anything except water. His mouth had been dry for hours, ever since he'd taken off from Miami, and he doubted anything would quench his thirst.

But he couldn't hang around the airport. He needed to distract himself from the mission ahead of him. And he had to make sure he did nothing that might arouse anyone's suspicion.

They had warned him about that. He had to act perfectly normal, as if he hadn't a care in the world. *Painfully* normal, was the way his contact had put it. Like any ordinary Joe out to enjoy himself.

So rather than look weird by hanging around the airport for an hour, when he could just as easily have left again as soon as he refueled, he chose to cover the delay with a perfectly ordinary trip for food.

It had surprised him to be tapped for this mission. It wasn't as if he were anyone special. And he'd lived in this country for so many years, since he was four, that it was surprising they would trust him.

But he'd flirted around the edges of the group for a while, seeking some purpose in his life, some sense that he would accomplish important things. Martyrdom hadn't been in his mind, ever. Until the day they offered it to him.

How could he refuse? At once he had been filled with a sense of purpose and destiny that had overshadowed anything he had felt in his life before. It was as if the finger of God had touched him, had picked him out from all the other human beings on the planet, and said, "You are special to Me."

And here he was, at the long-awaited moment. He had to force himself not to glance at his watch, not to betray any impatience. Not to betray any fear.

Martyrs were fearless. Whispers of fear arose from the Evil One. They had told him so, and he must be strong in the face of temptation.

But he slipped once as he climbed out of the cab, and glanced at his watch. It was quarter to eight. Time to have something cold to drink, and maybe a small piece of pie or cake for the energy. He had to time his arrival back at the airport so he would have only enough time to climb into his plane and taxi to the runway at eight-fifteen. A quick flight after that, and he'd be over his target at eight-thirty.

"Keep it tight," they had said. "Don't give anyone a chance to observe you."

He'd done pretty well with that. Except for that nosy mechanic who wanted to fix his transponder. But he'd managed to handle that well, too, and he was sure the mechanic wasn't suspicious at all.

There wasn't any reason anyone should be suspicious. No one knew what was planned, and even so, everyone must be sure that his plane had crashed when he had shut down his transponder and dipped from the radar.

That had been the clever idea of his contact. "Mislead them," he'd been told. "Just in case someone suspects something. Mislead them completely."

And that was what he had done.

He sat at the lunch counter and ordered a large Coke and a piece of pie. Another glance at his watch told him he would have to call a cab in another fifteen minutes to make it back on time. No problem.

He lifted his fork and realized his hand was shaking. Quickly he put it down and glanced around, wondering if anyone had seen. The counter waitress gave him an odd look, then went back to talking to a customer.

He had to be more careful.

Besides, there was a good chance he wouldn't die. Not a huge one, but a good one. The flyover of the air base probably wouldn't be met with a challenge because it would happen so fast. He'd dump his load and be headed south before they knew what had happened. There was a possibility that the dump would cause such uproar and confusion that he could get completely away. They would certainly have trouble finding him, since he would fly low, off radar, and silently without a transponder.

But there was also the possibility he would die. That he would be shot down. He knew that and accepted it. The important thing was to dump his load.

But he was scared anyway. Very scared.

But not scared enough to stop.

Matt arrived at the airport at quarter to eight. He found the traffic controller, who pointed out the plane and then called the mechanic to go over and assist him.

The mechanic met him on the apron. "Hi, I'm Jim Leary. You must be the detective."

"Matt Diel, Tampa PD." They shook hands.

"That's the plane," the mechanic said, pointing to a nearby Cessna four-seater. "Same tail number we got the alert on."

"It certainly is."

The mechanic looked at him. "Was the alert a mistake?"

"No, it wasn't. But we had information the plane had crashed."

The mechanic looked over his shoulder. "Looks pretty good to me. And the pilot didn't act like he'd had any trouble. But the transponder is out. Maybe that's why somebody thought he crashed."

"Could be. Do transponders go out very often?"

"Not usually. They're pretty reliable."

"Lightning strike?"

The mechanic nodded. "That might do it. But it'd probably take out a lot more than the transponder if it did that much."

"I see. What can you tell me about the pilot?"

"Not much. Seemed like an ordinary guy. He didn't want my help, but that's not unusual." Leary half smiled. "Especially since it's a rented plane. He's not going to pay me to make repairs, is he?"

"Depends on how safe he wants to be. So he wasn't remarkable in any way?"

"Not that I could see. He paid for a refuel and filed a flight plan, then he took a cab somewhere."

"Can I see the flight plan?"

Leary nodded toward a nearby glass door. "In there. Just ask for it. It's no big secret."

"Thanks. But now I have a big favor to ask of you."

The mechanic looked surprised but nodded. "I suppose."

"I need a look inside that plane."

The mechanic shook his head. "Sorry, Detective, but I can't do that. He locked it. And besides, don't you need a warrant for that? I could lose my job."

Matt hesitated. He understood that Leary had no idea what was going on here. Nor could he explain it, given that he didn't know himself. Pushing the issue, when for all he knew this was some covert op headed for Cuba, could cause a lot of serious trouble.

"Look," said Leary, "is the guy some dangerous criminal?"

Matt couldn't truthfully answer that, and lying had never come easy to him. Finally, he said, "He could be."

Leary sighed. "Can't do it. Now if *you* wanna do it, I wouldn't necessarily have to stop you, you being a cop and all."

Matt hesitated. Which did he want more? To know what was on that plane, or to get his hands on the guy flying it?

Put that way, the answer was obvious.

"No," he said to Leary. "I don't want to scare the guy away, and I sure will if he comes back and finds me nosing around in his plane. I guess I'd better wait for him to show."

Leary nodded. "You need me for anything else?"

"No. Thanks, Mr. Leary." He headed for the flight office, and Leary headed back to the hangar.

The woman at the desk inside was pleasant enough, and once she saw his badge, she couldn't move quickly enough to pull the flight plan.

Matt scanned it, gleaning what he could from it. "He's heading straight for Jacksonville?"

The woman glanced at the plan. "That's what he says. Departing at eight-fifteen."

The time in the message had been eight-thirty. Maybe this wasn't the right plane. Or maybe the target was a fifteen-minute flight away. "Isn't it unusual to make a flight like this at night?"

"Why? If he's instrument rated, it shouldn't be a problem."

"Is there any way to find out if he is?"

"Well," she said, "you could ask him. He'd have his certificate with him. Checking with the FAA works, too, but it takes a while."

"Thanks." Giving her his best smile, Matt glanced once again at the plan. Victor Singh. The man had a name.

Anticipating being shot was hell, Brendan thought. Absolute hell. Nor was it the least comforting to remember that Jesus had suffered worse on Golgotha.

There didn't seem to be a thing he could do to prevent it either. Unless the man started talking, and they could get some kind of dialogue going, that small gun in that shaking hand was probably going to go off.

Brendan spoke, keeping his voice as gentle as possible. "Will you at least tell me your name?"

"Wayne Humboldt. Mean anything to you?"

Because of events over the last couple of days, it certainly did. Brendan felt a hard thud in his chest, not unlike a punch. "Tom," he said. "You're related to Tom."

"I'm his father."

That news didn't come as a surprise; in fact, Brendan had expected it from the man from the instant he heard the name. "I'm sorry," he said.

That seemed to light Humboldt's fuse. "Sorry? *Sorry?* Is that all you can say?"

Brendan spread his hands. "I'm very sorry that such a fine young man, with so much life ahead of him, chose to kill himself. I'm equally sorry that I didn't see it coming in time to counsel him against it."

"Well, isn't that comforting?" Humboldt said, his voice dripping sarcasm. "You're sorry."

"Would it be more comforting if I weren't?" Brendan asked. "I liked Tom. He seemed like a great kid. So much to live for."

"He *was* a great kid," Humboldt said. "But not the way you wanted him."

"How do you think I wanted him?" Brendan asked. This was getting easier. If he could keep the man talking, there was hope.

"Your kind disgust me."

"Priests?"

Humboldt stared at him. "Yes. Priests. Priests who diddle

altar boys and seduce young navy men into lives of degradation."

Brendan's chest became so tight that drawing a breath was difficult. Given all the ugly stories that had come out about the Catholic Church and its cover-ups of such crimes in the past few years, he could easily see how this man had reached that conclusion.

"I didn't—" his voice cracked, and he had to draw another painful breath, one that couldn't quite fill his lungs. The band around his chest grew tighter. "Believe me, Mr. Humboldt, I never, *ever* did such a thing."

Humboldt let out a bitter laugh. "And you really expect me to believe that? I'm sorry, *priest*, but the medical evidence said otherwise."

Brendan arched a brow in a silent question.

"Oh, you didn't know? They did an autopsy. Standard procedure in any suicide. His anal sphincter was torn, and they found semen inside him. So did you like fucking him, *priest*?"

Indeed, Brendan hadn't known. And in light of what had happened recently, this put an entirely different spin on things. Because what this man had described sounded awfully violent. Could Tom have been murdered, and it made to look like a suicide?

"Mr. Humboldt . . ." Brendan hesitated, seeking the right words through his own shock and fear. "Mr. Humboldt, I'm so sorry. That news must have been . . . unbearable for you."

"As if you care!"

"I *do* care. But . . . I swear before my Savior, I never had that kind of relationship with Tom, or with anyone else."

"Liar."

The word hung between them, and Brendan realized with

a sinking sense of dread that he probably wasn't going to be able to reason with this man. What proof did he have, other than his own word, that he had never done such a thing? And given all the scandals in the Church, he doubted his word counted for anything at all with Wayne Humboldt.

It was time for a new approach.

"Mr. Humboldt, what possible reason would I have to murder your son?"

"Murder? He wasn't murdered. He shot himself."

"That's what they'd like you to believe," Brendan said. He fell silent, letting the words sink in. In the next room, the phone rang again.

"Dammit!" Of all the times to have to take a detour because of road construction. Of all the times to hit every single red light between here and forever.

Chloe swore loudly and reached for her cell, calling Matt.

"Diel," came the familiar voice. The transmission was crackly and weak.

"Father Brendan's in trouble," she said, wasting no words.

"How do you know?"

"I made him promise to answer the phone this evening so I could keep him posted. He's not answering."

"The idiot probably went out on a sick call. Cripes, Chloe, don't make a mountain out of a molehill yet. I'm over in St. Pete at the airport. I've found our plane, and I'm waiting for our pilot."

"Great. But Father Brendan—"

"I'll have somebody check, okay? But I'm sure he's all right. This isn't the first time he's jumped the corral fence."

"Matt, he *promised* me. Father Brendan doesn't break promises."

"Gotta go. I'll call somebody to check. But I think . . ." He was gone.

She'd be there before anyone else regardless, Chloe realized. But if there was trouble, it would be nice to know that backup was on the way. At the next light, she leaned over and checked her glove box. The Glock was still there. She had a license to carry, being a defense attorney with some unsavory clients; but she hadn't pulled out that gun once, except to clean it and replace the ammo, since she left the force.

She pulled it out now, keeping it in her lap so that no one would see it. It was loaded. A round in the chamber. Nine millimeter hell. The worst of it was that it still felt familiar in her hand. Even comfortable.

The light changed, and she was on the homestretch at last. She just hoped she got there in time.

The man walking across the apron looked innocuous enough, Matt thought. Small, dark, ordinary. Wearing the Florida uniform of shorts and a polo shirt. Carrying nothing except a large soft drink in a paper cup.

Passing him on the street, Matt would never have given him a second glance. Now he waited until he was sure what plane the guy was headed for.

Then he stepped out from the shadows.

"Murdered?" Humboldt asked.

Brendan nodded slowly. "That would be my guess. It seems to be how these people work."

"What people? Fags?"

"No," Brendan said. "Actually, from what a friend of mine says, sex crimes tend to be much . . . worse. But these people . . ."

"What people?" Humboldt asked again.

"You tell me," Brendan said, looking directly into the man's eyes. "You tell me what kind of people would rape a promising young sailor, then kill him and make it all look like a suicide."

Humboldt shook his head. "You're looking to confuse me, aren't you?"

"I'm looking for the same thing you are. The truth."

"I know the truth. You killed him."

Brendan leaned forward. "Mr. Humboldt, if I'd done what you say I'd done, do you really think the navy would have kept it a secret? Do you think they didn't check everything in your son's apartment to see if anyone else had been there? My fingerprints are on file because I was in the navy. They'd have identified them if I'd ever been in there. And semen carries DNA. It wouldn't have been that hard a case to prove, if it were true."

Humboldt's eyes were blinking rapidly now, a sign of his distress. That could be good, or it could be bad.

"I knew your son, Mr. Humboldt. And it was no secret. His name was in my appointment calendar more than once, and he got time off work to come in for counseling. His commanding officer had to know he was seeing me. If there'd been the least evidence that we had contact outside the chapel, they would have been all over me."

Humboldt's hand was shaking again, and his knuckles were growing white. If he squeezed too hard, it was going to be all over. But Brendan couldn't afford to think about that now. He had a wedge, and he had to keep hammering it, to save both himself and Tom's father from this terrible poison.

"Yes, I was counseling your son, Mr. Humboldt. He'd gotten involved in something that sorely troubled him. Some kind of consipiracy."

"Hiya," the man said casually. He was a cop, Victor could tell. Cops had a certain walk about them, even in plain clothes. Victor nodded to him and made as if to continue his preflight checks.

"Great evening for flying, isn't it?" the man asked.

Victor looked up at the darkening sky. "Looks to be."

His mind was whirling a mile a minute. A cop. Here. That damn mechanic had said something. He took a deep breath as he flexed the elevator panels. There were a million reasons a cop might be here. Airport security had been beefed up lately. Everyone knew that. Especially here in the Tampa Bay area, where a teenage boy had recently committed suicide by crashing a private plane into a downtown bank building. So yes, it made sense that he might run into some federal rent-a-cop.

Except this man didn't look like a rent-a-cop.

"Can I help you with anything?" the man asked.

"Have you done any flying?" Victor replied.

The man shrugged. "Not since Afghanistan. And I flew Blackhawks then."

The man was lying, and Victor knew it. He didn't have the cut or carriage of recent military. Nor could he have risen through the ranks fast enough to be plain clothes by now. And he *was* a cop. It was in the casual sweeps of his eyes, not darting nervously yet still taking in detail. Victor's father had had those eyes. Cop's eyes.

"I prefer fixed wing," Victor said. "At least if the engine cuts out, you can glide. A helicopter has the glide ratio of a brick. And even if you can autorotate, your odds aren't very good."

"That's true," the man said.

By agreeing, he'd taken Victor's bait. The truth was that even if a helicopter's engine stalled, the blades still had a lot of momentum stored up. That was why they kept whirling after the aircraft landed and the pilot turned the engine off. At flight speeds, the blades would continue to whirl fast enough to let the pilot land the chopper safely. That was called *autorotation*. A former military helicopter pilot would have known that. Now Victor was sure the man was lying.

But that didn't answer the question of how to get rid of him. Act natural. That's what he'd been told, again and again.

"Come to think of it," Victor said, "you could save me a couple of minutes. Could you check the ailerons for me?"

It had been either that or the landing gear, and Victor did not want this man snooping around the bottom of the plane. The flight controls out on the wingtips would keep him farthest away from anything that looked suspicious.

The man walked over to the left wing and flexed a flap. Not an aileron. He obviously knew nothing about airplanes. But Victor was hardly in a position to call his bluff. Victor checked the landing gear and glanced up at the gas release nozzle. Everything was fine. Just dupe this cop for a few more minutes, satisfy his curiosity, and send him on his way.

Then Victor would fly into history.

CHAPTER 24

The twilight was deep by the time Chloe reached the rectory. None of the security cops was in sight, and for a few precious seconds she debated whether to go hunting for one. Then she decided that might waste too much time if Brendan were in trouble.

Hefting the Glock, she hesitated. There was no way for her to carry the gun invisibly. Finally, she tucked it up under her cotton blouse, holding it close to her midriff.

Then she climbed out of the car, glancing casually around. The street was quiet. Not even somebody out walking a dog. There must, she thought, be something really good on the tube tonight.

Walking as normally as she could while holding a gun to her middle, she climbed the rectory steps and tried the front door. Locked.

She hesitated, wondering if she should try to break in. But she was feeling awfully exposed on the front porch. Anyone might be watching from neighboring houses; if she broke in, the cops would be called.

Now that might be a good thing. But it could also be a very bad thing for Brendan if he were inside and in trouble.

She didn't want to do anything that might cause a killer to panic.

So she backed away from the door, turned around, and descended the steps. If the church was locked, she'd go around the back way and enter the courtyard.

But the church wasn't locked. Merv was in the hospital, and whoever was supposed to be doing it for him hadn't done it. Brendan? Possibly. He was always quick to volunteer to step in where help was needed.

And he wasn't the type to forget to do something he'd promised to do, whether it was answering a phone or locking the church.

She stepped into the cool interior. None of the lights were on, so the church was dark inside, almost nightlike. She used the flickering sanctuary lamp to guide her.

Her heart was beginning to hammer hard. She hadn't felt like this since her days as a cop when she'd had to follow a perp into a building. Back then she'd had backup. Tonight there was just her. It wasn't a comforting thought.

She didn't genuflect this time; God would understand. What He might not understand was the gun she was carrying. It was out now, a comfortable, familiar weight in her hand. An obscenity within the walls of this church.

The sacristy was empty. Brushing against racks of robes, hearing them whisper as she passed, she headed for the courtyard door. It, too, was unlocked, and she passed through it, wincing when a hinge creaked. It wasn't that loud a sound, nor one that was unusual at this time of day, but she winced anyway. What she wished for right now was total silence.

She slipped across the courtyard, the gun held behind her

back so that if someone glanced out the rectory window, he would not see it. If.

There was a light shining dimly near the back of the building. Curtains filtered it, concealing whatever was happening inside. No other lights were on. Standing stock-still, she listened. Voices? She couldn't be sure.

She reached the side door of the rectory and tried the knob. It wouldn't turn, dammit. But in the hushed twilight she saw something around the jamb. Bending to see better, she drew a sharp breath. The door had been jimmied.

And when she pushed on the door, it swung open.

Matt saw the flicker of recognition in Victor's eyes. The bluff hadn't worked; Victor had figured it out. The question was, was he armed? Matt figured he probably was. There were too many variables in Victor's plan. A weapon would be an essential precaution. But where did he have it? Matt hadn't seen any bulges around his ankles, and the man wasn't wearing a coat or anything else that could hide a gun.

In theory, he had enough to search the plane, even without a warrant. It was on the watch list, and he was sure the *Carroll* Doctrine would protect him. Especially in the current legal climate. But there were problems as well. He was out of his jurisdiction. The watch had been canceled. And so far, the man hadn't done anything that provided grounds for reasonable suspicion, let alone probable cause.

No, Matt needed more. Enough that the case wouldn't be thrown out for faulty procedure. Because he needed this guy to roll over on his bosses. That wasn't going to happen if his lawyer took one look at the facts and saw an easy dismissal.

But how to bait him out, without having him reach for the weapon Matt was sure he had?

"So you're flying to Jacksonville tonight?" Matt asked.

Victor's eyes narrowed for a split second before he smiled, and said, "Sure am. Business meeting tomorrow."

So okay, Matt thought. *I know, and you know I know. Let's dance.*

"Pretty town," Matt said. "Well, the riverfront is nice, anyway."

"That's what I hear," Victor said. "This is my first trip there. I usually work south Florida."

"Lauderdale or Miami?"

"Lauderdale, mostly," Victor said. "Sales."

Matt made a face. "I hate Lauderdale. Been there three times and my car broke down all three times." It wasn't true, but it forced the conversation.

"I guess," Victor said. "I usually rent a car."

Matt had circled around the nose of the plane to approach the man from behind. "Well, of course, owning an airplane."

"It's an expensive convenience," Victor said. "But time is money in this business."

"But you don't own this one."

Victor stiffened and turned.

"This aircraft belongs to Vreeland Aviation, in Maryland," Matt continued, his voice level. "Rented to Lance Brucon two weeks ago. Shame what happened to him."

Victor couldn't quite conceal the look of surprise.

"But you didn't know, did you?" Matt asked. "They made a real mess of him. We needed dental records to identify him."

Victor had his back to the fuselage now, his shoulder pressed up against a wing. Nowhere to go.

"Did you really think they'd let you live?" Matt asked. The bluff was working. "We know all about your background, Victor."

In truth, he had no idea about this man's background. All he had was a name. But the mere mention of Brucon's name made Victor's eyes widen a bit.

"I . . . I'm just a salesman," Victor said. "I sell machine parts for carnival rides."

Matt nodded. It was a good cover story. Odd enough to believe without there being an obvious way for a casual listener to check it out. Who knew who supplied those parts? But somebody had to. His was a professional cover story, no doubt about it.

Matt inched a bit closer. Another foot or so and he'd be too close to Victor for the man to reach for a concealed weapon.

"And I'm sure that, if I knew who made carnival rides and took the time, I'd find employment records. Your employers seem to do good work."

"We make excellent machine parts," Victor agreed.

"Your employers don't make machine parts. You know it, and I know it. And as parts go, you're expendable. They proved that with Brucon. You have two choices, Victor. You can go along my way, or you go out their way. And those are the only two choices you have left."

Matt saw that he'd pushed too hard. Victor nodded, but it was a predatory nod. His hand rose as if to scratch the back of his neck, and Matt realized that was where the gun was hidden.

Matt was already reaching for his own gun when he

heard tape tear away from skin. He drove his left shoulder hard into Victor's chest, pinning him to the side of the plane, as he drew his own gun and jammed it into Victor's ribs. There was no way Victor could aim his own gun. But he could fire it. Right next to Matt's left ear.

The tiny report of the twenty-two, barely audible a hundred feet away, sounded like a whip cracking against Matt's eardrum. The world swirled for an instant, and in that instant Victor shoved him away.

Matt fought the insistent whine in his ear, trying to focus, to bring his weapon to bear. Victor was quick. Matt saw the flash and felt the sting against his side. That was a miss Victor would not repeat.

Matt leveled his gun and fired, the report of the 9mm explosive. Victor had gotten off the first shot, but the 9mm parabellum round could do a lot more damage. And did. It punched through Victor's sternum, mushrooming as it hit bone, and blew a two-inch hole in his heart.

Victor slid down slowly, his eyes already vacant.

For the first time, Matt felt the wet burn in his side. As the sound of sirens grew in his right ear, the world turned dark.

"Why'd you kill Steve?" Brendan asked. "He had nothing to do with anything."

Humboldt hesitated, then shrugged. "Everybody said he was like a son to you. I wanted you to know what it felt like."

A heavy sorrow settled in Brendan's heart, heavier than the fear he was feeling. A weight equal to the world. "He *was* like a son to me."

Humboldt nodded. "So now you know."

"But what I don't get," Brendan said, "is why you crucified him."

"I didn't."

Something slipped along Brendan's spine, something like the awareness of a presence. Something he occasionally felt when deep in prayer, that feeling of being cradled in love and light. And it was so out of place that for a few moments it stunned him.

"I didn't do that," Humboldt said again. "I'd never blaspheme like that."

Oddly, Brendan believed him. And the warmth now encircled him, enveloping him. He was not alone. And neither had Steve King been alone.

Chloe eased down the hallway toward the light, Glock at the ready. She could hear the voices better now, murmurs mainly. Brendan's and someone else's. He wasn't alone.

Then she heard a question that made her freeze.

"What's all this crap you were giving me about a conspiracy?"

"I'm just telling you what your son told me, Mr. Humboldt."

Chloe's heart slammed. Holding the Glock in both hands, she eased farther along the hallway to the partly open door through which light spilled.

"And," Brendan continued, "there's evidence of conspiracy right now. Somebody moved Steve King's body after you shot him. You know that. Did you ever ask yourself who?"

If there was an answer, Chloe couldn't hear it.

"I fear Tom was right, Mr. Humboldt. There are forces at

work here that neither you nor I know about. The more I think about it, the more I think your son was murdered. Can I ask you a question?"

If the man gave an answer, it was inaudible. Regardless, Brendan plunged on.

"Mr. Humboldt, did you get the idea that I was responsible for your son's death on your own? Or did someone else suggest it?"

The silence that followed was so profound that Chloe could hear the hammering of her own heart.

"My God . . ." said a strangled voice.

It was her moment. She burst through the door, gun at ready, and aimed straight at the man she assumed was Mr. Humboldt. "Drop your weapon," she said.

The man looked at her, not responding.

"I said drop it. Because believe me, you can shoot one or the other of us, but not both. Now drop your weapon!"

The twenty-two pistol tumbled to the floor, and Humboldt put his head in his hands.

Chloe kicked the gun away, keeping her bead on Humboldt. "Father, call the police *now.*"

He didn't move.

"Father, *call the police!*"

He turned his head and slowly raised his gaze to her. "I'm not going to press charges for this."

"Now wait—"

"You wait," he said firmly. "This man was driven past the point of sanity by someone with an agenda, and I'm not pressing charges. As far as you know, we were just having a discussion."

"At the end of a gun? No way, Father. The choice is out of your hands. Now call the police. You know damn well he killed Steve. And if you want to plead for mercy in his behalf at trial and sentencing, be my guest. But I saw what I saw, and if you don't call them, I will."

"Call them," Humboldt said, lifting his head. Tears streaked his face. "Call them. I'll tell them everything I know."

EPILOGUE

Healing wounds itched like the devil. A hundred times a day, Matt wanted to scratch the scabbed-over crease in his side. He'd lost his spleen, but other than that, and the damn itching, he was doing fine. Even his hearing was recovering, albeit slowly. There were still too many crickets in his ear.

He arrived at Chloe's house bearing gifts. What was that line about being wary of Greeks bearing gifts? The thought made him smile. She'd *better* be wary, because he was on the hunt now.

He carried flowers and a bottle of wine. The look on her face when she opened the door made him want to grin from ear to ear. He never thought he'd see her delighted.

"Come on in," she said. "Let me put these in water."

Then embarrassment struck him as he realized Brendan was sitting in Chloe's living room, wearing mufti and sipping a cup of coffee. He paused, hoping his cheeks didn't show the heat he felt in them. "Evening, Father."

"Just Brendan, please. I'm off-duty." Brendan smiled that engaging smile that had been absent for weeks now. "Go on. Don't mind me."

Matt hesitated only a moment longer, then followed Chloe into the kitchen and watched as she filled a vase and trimmed the stems. He put the bottle of wine on the counter.

"Sorry," he said. "I didn't know he was going to be here."

"He just dropped in. Why should you be sorry?"

He nodded toward the flowers. "Sorry if I embarrassed you."

"You didn't. But he'd probably like to hear what's going on as much as I would. Come on. Let's rejoin him."

He followed her again, like a puppy on an invisible leash. The thought made him squirm a little. He wasn't exactly used to this.

Chloe sat on the couch at the opposite end from Brendan, and Matt took the easy chair.

"So any new news?" she asked.

"No. We're still dead in the water on who was behind this mess. The lab did confirm the plane was carrying a cargo of chlorine gas and a smudge pot full of old tire shavings. He'd have dumped a very smelly, very deadly gas. And we found notes and sketches in Victor Singh's apartment. His target was MacDill. Probably Central Command headquarters, judging by the notes he'd made."

"My God! Matt, that would have been awful."

"I'm not sure. The heavy smoke from the rubber would have made it hang around for a few minutes, but at that time of night, there wouldn't have been many people walking around. And there's usually a pretty good sea breeze by then."

"So he was a stupid terrorist."

Matt shook his head. "Between you, me, and the gatepost, I think it was planned that way. Nobody will listen to me, but I think this was only *supposed* to look like a terrorist attack."

"Why do you say that?"

"Because the trail on Lance Brucon ends with the word 'classified.' And because somebody from the government e-mailed the photo that tipped us to all of this."

Chloe was silent for a few moments. "That's a chilling thought."

"I agree. But it's all speculation. We'll never know. Just like we'll never know who crucified King. How's that going, by the way?"

Chloe shrugged. "You know privilege is involved."

"I know. I know. I'm just surprised you're defending Humboldt."

Brendan spoke. "I asked her to, Matt."

Matt shook his head. "You're a little too Christ-like, Father."

Brendan cocked his head. "That's a good thing in a priest, don't you think?"

"Maybe." Matt plucked a grape from a bowl on her counter. "I hate cases like this, where you never learn what really was going on. Where you just have to spend the rest of your life wondering."

Chloe sighed. "Me too."

Brendan shook his head. "The thought that government black ops might have been behind this is appalling. I thought things like that happened only in novels."

"I would have said so, too," Matt agreed. "But you were in the navy. You probably heard things."

"I did." His gaze grew distant. "Things that might be better forgotten, given what's happened here."

Matt plucked another grape. "My guess is that they

wanted you gone because you might remember something and put two and two together."

"Like what?" Chloe demanded.

Brendan started to get that stubborn, I'm-not-going-to-say-a-word look, then sighed. "If I say anything, it stops here. I don't want the two of you in danger. I'm serious. You're not to pursue this in any way."

Matt was about to insist he wasn't going to make any such promise, then realized it wouldn't matter. If he tried to take on the government, he was apt to wind up as dead as Steve King or Victor Singh. "Okay."

Chloe nodded. "I agree."

"Understand," Brendan said, "that I'm piecing this together from a really fractured discussion and a distant memory. But . . . I got the impression from Tom Humboldt that some government operation had gone awry. That its purpose had become strengthening its own hand rather than its original mission."

Matt whistled quietly. "I could see that. I could honestly see that."

"How so?" Chloe wanted to know. "What could they possibly hope to accomplish by attacking their own country?"

"Easy," Matt said. "More funding. More power. Martial law. Expansion of our antiterrorist operations. I could see lots of reasons."

All three of them sat silent for a long time. Finally Chloe spoke. "That gives me the willies."

"Me, too," Brendan admitted.

Matt realized his ordinary level of paranoia was rising through the roof. "Listen," he said, "let's not talk about this anymore."

Chloe's head snapped around to look at him. "This is a free country."

"Yeah. And they can listen through closed windows. If they're still watching us, we don't want to make them nervous. So enough of this. We'll never really know what happened, and we'll sure as hell never prove it."

Brendan nodded. "I agree. I shouldn't have said anything."

"So," Matt said firmly, "how are you doing? Are you getting past this?"

Brendan smiled sadly. "Yes, I am. Steve is safely in the arms of God, and Wayne Humboldt . . . I pity that man. He was mercilessly used and now his life is truly ruined."

Matt almost gaped at him. "He killed Steve King. That young man was innocent of anything."

"I know. But I also understand the twisted emotions that led Humboldt to do it. They broke him. That's the long and short of it. They twisted the knife until he snapped. I pray for him, Matt, and so should you."

Brendan left a few minutes later, wishing them a good evening. Chloe and Matt stood at the door watching him vanish into the twilight. Brendan walked jauntily, not as jauntily as before, but it was an improvement over the past weeks. It was clear he had settled in himself, and settled with God, and was glad to be back to being a full-time priest.

"He's amazing," Matt said as Chloe closed the door.

"Faith will do that."

"Quit pushing."

"Aw," she said, an impish smile on her face. "And here I was going to ask you to go to Mass with me on Sunday."

He looked as horrified as if she'd suggested shoving

splinters under his fingernails. "You know I'm not one for that organized religion stuff."

"I know. But it sure wouldn't hurt you."

"Shit. Cut it out."

"Okay." She laughed. "How about some of that wine you brought?"

Once again he trotted after her like a puppy, into the kitchen. "I read where you filed an insanity plea on Humboldt."

Chloe merely looked at him, her gaze warning him off.

"There's no way he was legally insane, Chloe. He was aware of what he was doing. And he knew it was wrong."

She shrugged. "He's my client. I have to try. And you know I can't talk about it."

"Okay, okay. Let's discuss us instead."

Slowly her face softened. "Okay. What do you want to discuss?"

"Do you like champagne, and how big is your bed?"

Chloe laughed then, a belly laugh so deep that it seemed to drive all the darkness out of the world.

Now, if he could just keep her doing that . . .

ABOUT THE AUTHOR

RACHEL LEE, winner of numerous awards for her best-selling romantic fiction, is the author of Silhouette's #1 miniseries, Conard County. She also writes lighthearted contemporary romances as Sue Civil-Brown. But suspense fiction that zings like a high-tension wire with excitement and passion has become her signature style. As *Romantic Times* says, Rachel Lee is "an author to treasure."

THE EDITOR'S DIARY

Dear Reader,

D₀ we ever follow our mothers' advice? With our two Warner Forever titles this May, you can laugh at the hilarious advice of an eccentric mother or get a chilling reminder of what our mothers always warned us about. But definitely follow *our* advice when we say that reading two great romance novels is even better than reading one!

Janet Evanovich says, "Every girl from 18 to 80 will love Leanne Banks's SOME GIRLS DO. The best feel-good book you'll read this year!" We just know you'll agree. So throw yourself into the madcap adventure of Katie Collins and Michael Wingate. When personal assistant Katie must find a suitable husband for the daughter of her tycoon boss, she is forced to work with bodyguard Michael, who drives her out of her sensible shoes. But it's only when Katie takes the non-traditional advice of her late mother— "Every once in a while, you meet a man worth the trouble he's going to cause you"—that Katie takes the bull by the horns . . . and discovers why some good girls do want to be bad sometimes. . . .

Should a heart-pounding suspense be your choice of indulgence, why not curl up in your favorite chair with **LAST BREATH** by **Rachel Lee**. Father Brendan Quinlan is a popular pastor at St. Simeon's Parish whose world is turned upside down when he's suspected of murdering a young man attending his church. Private investigator Chloe Ryder takes on the case to prove Father Brendan's innocence, all the while butting heads—and hearts—with police detective Matthew Diel. Have some hot tea nearby to ward off the chills rolling down your spine. According to *Publishers Weekly*, "Lee skillfully constructs a suspenseful story—with romance in all the right places."

To find out more about these May titles, the authors, and Warner Forever, visit us at www.warnerforever.com.

With warmest wishes,

Karen Kosztolnyik

Karen Kosztolnyik, Senior Editor

P.S. Summer is just around the corner, so start your beach reading list early with these upcoming titles: **Mary McBride** presents the perfect hero with a wounded heart in the wonderful romantic comedy **MY HERO**; and **BACK ROADS** is Susan Crandall's debut novel about a young woman from a small town who yearns for a new life—it's women's fiction at its best.